M000304920

Dangerous Currents

Kathryn Knight

Wicked Whale
Publishing

This book is a work of fiction. Names, characters, and incidents are the product of the author's imagination or are used fictitiously. Any resemblance to actual events, locales, or persons living or dead, is coincidental.

Copyright © 2018 by Kathryn Knight

Cover & Interior Design: Wicked Whale Publishing

All rights reserved. In accordance with U.S. Copyright Act of 1976, the scanning, uploading and electronic sharing of any part of this book without the permission of the publisher / author is unlawful piracy and theft of the author's intellectual property. If you would like to use material from this book (other than for review purposes), prior written permission must be obtained by contacting the publisher at wickedwhalepublishing.com. Thank you for your support of the author's rights.

Knight, Kathryn
Dangerous Currents / by Kathryn Knight

Summary: When Malorie Montgomery returns to Cape Cod, romance reignites just as a killer sets her in his sights.

ISBN: 978-1-7322522-1-9

Wicked Whale Publishing
P.O. Box 264
Sagamore Beach, MA 02562-9998

www.WickedWhalePublishing.com

Published in the United States of America

Dedication

To Kate, Jen, Jen, and Janet, and nearly forty years of
friendship. I love you ladies.

Chapter One

Despite the warmth of the day, a chill passed through her as she stared at the ocean. The morning sun shimmered across the water, creating silver sparks on the rippling waves. It should have been a peaceful view. Relaxing. Instead, it stirred a chord of anxiety deep inside her.

Tightening her grip on the leash, Malorie Montgomery glanced down into the eager eyes of the dog sitting by her feet. He was waiting for her command with what appeared to be his last ounce of restraint. The quivering muscles beneath his black fur revealed his excitement over exploring a new location. He lifted his hind legs a fraction of an inch before sitting back down on the wooden deck with an impatient thump.

A smile tugged at her lips. "Are you ready, Brady?" she teased, scratching behind one floppy ear. She'd named him after Bradic Place, the street address of her London flat.

Her former flat, now. She'd given up her lease when she'd decided to move back to the States. And now here she was, on the sandy shores of Cape Cod, the curved strip of land jutting out from the rest of Massachusetts like an arm bent at the elbow.

The town of Ontoquas occupied a southwestern slice of the peninsula, and her family's beach house boasted a breathtaking view of the stretch of the Atlantic known as Vineyard Sound. On a bright, nearly cloudless day like today, it was clear enough to see the island of Martha's Vineyard in the distance.

A lone boat bobbed in the ocean, its crew too far away to make out. The beach was similarly deserted. That wasn't unusual, this early in the morning in June, but the sense of isolation was surreal.

Brady's body wiggled again, his mane of fur tickling the skin of her thigh. She brushed the spot with her fingertips, plucking a few crinkled hairs from her tight workout shorts. "Okay, then," she said, bracing herself. "Let's go!"

He launched himself down the wooden steps, and she scrambled to keep up as the extendable leash zipped out of the red plastic handle to its maximum length. Brady plowed straight ahead, pulling her across the beach toward the group of tiny birds near the shoreline.

She dug her sneakers into the sand and yanked on the leash, her heart fluttering like the fleeing birds. "No, boy," she called as she reigned him in. Her arm jerked with the sudden stop in momentum. *Ow.* That was going to be sore tomorrow. But she wasn't ready to get that near the water. Not yet. There was plenty of time to deal with her demons later.

There was plenty of time to continue to ignore them, too. It had worked well enough so far. She adjusted the strap of her white tank top and rubbed her shoulder absentmindedly. Or had it? Her gaze slid along the row of neighboring houses before she could stop herself.

Pain seared her chest as her eyes snagged on the deck of the fifth house from hers. Dean's house. She shook her head, biting down on her lower lip. No. If she was going to live here, she needed to adjust her thought process. It was Mrs. Walters' house. Or at least it used to be. It could have changed hands several times over the six years she'd been away, for all she knew.

Her grip tightened on the leash, and Brady's impatient tugs rattled her joints as he veered left, following the direction of her gaze. "Hang on," she murmured, forcing her attention away from the wide windows of Mrs. Walters' house and back to the familiar stretch of sand that belonged to the exclusive Sandalwood community. Beyond a half dozen more spacious oceanfront houses, chairs owned by the private beach club where she'd worked those last few summers sat stacked under awnings. Additional houses lined the dunes on the far side of Sandalwood Club. Past the last gray-shingled home, the beach tapered to a thin strip of land sheltering Ontoquas Bay; on the other side of the water, pine trees clustered like a green army on the shores of Cotuit and Osterville.

She turned away, pulling Brady in the opposite direction. Her house sat on the very last buildable lot on this end of the Sandalwood development, and as they walked beside the barrier dunes, the beach grew narrow, giving way to the marshy woodlands surrounding the Ontoquas River. Brady zigzagged in front of her, trying to smell every clump of seagrass to their right and every washed-up horseshoe crab shell to their left while simultaneously maintaining his forward motion.

A seagull cried overhead, and she jumped. God, she was on edge. She rolled her eyes. It was supposed to be calm and relaxing here, after the frenetic pace of London. But the long flight, followed by a two hour drive from Boston, had teamed up with the time change to wreak havoc on her system. She'd managed to unpack enough to settle in before falling asleep on the couch last night; she'd then awoken in the predawn hours, confused and sore. Eventually, she had given up on sleep and taken Brady out quickly in the darkness, promising him a legitimate walk once the sun rose. A yawn escaped as she massaged the tight muscles in her neck. Maybe she could sneak in a nap later.

And why couldn't she? Her empty schedule was almost depressing. She heaved a sigh as she followed Brady along the trail leading into the woods. Maybe coming here had been a mistake. But what choice did she have, really? The plan that had been in place as far back as she could remember—a lifetime devoted to ascending the ranks at Montgomery Wealth Management—had imploded a month and a half ago. The fact that she'd never been one hundred percent certain it was the life she actually wanted meant little when compared to the fact she had no alternate plan.

Then Julia had asked for help, and the initial seed had been planted. Her family's beach house was still here, a rent-free option for her on the opposite side of the Atlantic from her father; a familiar place where she could start fresh and get her feet back under her. She could help her best friend with the challenges that would come with starting up an ambitious charitable project. Her business background would be invaluable to the process—or at least, that's what Julia told her.

That would all be volunteer work, of course. But she'd managed to find a paying job teaching introductory business classes at the local community college. The money wasn't great, but it would be enough to buy groceries without having to ask her father for any additional support. And that was important in terms of maintaining the last fragile shreds of her pride.

A fork in the trail split the dirt path in two directions, and she shook her head slightly at the metaphorical significance. "This way," she said, pulling Brady to the left. The other path led toward the river; with its wider clearance and smoother surface, it was the route more frequently chosen by walkers and joggers. And she didn't really feel like seeing anyone right now, even in passing.

This trail came with its own set of drawbacks, however. It wound its way closer along the shore, leading eventually to the spot where she and Dean used to leave the narrow path and slip into the woods, picking their way through the pines and underbrush toward an isolated clearing. Their private retreat, away from the rest of the world.

Ancient history. With a forceful shake of her head, she tried to focus instead on her to-do list for the day. Finish the last of her unpacking. Dust. Change lightbulbs. Call Julia. Do a more thorough grocery store trip. Hopefully take that nap at some point.

She pulled in a deep breath, filling her lungs with the mossy, brine-filled air. But the distinctive scent brought its own set of memories. Long conversations under the stars. Shared secrets and stolen touches. And then passionate kisses, when the force of their attraction could no longer be denied.

Stop. Just stop. She clutched her stomach with her free hand as the sting of betrayal burned through her. She was not going to let this happen every time she left the house. She was stronger than that. She had to be.

Yanking on the leash, she pulled Brady back onto the trail and turned her attention to a grocery list. What would she need for meals? Her cooking skills were seriously rusty. Living in Mayfair, she'd been in walking distance to Shepherd Market, with its variety of pubs and restaurants, as well as a Tesco featuring a well-stocked section of prepared foods for quick purchase. And before that, she'd dined on campus, in one of the university cafeterias.

She'd mastered a few easy recipes in high school, out of necessity. It would come back to her with a little practice. Besides, she'd only be cooking for one, and it was unlikely Brady would criticize her efforts if he received any leftovers. Once she'd become more comfortable in the kitchen, maybe she could invite Julia and her boyfriend Pete over. Eating alone night after night was sure to get depressing, eventually.

Brady lunged toward a thick tangle of brambles, and a rabbit dashed from its hiding spot, fleeing into the woods. She stumbled forward as Brady took off in pursuit, the leash slipping from her grip. His sharp, excited yips rang out as the red plastic handle of the leash trailed behind him, bouncing through the underbrush.

Crap! "Brady!" she called, shaking her stinging wrist. "No!" She plunged into the woods after him, wincing as thorny vines tore at the bare skin of her legs. This was bad. Very bad. Brady didn't know the area, at all. They'd been here a total of fourteen hours. He would have no idea how to find his way back to the house. He was still wearing a tag with their London address, for God's sake.

She jumped over a fallen tree, cursing as her ankle twisted when she landed. Obstacles shouldn't be a major challenge for a former gymnast, but the ground was uneven, and she wasn't being careful. It was her bad ankle, too. And now she'd lost sight of him completely. *Damn it.* "Brady! Come!"

Panic burned through her veins, fueling her muscles. She continued calling out, but her cries went unanswered. It was all she could think to do, even though she really didn't expect him to return to her while there were rabbits to chase and new smells to explore. When she'd adopted him a year ago from the animal shelter, she'd had every intention of working with her new dog until he obeyed her commands without question. She'd even purchased several books on training methods and highlighted important passages. But, as usual, her hectic work schedule interfered with her plans, and taking Brady for brisk walks through one of the nearby parks took precedence over tedious training sessions. Any downtime beyond that was usually spent at the gym, followed by lying on the couch, reading or watching TV, eyes drifting shut, with Brady snuggled up with her, doing his impersonation of a 40-pound lap dog. After a year, "sit" was as far as they'd gotten, and even that depended on the level of distractions in their vicinity.

No, he wasn't the most well-trained dog, but that wasn't his fault. And while he wasn't always obedient, he *was* sweet and loyal, and she loved him fiercely. In many ways, he was her best friend. A fresh wave of terror crashed over her as she pictured him lost in the woodlands for days, hungry and scared. These woods were part of the Waquoit Bay Reserve, encompassing nearly 2800 acres of land and water.

In addition to the ocean border, there were several ponds, the river, and Waquoit Bay. Could Brady even swim, if he found himself in the water? What if he encountered a coyote hungry enough to attack something its own size?

A trio of frantic barks echoed in the distance, and she stumbled to a halt, throwing out her arms to keep her balance. She froze, scanning the spaces between the trees, listening. Her breath came out in labored gasps, and she clutched at a stitch in her side as she fought to hear above the thunder of her pulse. A mosquito whined in her ear.

There. A faint rustle of movement through the underbrush, the chattering of an anxious squirrel. Up ahead and to the right, past a thick cluster of pitch pines. She forced herself to pause for a moment and get her bearings. Her wild route had taken her across one of the main trails at one point, and closer inland, away from the river. Good—maybe that would make it easier to find her way back to civilization. Once she found her dog, of course.

She broke back into a run, praying the noises she'd heard were Brady, and that he'd stay in one place long enough for her to get there. *Please*, she begged silently. *I deserve a little luck.*

A movement caught her eye, a flash of black amidst the muted shades of brown and green. *Stay.* She pumped her arms, barreling up a little incline and knocking a low limb out of the way before it smacked her in the face. From her vantage point, she could see him now, investigating the detritus of the forest floor. His feathery tail swayed as he dug through layers of pine needles, oak leaves, and sandy dirt.

She just had to get there before he lost interest in whatever it was that had held his attention for this long. And without spooking him or turning this into a continued game of chase. Picking her way down the slope, she carefully avoided a thick knob of roots jutting from the ground. The pain in her ankle was gathering force, sending up warning flares every time she put weight on her right foot. She'd have to ice that later. Add one more thing to the to-do list.

"Hey, Brady," she called out casually, as if she was surprised to have bumped into him during her leisurely jog. "What did you find, boy?"

Almost there. She approached him with slow, deliberate steps, ready to pounce if necessary. But he was ignoring her, intent on his activity. His head was down, and the black cord of the leash trailed from his collar in a diagonal line. A patch of the red plastic handle blazed beneath a pile of decaying leaves Brady had unearthed.

She focused on the splotch of crimson as it wiggled with his movements. Angling around to the side, she coiled, prepared to grab it. Then her eyes caught on an odd-shaped rock jutting from the clumps of soil and vegetation.

Not a rock. Her breath came out in a rush as she reeled backwards. It was a foot. A human foot, limp and waxy, the skin a mottled blue-gray.

She screamed.

Chapter Two

Oh, God. She clutched at a tree, grabbing onto the sturdy trunk to keep from collapsing. Bile bubbled in her throat, and she squeezed her eyes shut as she leaned her forehead against the rough bark. She could not have just seen that. It was her tired mind playing tricks on her. With a deep breath, she dragged her eyes open.

Her scream had apparently alerted Brady to her distress and brought him to her aid. He stood beside her, his dark eyes full of concern as he stared up at her. "It's okay," she managed, reaching out to stroke his head with a shaky hand. But was it okay? She was going to have to look. Swallowing hard, she slid her fingers around Brady's collar and held on tight, using her other hand to reel the handle of the leash toward her like a bizarre scarlet fish. She kept her gaze glued on it as it bumped across the uneven ground. Anything to avoid seeing what lay beyond.

The leash handle came to a stop near her sneaker and she stared at it. She didn't want to touch it, after what she'd seen beside it. With a grimace, she picked it up gingerly and fixed the retracting mechanism. Okay. At least she had Brady.

Her sweaty fingers tightened around the leash. She took a step toward the disturbed leaves, her heart slamming against her chest. The frenzied thud of her heartbeat reverberated through her skull with enough force to produce an echoing tempo in her ears.

Wait—that was the pounding of footsteps. More sounds registered over the rush of blood in her head: the cracking of twigs, the crunching of leaves. Someone was coming. Instinct screamed at her to hide, and she slipped behind the pine tree. No good. She was slim, but the trunk of the scrub pine was not enough to conceal her. She cringed as Brady let out a warning bark.

"Hello?" a man called out. "Is everything all right?"

Just someone out on the trail. A jogger or walker. Someone had heard her scream and had come to help. That was all. Her muscles turned liquid as some of the adrenaline holding her upright dispersed.

She suddenly felt ridiculous, hiding behind a tree, until she remembered there might be a body—or at least a foot—15 feet away. "Over here." She'd meant to yell, but the words came out in a rasping plea.

A figure raced toward her, his long strides covering the distance quickly. "Are you all right?" he repeated.

That voice. Her breath caught. *Dean.*

No. That was absurd. Hysterical laughter gathered in her lungs. First, her mind had created a grisly mirage. Now, she'd conjured up her old boyfriend to save her.

Dread crashed over her as the realization hit. *It was happening.* Just like that. With a moan, she doubled over, clutching her stomach. The leash pressed into her belly as she fought to gulp in air. Brady whined and nuzzled her side before pulling away, straining toward the approaching man.

That part was real, anyway. *Get yourself together.* A stranger was about to witness her having a nervous breakdown in the middle of the woods, her face dripping with sweat, her legs and arms scratched and bleeding. She straightened, brushing the sticky strands of hair that had escaped her ponytail out of her eyes.

"It's okay," she murmured to Brady, clutching his leash in her damp palm. Louder, she shouted "Everything's fine" as she turned to the man. "I thought—"

It *was* him. Dean. Recognition slammed into her, nearly sending her reeling again.

He slowed to a stop, his gaze moving between her and Brady. "Mal?" Her nickname rang out like a horrible accusation. "Is that you?" His arms slowly dropped to his sides as he stared at her.

This could not be happening. Her trembling fingers drifted over her mouth as she studied his features in the shafts of sunlight filtering through the trees. A hint of scruff now covered his jaw. His cheekbones were sharper, the planes of his face more pronounced. His dark hair, tousled by his sprint through the woods, was a bit shorter than in high school. But it was definitely Dean Slater. The 25-year-old version of him, anyway.

She nodded. "It's me." Brady had already headed over to greet his new acquaintance, and she watched Dean lean forward and offer his hand as she searched for words. Any words.

"What…what are you doing here?" Not great, but they were words.

"I was jogging, and I heard someone scream. What happened?" He raked his gaze over her body, lingering a beat too long on her legs before meeting her eyes again.

She glanced down at her bloodied shins, trying to picture what she must look like. Not good. And why was she thinking about her appearance, anyway? The important thing was what she'd seen—or what she thought she'd seen. A shiver traveled up her spine as the gruesome image flashed through her mind.

Clearing her throat, she gestured toward the area where Brady had been digging. "My dog—Brady—got away from me. And when I found him, I thought I saw…" Her gaze landed on the hint of white among the damp, moldy leaves. "I think there's a body over there. Or…part of a body." She shuddered, pulling her forearm across the beads of sweat still rolling down her forehead.

His green eyes darkened as his muscles went rigid. "Stay here," he ordered, taking several long strides in the direction she had indicated. He sucked in an audible breath. "Shit." Shaking his head, he squatted slightly before standing back up. He scrubbed at his jaw as he returned to her. "It's a woman."

Oh, no. "Is she…?"

"She's dead. No question."

She pressed her fingers to her mouth. "An accident, do you think?"

He shook his head. "I don't think so. It looks like she was buried. Although not very deep."

The edges of her vision turned gray. "I just...I think I need to sit down for a sec." Right here seemed like a good spot. The forest floor tilted sickeningly, and her knees buckled.

"Whoa!" Dean's hands shot out and caught her around the waist. "Easy there." He pulled her toward him, turning her away from the makeshift grave and curling an arm around her back. "Let's go a little farther away," he said as he took the leash with his free hand. "This could be a crime scene."

He hauled her toward the little hill like a ragdoll, and she swallowed back her humiliation and focused on staying on her feet. Despite the layers of fabric separating their skin, her flesh burned where their bodies connected. After all these years, she was in Dean's embrace again—and on some level, it still felt right. Fresh anger welled up even as a tiny traitorous part of her leaned into his solid form.

Pathetic. "I just need to sit for a minute," she repeated, ducking away from him. She landed hard on the spongy ground, desperately hoping the move looked more graceful than it felt. She pulled her knees into her chest and locked her arms around her shins, sucking in air as Brady licked at her face.

Dean loomed over her, his forehead rippled with concern. "Are you okay?"

"Uh huh," she managed, meeting his gaze before dropping her forehead to her knees. Maybe this was all just a dream. Maybe she was actually back at her house, still sprawled out on the couch in a deep sleep. It wouldn't be the first time Dean took a leading role in her dreams. Not by a long shot. She willed herself to wake up as her jagged breaths warmed the tops of her thighs.

Dean cleared his throat. "We need to call the police."

She peered up at him. "Yes. Okay. Do you have a cell phone?" Hers was back at the house, sitting on the kitchen island.

"No." He held out his arms as if to prove it, his damp gray T-shirt stretching across his wide chest, the red handle of the leash still gripped in his left hand. Brady was now lying between them, panting.

"He must be thirsty," she said, tipping her chin toward the dog. "I need to get him back to the house. Then I can call the police." Summoning her last ounce of strength, she pushed herself to standing and reached for the leash.

He raised his eyebrows. "Do you even know where you are? Where are you going to tell the police to look?"

It was a fair point. She was still so disoriented; none of this felt real. She snatched the leash from him, her fingers brushing against his as she reclaimed it. "Do *you* know where we are?"

"I have a general idea. There's an access road not far from here." He set his hands on his hips, tilting his head away from the way she'd come.

"A road? In here?" She scanned the tree line for a break in the seemingly endless expanse of pitch pines and scrub oaks.

"Just a dirt road, for emergency and maintenance vehicles. If we head that way, you can wait there, and I'll get my truck and pick you both up." He nodded at Brady.

She bristled. "We can walk."

He shrugged. "Suit yourself." Turning his back to her, he retraced his steps toward the makeshift grave. He examined the area one more time, making a wide berth around the body, noting landmarks, and squinting at the strengthening sun to get his bearings. Then he reached behind his head and pulled off his T-shirt.

What the hell was he doing? She stared at the tanned skin of his back. His muscles rippled as he tore the cotton shirt into thin strips. To her dismay, a tiny thread of desire pulsed in her belly. Grinding her teeth together, she pulled her gaze away.

Damn it. How could he have this effect on her after all this time? After what he'd done? And after she'd just discovered a dead body?

She was just in shock. That was all. That, and the fact that she hadn't been with a man for quite some time.

"I wish the material were brighter," he said as he tied one of the gray strips around a narrow tree trunk. He glanced at her white shirt before tying another one to a low branch.

"I'm keeping my shirt on, thanks." It wasn't much, just an old, plain white tank top with thin straps and a shelf bra. Something she once wore under work suits. But she currently had nothing on underneath. "I'm sure that will be enough." She nodded at his efforts, resisting the urge to praise his idea to mark the scene for authorities.

He left one more on the far side, then stuffed the rest of the shirt pieces in the pocket of his black gym shorts. "We'll head up toward the access road, and I'll leave a few more markers to show the way we came." He checked the sun again, nodding to himself. "You ready?"

She'd never been more ready to leave a place in her life. On the other hand, she was about to endure a long, awkward walk with the man who had not only broken her heart, but ripped it into shreds like the sweaty gray T-shirt. She pressed her lips together, immediately ashamed of her train of thought. At least she was alive. The same could not be said for the unfortunate woman lying 20 feet away in an unmarked grave.

"Ready," she answered, tugging on Brady's leash. She sighed inwardly. Let the awkwardness begin.

Chapter Three

He led them through the woods, in a southeastern line, he told her, as if that meant anything to her. Obviously he'd forgotten how bad she was at directions. Her throat was a desert, and she swallowed against her thirst. She had tried to forget everything about him over the past six years, and she thought she'd succeeded. But now, as she walked behind him, memories were creeping in. She hadn't forgotten everything— she'd just buried it.

Ugh. Poor choice of words. She grimaced as another horrifying thought popped into her brain. "Um, Dean? I didn't see the whole body." She'd been too busy screaming. But she was glad, now that she thought about it. The last thing she needed was a mental picture like that haunting her. "Brady didn't…do…anything to it, did he?" *Please say no.* Her stomach roiled as she recalled his tongue lapping at her face.

He turned back to her, holding a low branch out of the way. "No, I think he just dug her up. She's not in great shape, but she's…intact. No blood that I saw, although she had clothes on. I'm no expert, but I don't think she's been there that long. Other animals probably would have got to her."

She shuddered. She probably hadn't needed those details, but she was glad Brady had only helped to find her. "I wonder what happened."

"I don't think it was a natural death. She was young. Our age, maybe younger. And it looked like there was bruising around her neck...so..." He let the sentence drift off. "I guess we'll find out once the police have investigated."

She nodded, even though he couldn't see her. Her legs were on fire, sore muscles burning within, torn skin singing with pain each time a bramble slapped against her. The dirt road was visible up ahead, and she considered waiting there for Dean like he'd suggested. But she knew her pride would win out. Anyone else, she'd admit she needed a ride. Not with Dean, though.

The woods gave way to the rough access road, and she breathed a sigh of relief. At least the branches and brush would no longer be clawing at her with every step. Even Brady looked worse for wear, his tongue hanging out, his normally sleek black fur crusted with thorny twigs and bits of leaves. For the first time ever, his boundless energy appeared to have hit its limit.

She quickly discovered the drawbacks to their new terrain, however. They'd walked single-file through the wooded area, Dean picking the path of least resistance as he led them out. It had been easy to avoid conversation. Now, there was plenty of room to walk side-by-side; he'd even shortened his stride to avoid leaving her behind. She didn't fool herself that this kindness had anything to do with her—it was just a vestige of the chivalry his mother had instilled in him. Her chest tightened at the thought of Mrs. Slater, and she searched for something else to occupy her mind.

The silence seemed to expand in the open space. Even the bird calls faded, despite the endless acres of trees attempting to reclaim their territory on either side of the narrow road. Did the lack of conversation bother him? She couldn't stand it much longer. Besides, anything was better than focusing on her exhaustion and thirst. Not to mention the dead woman they'd left behind and the police interrogation they had to look forward to.

Kicking a small rock, she slid a glance in his direction. A sheen of perspiration covered his bare skin, and layers of hard muscle lined his chest and arms. Bloody hell. This wasn't fair. "Um…do you know how much longer?"

He slapped at a mosquito on his shoulder. "Less than a mile, I think. Maybe another 15 minutes. This will bring us out to Lady Slipper Way."

That was near the back entrance to Sandalwood. She could make it.

"Malorie…what are you doing here?"

The question caught her by surprise, although there was no reason it should. The bigger surprise was that he'd waited this long to ask her. She'd just assumed he didn't care one way or another. "I…live here now. I mean, again. I moved back."

His steady pace faltered for the briefest of moments. "I thought you lived in Europe."

"I did. After uni, I lived in London for two years. I just moved back." She tugged Brady away from a clump of weeds. "Yesterday, as a matter of fact."

"Oh." He reached behind his head to rub the back of his neck.

She fought to keep the anger out of her voice. No need for him to see how his reaction to her presence here cut her to the core. Besides, he didn't own rights to the Cape. It was *her* family who owned property in nearby Sandalwood. Not his. "Do you come here a lot? I mean, to run?"

He lifted a shoulder. "It's convenient."

A pit opened up in her stomach. What did he mean by that? She licked her dry lips. "Where are you living now?"

"Sandalwood."

Her jaw dropped open. He...lived in Sandalwood? *Oh, God.* Ontoquas was a small Cape Cod town, and Sandalwood was an even smaller community. She would run into him all the time. This could not be happening.

"So you liked living there enough to buy a house?" It was mean, but she couldn't help it. Money and status—or lack thereof—had always been a perilous chasm stretching between them. Sometimes she told herself that's why he did what he did. But in her heart, she knew the truth: he had just been using her, all along. Her family's wealth and reputation had only made the eventual conquest that much more fun.

He laughed, the sound bitter and hollow. "I work for a landscaping company. I can hardly afford to buy a house in Sandalwood."

"But..." She frowned, rewinding his earlier words in her head. Hadn't he just said he lived in Sandalwood? Realization dawned on her...perhaps it was a similar arrangement to the one that brought them together the year they met.

But that had been late August, when the summer residents were closing up their houses for the season. This was June. It didn't make much sense, but maybe he was staying in the very same house he'd lived in for nine months during their senior year of high school. Maybe Mrs. Walters had just decided not to use the house this summer. She ventured a guess, since it didn't seem like he was going to help her out. And it was important to know exactly where he lived in terms of figuring out how to avoid him. "So Mrs. Walters gave you the house for the summer?"

"Mrs. Walters gave us the house, period. She passed away about four years ago, and she left the house to my mother in her will."

Malorie blinked, struggling to process this turn of events. This day just kept growing more and more bizarre. "Wow. That's so amazing." That kind of generosity *was* amazing, despite the negative impact it would have on her own life.

Her forehead tightened as her choice of words registered. 'Amazing' wasn't exactly the right way to respond to a woman's death. She blew out a breath, dragging her fingers through her ponytail. "For your family, I mean," she added hurriedly as she dropped a tiny twig to the ground. How did that get in there? She truly dreaded facing a mirror. "I'm sorry to hear about Mrs. Walters, though. She was such a nice lady."

In truth, she wasn't sure she was even remembering the right woman. Mal had spent her childhood and teenage summers at Sandalwood, but she hung out with the kids at the beach club. That's how she met Julia. But Mrs. Walters *had* to have been nice, right? She'd opened her beautiful summer house to a struggling family after their mobile home burned to the ground.

"She definitely was nice…a one-of-a-kind lady. But the cynic in me can't help thinking she also took a little pleasure in delivering a final parting shot to her son. Apparently he couldn't be bothered to give her a call every once in a while, much less visit her. My mom said she and Mrs. Walters used to talk about it a lot."

Somehow they were now actually having a civilized conversation. And for some inexplicable reason, she wanted to keep it going. "Well, maybe part of her motivation was to make a statement to her son, but I bet it had more to do with what a wonderful and loyal employee your mom was. I mean…she must have worked for her for like twenty years by that point, right? That's a long time, even if they only saw each other during the summers. I'm sure they developed a strong bond."

"They did…especially after Mr. Walters was gone. Still, it's not exactly the kind of bonus most people give their cleaning lady. My mom didn't exactly feel comfortable with it, but she swallowed her pride because she knew it was a better place to raise her family. She'd do anything for her kids."

She nodded. "I remember." The Slaters never had an easy life, but Mrs. Slater was completely devoted to her sons. Malorie could recall being envious of that kind of unconditional love from a parent.

"It did take the residents of Sandalwood a little time to adjust."

Her lips twitched as she tried to stifle a giggle. "I can imagine." Overhead, an osprey chirped a series of whistling calls as it soared across the sky.

He chuckled with her for a moment, shaking his head. "I mean, after the fire, people just chalked it up to an eccentric and lonely old lady opening her second home to a family in need. A temporary situation during the off-season. Everyone in town was offering extra clothes and gift cards, so offering shelter— even for the entire time we were homeless—didn't seem all that odd. But when we moved in permanently, things were a little tense."

The road angled, and the dull black of asphalt appeared ahead. *Oh, thank God.* They were almost out of the woods— literally, anyway. "I'm sure your mom won everyone over. She's an honest and hardworking woman."

"Thank you. She's gone now, too. She passed away last year."

A lump swelled in her dusty throat. Mrs. Slater had always been so kind to her, so welcoming...her hearty hugs so different from her own father's treatment of Dean. And while she would never forget the pain Dean had caused her back then, she was truly sorry for his loss. Squeezing her eyes shut, she swallowed hard. "I'm so sorry," she managed finally.

"Pancreatic cancer. It was fast."

She nodded weakly as they turned onto Lady Slipper Way. At least she knew where she was now. This road circled around to the back entrance of the community; they only had to walk down to the corner and then cut through a path on the next street that led to the beach.

There didn't seem to be anything left to say. The tenuous sense of intimacy created by their isolated surroundings dissolved with the appearance of civilization. So she pretended to admire the houses as they walked along the side of the road.

Although the houses along Lady Slipper Way could not boast ocean views, they were still stately homes just as large and impressive as the beachfront houses. The majority were luxurious versions of the contemporary Cape Cod style: elegant structures with pitched rooves, wooden shingles, dormers, Palladian windows, and two-car garages. Wide white columns and decorative stonework embellished many of the exterior designs.

Front yards were similarly well-maintained. Bright clusters of pastel blooms burst from hydrangea bushes in shades of pink and blue. Sea grass rose up in majestic fountains beside decorative gray boulders, and lush rose bushes climbed on white fences and trellises. Heavy urns of artfully arranged plants dotted porches and walkways, and window boxes overflowed with trailing vines and colorful flowers.

The silence spun out as they entered the path that cut between two houses, so she turned her attention to what she could see of the backyards. Raised decks, swimming pools, and gazebos surrounded by emerald green lawns. It was hard to believe the majority of these were only summer homes. At least her family's summer home would now be her full-time residence, at least for the near future as she figured out what her next step would be. And she was grateful it was available to her, even if it meant living five doors down from Dean.

The path brought them to Beach Plum Drive—her road. *Their* road. The houses here backed to the private beach, where sprawling decks sat upon sand dunes dotted with clumps of spidery grass and thorny masses of beach roses with bright fuchsia flowers and red fruit. Wooden stairways descended the gentle slopes to bring residents to the stretches of smooth sand below, where the small waves deposited rocks and shells in wide bands that corresponded to the tides.

Her house was to the right, where the road ended in a cul-de-sac partially flanked with the woods. She cocked her head in that direction as they slowed to a stop. She really didn't know what to say, but the situation seemed to call for something other than parting ways after everything that had happened with no goodbyes.

"Well. Glad we made it." She took a step away, fighting the instinct to thank him for responding to her screams. He didn't deserve her thanks.

He nodded, running his fingers through his hair. The sun had already painted streaks of copper through the unruly dark brown strands. "I'll call the cops as soon as I get home. They'll probably want to talk to you too. Will you be home?"

She almost wanted to laugh, given the fact there was literally nowhere else for her to be. Except maybe Stop and Shop. "Yes."

A flicker of concern passed over his face. "Is anyone in your family with you?" His tone took on a rough edge. "Your father?"

"No. I'm alone." The moment the words left her mouth, she realized how true they were. In every sense. Biting her lip, she reminded herself that she had Julia, and the promise of Friendship Farm. She hurried on, anxious to move past the sad statement. "My parents…got a divorce. And then my father remarried, so he lives in London full time now. That's where most of his clients are anyway. He originally hung on to the house here to maintain residency and avoid the higher income taxes over there. But now he doesn't want to be away from Holly and the twins, so he sort of forgot about this house."

It was the wrong thing to say. She cringed inwardly as his features hardened. Most people did not forget about lavish waterfront houses. But Russ Montgomery had worked hard for everything he had.

"I'll give the cops your address," he said as he turned his back on her.

"Thanks," she replied, before she could stop herself. But he was already walking away.

What was his problem? She shot him a nasty look as she pulled Brady toward the house. What had she ever done to him? Not a damn thing, except hand him her heart and her trust. He was the one who'd tossed it all aside as soon as he'd gotten all he really wanted from her.

Nothing he does can hurt me anymore, she told herself firmly. But tears pressed against the back of her eyes as she trudged down the street.

Chapter Four

What a shit storm. He scrubbed a towel through his wet hair and then jammed it into the hamper with unnecessary force. How had a peaceful run on his morning off resulted in this? The discovery of some poor woman's body dumped in the woods. By none other than a woman he never expected to see again. Pulling a fresh shirt over his head, he jogged down the stairs. The cops were on their way. He grabbed a bottle of water from the fridge and paced around the kitchen, unable to sit still. His relationship with the police had never been what anyone would call positive. Of course, he had only himself to blame for that. Himself, and the male members of his family. Breaking the law was somewhat of a family tradition among the Slater men. Despite the fact that he'd done nothing wrong—and hadn't in quite a long time—old associations were hard to break, and he wasn't looking forward to the encounter.

He wandered outside and sat on the stone front steps to wait. Even after living here four years, it was still hard to believe he owned this house. He and his younger brother Matt were probably the unlikeliest residents Sandalwood have ever had. Two young men in their twenties were hardly considered desirable neighbors in this exclusive community—especially when they were the sons of a local cleaning woman and an incarcerated drug dealer whose former family home had been a doublewide. He'd never given a damn what anyone thought of him, though, with the exception of his mom.

And, at one point in his life, Malorie Montgomery.

She'd been the most important person in the world to him, once. He'd been 18 when they met, a year older than her but heading into the same 12th grade class at the high school as she was; he was a little late getting to his senior year due to a mandatory encore attempt at freshman year. He wasn't stupid…it was just hard to do well when you didn't try. Malorie had known that about him. She'd seen things in him no one else ever had, and although he'd been with other girls before they met, he'd never loved anyone like he had loved her. And, he admitted to himself with reluctance, he had never loved anyone like that since.

But part of him had always known he wasn't good enough for her. Even without her father spelling it out for him. He'd just made the mistake of believing Mal was strong enough to endure the challenges they'd face. And the mistake of believing that she trusted in their love unconditionally. A fresh wave of betrayal burned through him, and he took a healthy swig from his water bottle. Whiskey might be a better solution, but that might look a bit strange at 10 a.m., especially when discussing a possible homicide with cops. Then again, if they had any idea of what he'd already been through this morning, they'd probably understand.

By the time the detectives pulled up in an unmarked car, followed by a patrol car also carrying a pair of officers, he was almost relieved to have the distraction. He guzzled the rest of his water before pushing himself up and striding down the walkway to meet them. Directly across the street, a face framed in curly white hair appeared in the large bay window facing out to the street. Dean sighed inwardly. Mrs. Clancy. The rumors involving the arrival of law enforcement at the Slater brothers' house would begin any moment now.

A detective climbed out of the passenger seat and approached Dean, hand extended. He was older, maybe in his forties, with salt-and-pepper hair and pockmarked skin. "Detective Charles Rayburn," he said, shaking Dean's hand with a firm grip. "If you don't mind, we'd like you to take us directly to the closest access to the area where the body is located, so the officers can begin securing the scene. Then we can return here to just ask you a few questions, before we head over to…" he checked the spiral notepad he'd pulled from his suit pocket, "Mrs. Montgomery's residence."

"It's 'Miss'." His brow furrowed. How was that his first response? And how would he know, anyway? She hadn't been wearing a ring, but she also hadn't been carrying a cell phone. All signs pointed to an intent on her part to take a quick walk with her dog—probably not an occasion she normally dressed up for. Had she been wearing any other jewelry?

Whoa. He reined himself in. What on earth was wrong with him? "I mean…I don't think she's married. She could be." An odd sensation passed through him as he realized this, and he dragged a hand through his damp hair, willing his muscles to relax. "I don't really know her. That is…we used to know each other, in high school. She just moved back. If she's married, I probably gave you the wrong last name."

Detective Rayburn gave him a strange look before glancing down to make a note in his book.

"But, sure, we can head over," he continued hurriedly. "It's not far to the access road from here, and like I mentioned on the phone, I tied pieces of material to a few trees to mark the site."

God, the way he was babbling, he was probably going to land himself at the top of their list of suspects. Detective Rayburn opened the door to the backseat, and Dean slid inside the car, greeting the detective behind the wheel. This cop was younger than his partner, with closely cropped blond hair that exposed large ears. His last name, Yarborough, rang a bell, and Dean wondered if they'd gone to school together at some point. Dean didn't really remember the majority of his classmates, especially those outside the circle of degenerates he'd hung out with. Except Cherry Jones, his mom's best friend's daughter who had been more like a sister. And Malorie, of course.

Damn it to hell. Leaning forward, he offered directions to the detectives, and they pulled away from the curb, the patrol car behind them. Then he pressed himself back into the cool vinyl seat and closed his eyes. He had a feeling now that Malorie was back, she was going to drift into his thoughts with alarming frequency, slipping through the cracks of the barricade he'd erected long ago. And he didn't like the idea of that. Not at all.

Chapter Five

The shower had not been nearly long enough to erase the stress of the day so far. But she'd figured the police were coming, and she'd raced through it, cursing her failure to notice the lack of adequate products before she stepped gratefully under the stream of hot water. An old bottle of shampoo had served as soap as well as she scrubbed off the sweat and dirt of the morning.

Her appearance after the ordeal in the woods had been just as terrifying as she'd imagined. She wiped the steam from the mirror to check if things were any better. Her face had escaped any scratches, at least, although the skin beneath her eyes was still shadowed from lack of sleep, and aside from the dark circles, the rest of her complexion seemed devoid of color. Even her lips seemed pale.

Dean used to say she was beautiful. But then, Dean was a liar. And she'd been a fool to believe him, about that or anything. Her looks were unremarkable—attractive enough, but nothing special. Everything about her was medium. She stood at 5 feet, 5-and-a-half inches. Average build, not whip thin like Julia, but not overweight either. Long brown hair that was neither a light chestnut nor a rich dark chocolate, but somewhere in between. The heavy waves hung down to the middle of her back in no particular style. Her eyes were hazel, somewhere in the mossy neighborhood between brown and green.

She located an ancient bottle of hydrogen peroxide and swiped it on her cuts, then hurriedly dressed in a pair of tan walking shorts and a bright purple top she hoped would make her appear alert and competent. Julia had sent her a text, and she responded with a suggestion to come over later, around 4:00. She wasn't about to attempt to explain everything that had happened via texts and emoticons, or even a phone call. It could wait until she could see her friend in person.

A series of rapid knocks sent Brady into a frenzy, and she snatched a hair tie from the bathroom vanity before rushing down the stairs. Pulling her damp hair into a knot, she hurried to the front hall, where Brady was standing on hind legs in order to see out the windows framing the door. "All right," she muttered, grabbing his collar as she opened the door. A pair of men in summer-weight suits greeted her, the older one eyeing Brady warily.

"Ms. Montgomery?" he asked.

"Yes."

"I'm Detective Rayburn, and this is Detective Yarborough. May we come in? We need to ask you a few questions about the incident this morning. It shouldn't take long."

"Of course." She yanked Brady back and gestured them inside. "He's fine," she said, tipping her chin toward her straining dog. "He's just excited. But I can put him in another room if you'd like."

Detective Yarborough exchanged a look with his partner, then said, "He can stay." With a slight tug on his slacks, he crouched down and ran his hand over the wavy hair around Brady's neck. Clearly, one of these men liked dogs more than the other.

"Where can we talk?" Detective Rayburn asked, ignoring Brady as he sniffed at his legs.

Malorie gestured down the hallway toward the great room, which extended the entire length of the back of the house and featured a wall of windows and a set of French doors leading to the deck. The open floor plan allowed access to the impressive space from both sides of the staircase, either via the kitchen or through a long hallway, past the downstairs bath, her father's study, and the narrow mudroom with a coat closet and an entrance to the garage. She led them down the hall, Brady's toenails clicking on the hardwood floor.

"Can I get either of you anything?" she asked, directing the question mainly to Detective Yarborough, who she favored with a smile. She much preferred people who liked dogs, and he seemed to have met Brady's approval.

The great room, while one open space, was divided into three sections: a dining table to the left, off of the kitchen, a sitting area in the middle with couches and chairs grouped to take advantage of the view, and more couches on the right-hand side facing a television above the stone fireplace. She motioned them toward the middle of the room, taking a seat on the white couch. A few crinkly black dog hairs were already stuck to the fabric, and she brushed at them with an ineffective sweep of her hand.

"No, thank you," answered Detective Rayburn, lowering himself onto a striped chair in hues of blue and beige. He pulled a notepad and pen from inside his suit. Detective Yarborough echoed his partner before taking the matching chair and producing his own notepad.

"As I said, this shouldn't take too long. We've already spoken with your friend, and he took us to the scene."

"He's not my friend," she corrected, crossing her legs. Angry welts and jagged scratches crisscrossed her skin like a bizarre crimson roadmap. She cupped her hands over her knees.

Detective Rayburn raised a bushy brow at her. "Sorry. Your neighbor, Mr. Slater. He called in the report, and gave your name as the other witness. Is that correct?"

Her foot bobbed spasmodically, and she ordered her muscles to relax. She wasn't in any trouble. "Yes, that's correct."

"Okay, can you give us your full name, with the spelling, and your permanent address?"

"Sure." She spelled her name out. "And this is my permanent address now, actually. Seven Beach Plum Drive. I was living overseas, but I just moved back. This house has been in our family for many years, but we've mostly used it as a summer residence in the past." She chewed on her lip to stop her nervous chatter.

"And why were you out in the woods this morning?"

"I was walking my dog, Brady." At the sound of his name, he peered up at her from his spot by her side.

"What time was that?"

"We left the house a little before eight, I think."

"You're familiar with the conservation area, then? Have you been there before?"

Warmth flooded her cheeks as memories of some of the things she'd done in those woods flashed through her mind. She and Dean, slipping through the trees to meet up at the clearing. Kissing beneath a canopy of leaves and stars. Clinging to each other on a bed of pine needles, their bodies aching with desire. She dropped her gaze to Brady and scratched behind his ear. "Well, not recently, since I just moved back yesterday. But we spent our summers here, and I lived here during my senior year of high school, so, yes...I've walked through there quite a bit over the years. But I've never been to the area where the body was."

Detective Rayburn glanced at his notes. "What brought you there today?"

She dipped her chin toward Brady. "My dog went after a rabbit, and he got away from me. I chased after him, and that's where I found him."

"With the body?"

"Yes. I mean, I think so. I actually didn't look at the entire body." For that, she was grateful. That kind of trauma could have devastating consequences. What she had seen was bad enough. "I saw a foot," she continued, her voice cracking with the grim words, "and I...sort of freaked out."

"It can be very distressing, that sort of thing," Detective Yarborough interjected, offering her a supportive smile. The tips of his ears turned pink as she smiled back weakly.

"It was. I screamed, and backed away, because I felt a little sick. Then I heard someone running through the woods, and Dean showed up. He heard my screams."

"What direction did he come from?"

"I'm not very good with that kind of thing, especially because at that point, I was a bit turned around. I was coming from a trail closer to the ocean, and he came from a different direction. From one of the other trails near the pond, I think. Sort of diagonal from how he led us out to the access road."

Detective Rayburn scribbled in his notebook, twisting his mouth to the side. He looked back up. "So you didn't touch the body, correct?"

"No. Like I said, I didn't even really look at it. But…my dog may have touched it. He definitely did some digging." Her stomach curled into a queasy knot. Outside the window, a seagull landed on the deck railing.

"Did Mr. Slater touch the body?"

"I don't think so. He just went over and checked, after I told him what I saw. Then he took off his shirt and ripped it into pieces to mark the area." She reached behind her head to adjust her hair, trying not to picture Dean's muscled torso. "Neither of us had a cell phone, so we headed back so we could report what we found."

"Did you see anything else unusual? At the scene, or on your way there, or on your way out of the woods?"

She cocked her head, replaying the events again in her mind. "No. Nothing." *Just the man I've tried to avoid thinking about for the last six years.*

Detective Rayburn nodded. "Okay. If you do think of anything, no matter how unimportant you might feel it is, please give me a call." He fished a business card out of his pocket. "And if you could just give us the best number to reach you should we have any additional questions, we'll let you get on with your day."

If this morning has been any indication, it should be a great one. She recited her cell phone number, accepting a business card from both detectives as they all stood. Detective Yarborough gave her a hopeful grin along with his. She couldn't tell whether he wanted to be the one she contacted about the case if she had any new information, or if he just wanted her to contact him, period. Either way, she didn't see it happening. Wrong time. Wrong girl. She'd sworn off dating after breaking it off with Harry last year. What was the point?

Closing the front door behind them, she turned and leaned back against it. Now what? It felt like several months had passed since they left the house this morning, but it was actually only a little after noon. She had four hours until Julia arrived. She could try to take a nap, but she felt too keyed up at the moment to believe she'd actually succeed in falling asleep.

Her stomach emitted a long, low growl, and she realized what she needed to do was eat. The only thing she'd had so far today was a banana before their walk. "Come on," she murmured to Brady, wandering into the kitchen. It would be slim pickings. All she had were the few items she'd stopped for on her way from the airport. And her rental car had already been too stuffed with suitcases and a dog crate—not to mention a dog—to fit in a large haul anyway.

She'd find something for lunch, then go to the store. After that, if she had time, she'd try to lie down. Rolling her shoulders back, she pulled open the fridge to see what she could find.

Chapter Six

Julia arrived a few minutes after 4:00, with homemade banana nut muffins and a bouquet of flowers. After hugs and introductions to Brady, they made their way into the kitchen, where Malorie poured them both coffee before she dropped her bombshell.

Julia sat in stunned disbelief, her coffee mug suspended in midair, her blue eyes wide. "You found *what?*"

"A body. The body of a young woman, left in the middle of the woods. It was horrible. The police were here earlier, asking me questions, which is why I asked you to come over later."

"That is awful. You should have told me earlier! I could have come over to support you." She finally took a sip of her coffee. "Jeez. Here I thought you put my visit off till the afternoon in some weird attempt to recreate your English teatime ritual over here." Her lips pursed in an apologetic half-smile. "Sorry. It's probably too soon for jokes."

Malorie shook her head forcefully, the motion reawakening the sore muscles in her neck. Tonight she needed to make sure she got sheets on the bed before she dropped from exhaustion. In London, it was already 9:00 p.m. right now. "No, no...to be honest, I could really use the laughs. But I do have a bone to pick with you first. I left something out of the story. Because I think you left out some important information when you were encouraging me to move back here."

"Uh oh." She twisted a lock of her sleek blonde hair around her finger, a nervous habit that apparently hadn't changed since high school.

"Yeah," Malorie said, her tone tinged with accusation. She folded her arms across her chest and watched Julia fidget on her stool on the other side of the kitchen island.

"Crap." Her delicate lips pressed into a thin seam as she pulled in a breath. She exhaled slowly, her tall form sinking on the stool, her shoulders slumping with guilt. "Mal, I am so sorry. What happened?"

She lifted her brows. "Guess who heard me screaming in the woods and cut his jog short to come check things out?"

Julia's mouth dropped open as her eyes went wide. "No. Seriously?"

"Why didn't you tell me he still lived in Sandalwood? A few houses away from me?" Brady stirred from his spot on the rug beneath the sink, his head lifting as the pitch of her voice rose with each word.

Julia shrugged, shaking her head rapidly, sending her dangling earrings swaying beneath her shoulder-length hair. "I don't know. While you were in England, it wasn't even on my radar. Who cares where Dean Slater lives? Our unwritten rule has pretty much been to never speak of him, and that's fine by me, after what he did to you."

"How about once you knew I was coming back?" She pinned Julia with a steady gaze. "A little heads up would have been nice."

Guilt flashed in her eyes as she looked away. "Yeah, I'm sorry about that. After what happened at your work, you were just so upset, and I didn't want to mention him and make things worse. I really thought coming home would be the best thing for you. And I'll admit, I really wanted you back here too. I was afraid that you might use him as an excuse if you knew he was still living here."

Her irritation softened a bit. It was hard to stay mad at Julia; besides, there were worse crimes than someone actually wanting her around. She sighed, letting her arms fall to her sides. "I get it. And I'd like to say knowing wouldn't have weighed into my decision, but it might have. Ugh. I can't believe I just said that. He should not have any impact on my life. At all."

"Exactly!" Julia slapped her hand on the granite countertop to punctuate her enthusiasm for Malorie's declaration. "But I swear, I was going to tell you right away. Today. Just so you could be prepared if you ran into him. How was I supposed to guess you'd accomplish that before 9 a.m.?"

A wry smile tugged at Malorie's lips as she reached for the flowers, still wrapped in their paper and cellophane. "Have you met me? That's the kind of luck I have." She opened the junk drawer to her left, which still held long-expired beach passes, faded menus, and several bits of sea glass. She'd collected it, once upon a time. Pulling out the scissors, she slit open the bouquet's wrapping and cut the rubber band at the bottom.

A swell of gratitude rose in her chest as she examined the arrangement more closely: chrysanthemums, asters, roses, and carnations in various shades of purple. Julia knew it was her favorite color. It always had been, for as long as she could remember. Her initial preference for the color was probably rooted in one of the happy memories from her childhood—of the lavender rosebushes she and her mother used to paint in the backyard of their Connecticut home, their easels side-by-side in the warm grass. The series her mother had done still hung on the walls in this house—proof that those good times actually did exist.

But the attraction to purple was solidified when her gymnastics idol, Carly Patterson, wore a sparkly violet leotard at the Athens Olympics. The posters depicting the cute all-around champion of 2004 that once plastered Mal's bedroom walls were long gone now, but the inspiration that had fueled her own passion for gymnastics during her teenage years had saved her, in many ways.

She shook her head slightly to clear the memories, returning her attention to the conversation as she snipped the ends off the flower stems.

"Well, we're going to change your luck," insisted Julia, the eternal optimist. "Starting with everything we're going to do to create Friendship Farm. I'm so excited you're here to help." She leaned forward, resting her elbows on the island. "Did I tell you we found a few promising properties?"

Friendship Farm was now Julia's passion. Her nephew, Ethan, had been diagnosed with autism at the age of two; in the five years since, it had become clear that, for him, interaction with animals led to significant therapeutic benefits. Horseback riding in particular had become a source of both comfort and communication, but the long drive to the closest therapy farm made frequent trips difficult.

Then Julia and Lauren, Ethan's mother, had inherited a large sum of money when their grandfather passed away. Julia, intent on helping her sister and unhappy with her teaching job, had come up with the ambitious plan to start their own program to give special needs children the opportunity to spend time with horses, riding and caring for them. The idea of taking on something so large in scope would dissuade many people, but not Julia. She was a force to be reckoned with once she set her mind to something, and she had some experience in this area, having grown up taking riding lessons and showing. She couldn't wait to combine her passion for horses with helping children like Ethan.

So Julia had begun looking at local horse farms for sale, setting the wheels in motion. Her hope was to launch a nonprofit charitable organization that also offered income-generating services, like boarding and lessons. If they were successful, the added bonus would be a new fulltime job for Julia, as charities were allowed to pay employees a reasonable salary.

It would be Malorie's job to set up the farm as a 501(c)(3) tax exempt nonprofit, and help wade through the murky laws involving earned income for charitable organizations. In addition, she would do the accounting and help with fundraising and grant applications.

Tackling all the financial aspects would be a large—and occasionally stressful—job, but for Malorie, it would be nothing compared to the high-pressure position she'd held in her father's business. Plus, she was thrilled her education would now be used to help children, as opposed to helping wealthy individuals become wealthier. And she'd get to work with her best friend to boot. She was thankful Julia was so adamant about having her onboard, and that she had so much confidence in her skills.

She'd met Julia when they were nine years old, and enrolled together in the summer camp offered at the Sandalwood Beach Club. They'd become fast friends, staying in touch while they were apart during the school year and slipping back into their close friendship each summer. When they outgrew camp, they transitioned to jobs at the Club, from junior camp counselors and snack bar attendants to lifeguards when they were old enough and had passed the required tests.

Julia's family was one of the few that lived in Sandalwood year round, and her parents, The Pearsons, still lived in their beautiful house overlooking the Sandalwood golf course. Julia now lived with her boyfriend Pete in an apartment near the gym he owned.

Malorie returned from the sink with a crystal vase. "You did mention all the potential properties. I can't wait to see them," she added as she slipped the stems into the water.

Julia bounced on her stool. "Me either! It's going to be amazing."

A smile pulled at Malorie's lips as her head shook in wonder. "*You're* amazing. I don't know where you get your energy."

Julia held up her mug in a mock toast. "Caffeine. And sugar," she added, turning the tray of muffins in a slow circle. She selected one and put it on her plate. "I really shouldn't eat this—I have that dinner with Pete and his family for his parents' anniversary. Are you sure you don't want to come? I'm sure they wouldn't mind."

Malorie gave her skeptical look. "They don't even know me. They might mind."

"Who cares?" Julia mumbled through a mouthful of muffin. "You can keep me from stabbing someone with a fork. And there will be cake." She wiggled her brows and licked the crumbs from her lips.

"Pass. Although it sounds truly tempting." Her smirk turned into a genuine smile. "But thanks, really. I'm just too tired to even think straight, much less carry on intelligent conversation. I've had…quite the day."

Julia nodded. "I get it. Just don't want you to be lonely."

Malorie's chest tightened. She'd realized long ago that she would be spending her life alone, for the most part. And she had decided that didn't mean she'd have to be lonely. But her heart warmed with Julia's concern. "Brady and I like our alone time," she pointed out, tilting her head toward the snoring dog. "And I can only hope to be sleeping that deeply as soon as my head hits a pillow." She circled around the island and wrapped an arm around her friend, squeezing gently as she laid her head against Julia's. "But I am so glad to be living somewhere I can see you every day now. Or every other day, maybe—I don't want you to get sick of me."

Julia laughed. "If it hasn't happened in the past 15 years, I don't think it's likely. You know I love you, Mal. Always." She stood and gestured to the French doors leading to the deck. "Let's switch to wine and enjoy the view." Striding toward the fridge, she paused, a concerned expression passing over her regal features. "Unless you don't have any wine, in which case I may be forced to reevaluate everything I just said about our friendship."

She huffed, rolling her eyes. "Please. I'm not an amateur." Crossing back toward the sink, she opened an overhead cabinet and pulled down a pair of dusty wineglasses. "Let's go." ***

An hour later, Julia left for her dinner, and Malorie considered her choices as she wandered back into the kitchen. It was 11:00 p.m. in London, and exhaustion had seeped into every cell in her body, turning her bones to lead. But she had to eat something beyond a muffin, and she hoped to stay up a little longer in order to speed the process of resetting her internal clock. After pouring a cup of dry kibbles into Brady's dish, she made a sandwich from the deli items she'd purchased. She cleaned the kitchen and, after some contemplation, made the bed in the master bedroom. This was her home for the near future; she may as well enjoy the bigger room with the nice master bathroom and the better view.

Returning to the kitchen, she eyed the wineglasses drying beside the sink. *Why not?* She normally tried to limit herself to only one glass—it was important for her health to avoid excessive alcohol. But today had been a seriously crazy day, and although her body was tired, her mind was still spinning. Two glasses over the span of several hours would hardly cause dire consequences. Pouring herself a generous glass of Chardonnay, she carried it out onto the deck, Brady by her side on his leash. She wasn't about to go on another chase. After securing the leash to the deck railing, she sunk into one of the wooden Adirondack chairs and gazed out at the ocean.

Tiny gray and white piping plovers raced across the shoreline, foraging for food as the waves retreated. Clumps of shells and drying seaweed lay in lines marking the tides. A few gulls sat farther in, resting on the sand as the breeze buffeted their feathers.

Not much had changed in six years. This stretch of beach looked exactly the same as it had that fateful day, when Dean Slater had entered her life. Right out there, in the sloping coastal dunes in front of her house. She closed her eyes, trying to block out the memories. But they came regardless, assaulting her heart in agonizing jolts.

She'd been huddled beneath the ledge created by the dunes, crying. The little cliff at her back had shielded her from the house while still allowing her to maintain a distance from the water. The repetitive slap of the shallow waves had even felt almost comforting from that far away. Almost. But her stomach had still flipped as she stared miserably at the endless expanse of ocean. With a shudder, she'd dropped her head to her knees, hugging her shins. A fresh series of violent sobs had bubbled up in her chest, and she'd allowed them to break free in staccato bursts.

It wasn't just Eric breaking up with her. She could handle that. It was everything leading up to that, all the changes she'd had to endure since the accident. And, yes, everything that had happened before the accident. Her whole damn life was a disaster.

Especially painful was the reason Eric had ended it. Not because he didn't like her anymore, or had lost interest. In the three months they'd been dating, they'd had a really good time. Perhaps she had behaved a little wildly, a little more rebellious than she normally would. Who could blame her? After what she'd been through—the complete truth of which she'd only revealed to Julia—she'd needed to act out, to push the boundaries a bit. And she'd wanted to fit in. But, in the end, she wasn't ready to abandon her own morals. Not the ones that she held because that was who she was, anyway, as opposed to those handed down by her father.

And so, when Eric had pressured her, told her that after an entire summer together, it was time to have sex, she'd balked. She wasn't ready, and she certainly didn't think she loved him. He'd given her the ultimatum, and she'd called his bluff, much to his apparent shock.

But he hadn't been bluffing, in the end. He didn't want to continue their relationship into senior year if they weren't going to "move forward" physically. Maybe he thought actually breaking up with her would change her mind. Admittedly, she'd wavered for a moment, as they argued this afternoon in his bedroom in the otherwise empty house. Adjusting to a new school senior year was going to be hard enough…she'd have Julia and some of the other kids who'd she'd hung out with during the summers, but she'd thought she would also have Eric by her side.

He drove her home when she stood her ground, pointing out that at least he was being honest. Apparently he cared for her too much to stay with her while potentially cheating on her with other girls. What a stand-up guy. If it was a last-ditch attempt to make her jealous, it hadn't worked. She'd even managed to remain dry-eyed throughout the car ride, using her years of practice at distancing herself from painful emotions.

But it *did* hurt. To be discarded in such a way brought all her doubts regarding her self-worth to the surface. A few months of therapy while she was healing from the accident had given her some insight into her fear of abandonment. And the therapist had made it pretty clear her feelings were justified. That didn't change the fact that her father wanted to put all the gossip and rumors behind them, if only to shield his family and his business from embarrassment. Once summer was just a few weeks away, he'd moved them to the Sandalwood house early. Then he'd told Malorie he was selling the Connecticut house, and that they'd live here permanently until the following summer, when if all went according to his new plan, they'd move to the United Kingdom for both her college education and his business. And to be closer to her mother, who had already been secreted away.

Lifting her head, she gulped at the salty air, trying to calm the spasms wracking her lungs. Her eyes landed on the thin gold bracelet Eric had given her last week, for no particular reason. Although now, in hindsight, she thought maybe she knew the reason. A fresh surge of anger swelled in her chest, and she pinched the clasp with trembling fingers. It dangled from her hand for a moment, glinting in the fading sun. Then she hauled her arm back and flung it into the dunes.

Crap. Immediately she regretted her impulsive act. Eric had spent money on that. What if he asked for it back? She should offer it to him, even if he didn't ask. And if he didn't want it, well, she could donate it or something. It was a pretty piece of jewelry that someone might appreciate. It didn't do anyone any good lying in the sand. In fact, it could end up harming wildlife, if it looked tantalizing enough to a bird or sea creature to eat.

With a heavy sigh, she pushed herself up, wiping her face with the back of her arm. This wasn't going to be easy. She squinted, trying to estimate how far she'd thrown the thing. So stupid. This was the last thing she felt like doing. Then again, it was better than sitting here alone, continuing to cry. And if she didn't find it now, she'd never find it.

Why did Julia's family have to go on vacation *this* week? She shook her head at her terrible luck as she began shuffling through the dunes, leaning over every few steps to examine the sand.

"Lose something?"

She spun around, a scream lodged in her throat. A guy stood behind her, his head cocked to the side. His green eyes widened at her reaction.

"Whoa." He pulled his hands from the pockets of his torn jeans, extending them in a placating gesture. "Didn't mean to scare you."

She finally released the breath she'd been holding. "You didn't," she said, rolling her shoulders back. She resisted the urge to take a step backwards. This guy looked out of place, with his tousled long hair and worn T-shirt, but he didn't appear to be an immediate threat. Besides, she wasn't far from her house. She suddenly wished her aunt, who supposedly kept an eye on her while her father was away, was actually home. It was a completely foreign sentiment. But Aunt Kay was likely hanging out in the luxurious ladies' card room in the clubhouse, as she usually did when she was here, playing bridge and putting cocktails on her father's tab.

"Clearly." A smile tugged at the corners of his mouth.

She sniffled, rubbing a knuckle beneath her eyes. "I'm just...having a rough day."

He nodded. "It looks that way. Are you all right?" His gaze traveled down her body, then back up to her face.

Her pulse skittered, and she wrapped her arms across her chest. "Yeah. It's just...life, you know?"

"I do know." His voice was leaden with solemn conviction.

It suddenly hit her. This was one of the kids from the family who'd been displaced by a fire. One of the Montgomery's neighbors up the street had offered her summer home to her cleaning lady and her sons. Aunt Kay had been grumbling about it to her father when he called to check in from London.

"Oh. Are you...were you the ones with the fire?"

A sound of assent escaped with a sigh as he shoved his hands back into his pockets. "Although I really can't take credit for starting it. That honor belongs to my brother."

Wincing, she covered her mouth with her fingers. "Oh, God," she mumbled as guilt crashed through her. Here she was, crying over the collapse of a three-month relationship. His freaking house had burned down, and his brother had started the blaze.

One muscular shoulder lifted beneath his T-shirt. "Yeah. I *told* him to quit smoking. It's not that hard. I managed it." He shook his head in disgust, pressing his full lips into a line. His features were angular, his tanned skin smooth with the exception of a thin scar on his left cheekbone.

Well. She didn't know what to say to that. From what she'd heard, they'd lost everything they owned. It made her current troubles seem ridiculously paltry in comparison. "I'm really sorry that happened," she finally managed, digging her bare toes into the sand.

"Thanks," he said with a resigned shrug. "Did you need help? It looked like you were searching for something."

"Oh. Yes. I'm looking for a bracelet. It's gold."

"Did you want some help finding it? I'm not exactly busy."

"Um...sure." Why not? He seemed nice enough. Hot, too, in a rough, dangerous way. And he probably went to her new school. Ontoquas was too small to have more than one public school system. Kids from all the economic areas in the town went to school together, unless their parents chose to send them to a private school in another town.

That had actually been her father's plan, but she had thrown a fit. Ontoquas High had a decent reputation, and Julia went there, along with most of the other kids she'd come to know over the years, who either lived in Sandalwood year-round or lived somewhere else in town and worked at the Club during the summer. The one saving grace in the whole process of changing schools her senior year was having some friends there already. In the end, she'd won that battle.

"Where were you last time you remember having it on?"

"Well, I had it on when I was sitting right over there," she said, gesturing to the little shelf of sand. "And then I took it off and threw it over here." She flattened her palm and made a wide circle, encompassing the slope of dunes and sea grass.

His eyebrows shot up, but his expression remained unchanged. "Okay." He cracked his knuckles as he surveyed the area. "We could set up sort of a grid system," he announced.

What? She nodded as though she fully understood. "Great. I'm Malorie, by the way."

He smiled. "Dean." A breeze ruffled his hair, and he ran his fingers through the dark, heavy waves. "Okay Malorie, let's see how good of an arm you have."

She laughed, and the sound startled her. Hadn't she been sobbing less than fifteen minutes ago? Her eyes still stung, and she pictured her red, swollen face with an internal grimace. Oh, well—nothing she could do about it now. Squaring her shoulders, she nodded. "Let's do it. I'm ready to hear about this grid plan."

He broke the area up into squares using rocks and driftwood, and sure enough, they found the bracelet. As they combed through the sand, they chatted. And in those waning days of summer, a fragile bond was formed, and they fell into a routine of searching each other out on the beach. With Julia away and Eric out of the picture, and work at the Club dwindling as the season came to end, Malorie found herself with countless empty hours to fill as Labor Day approached. She looked forward to the time she spent with Dean—he chased away the loneliness and helped quell her nerves about starting school.

Dean had seemed to need her just as much as she needed him. He was out of his element, devoid of almost all the possessions he'd collected over 18 years, and living in a neighborhood that really didn't want him. The family had one car, and since his mother worked days, Dean worked a late shift, bussing tables at a restaurant until close, a schedule opposite of most of his friends'.

They were each adrift in their own sea of uncertainty, and they found something to cling to in each other during those last few weeks of August. They were allowed to form a friendship in an isolated bubble, free of the constraints of their usual social circles. Then school began, and they discovered themselves in several classes together. By the time the leaves of the trees on the edge of the beach took on their initial yellow tinges, they were a couple.

Chapter Seven

He hadn't meant to kill her.

Things had gotten . . . out of control. But, damn, there'd been something incredible . . . liberating . . . about having that kind of control over another person. Over everything that happened, in that moment. *That* was power. A small, satisfied smile played across his lips as he drove down Route 28, his headlights slicing through the darkness.

So, yeah, killing her had been an accident. After he'd finished, and realized the pressure on her neck had left her not just unconscious, but dead, a moment of panic had set in. But then he'd realized he could solve this problem, easily. Confidence had replaced distress as his mind turned over the various solutions. He was once again overcome with a sense of control. He could do this. No one thought he could do anything right, but he would prove them wrong, even if he could never take the credit.

Granted, he didn't have a lot of time to think of all the possible options, driving around with a body in the front seat. He had stayed on the back roads, keeping the speedometer well below posted limits as he fought to sort out the jumbled thoughts ricocheting through his head. Sweat poured from his skin, creating puddles beneath his arms, causing his hands to slide along the wheel.

Then it hit him. He didn't need to bother with ropes and weights, or worry about waves or tides or the depth of ponds. Cape Cod was covered with huge swaths of wilderness. Isolated spots where she'd never be found. Even if she was, his DNA wasn't in any system. And dead women couldn't talk. In a way, this was less risky than letting them go after he'd raped them, which he'd done in the past.

Not that he'd ever really been worried about any of them reporting it. Junkies rarely sought out the police voluntarily. But he took a few precautions. Once he'd taken them to some lonely spot, he'd always hit them with a stun gun before zip-tying their wrists and slipping a ski mask over his face, just to be safe.

The only real challenge was timing—finding one of them hanging out alone in one of the dreary spots where druggies desperately waited to score. But that was part of the process. The excitement of hunting. Still, he hoped he'd get lucky tonight. Memories of how it had been with that last girl played out in his mind like a private porno: her eyes bulging wide with terror, her desperate struggles, her choked screams. And best of all, the way he'd come at the same time the life had been leaving her body.

He shifted in his seat, aroused. Pressure was building inside him, and he didn't want to go home frustrated. His pulse spiked as he turned down a dark street near the bus station, and he slowed down, his eyes sweeping the shadows.

He'd find his prey. He just had to be patient.

Chapter Eight

Pushing herself to stay up a little later had worked. Malorie managed to sleep until 5:00 a.m., which was reasonable. She brought Brady down the steps of the deck quickly, promising him a better walk after she'd had coffee. Once she had a steaming mug in her hand, she secured his leash to a deck railing so they could sit and watch the sun's journey above the water. Huddling in a fleece blanket, she relaxed in a chair, making a mental note to get to a pet store and buy a sturdy tie-out leash that she could keep out here. Something long enough to allow him to get down to the sandy backyard if he needed to relieve himself.

She'd been lucky enough to have a tiny little square of fenced-in space outside the bedroom of her London flat for when she didn't have the time or energy for a walk. There were no such enclosures here, and she doubted she could afford to have anything built anytime soon. She'd refused to cash her final paycheck after the fiasco at work. It was mostly a symbolic move, but it made her feel better. Until her new teaching job provided her with some checks, she'd have to live off the savings she'd amassed in the two years she'd worked at her father's company. It wasn't nothing, but it wouldn't last forever, either. Best to be frugal.

By the time they headed out for their walk, the sun had climbed higher in the sky, warming the salty air. The beach was still nearly deserted, though, this early on a weekday in June. The summer residents would begin arriving in earnest next week, in advance of the July 4th festivities.

She hesitated at the bottom of the stairs, swiveling her head from side to side. Neither direction looked especially appealing this morning. She wasn't going to avoid the woods forever, but yesterday morning's events were still too fresh in her mind. The scratches were still fresh on her skin. And a dull throb pulsed up her leg every time she put weight on her right ankle.

So, the beach it was. She'd have to pass by Dean's house, twice, but that was something she was just going to have to get used to. All she could do was hope he wasn't around.

Decision made, she toed off her sneakers. No need for shoes if she was going to stay on the beach. Praying Brady would stay focused on the dismembered crab he was sniffing for one more second, she balanced on one foot at a time to peel off her socks. The sand was still cool from the night air, and it rose between her toes in damp ridges as she crossed the sloping dunes, pulling Brady with her.

She rolled her neck, sending the heavy knot of hair she'd secured in a tie slipping downward. Pausing in front of the shuttered house of her next-door neighbor, she clamped Brady's leash handle between her knees as she fixed it. The next two houses appeared equally vacant, windows still closed up against the weather, decks empty of furniture.

She forced her attention out toward the horizon, where a narrow ledge of clouds hovered over the water as though floating on the surface. *Think peaceful thoughts*, she reminded herself. *Appreciate nature. Ignore the rest.* She blew out a breath. If only there was something slightly more distracting out there. A pod of dolphins. A diving osprey. Kayakers. Anything to keep her mind off the proximity of Dean's house.

This whole situation was really mucking up her fresh start program. It wasn't that she was going to allow him to hurt her every time their paths crossed. Yesterday had been a shock, for a number of reasons, and the renewed sense of betrayal had stung. But she could fight that—their relationship had ended long ago. Another lifetime.

Right now, it was more that she was dreading the awkwardness that would surely spring up every time they encountered one another in this small community in this small town. How was she supposed to act when she saw him? Ignore him? Effective enough, if not a little immature. But finding a body together changed things a bit. They'd already talked. Even if things were strained, they'd managed to be civil for the most part. So now what? A friendly long-distance wave if he was on the deck? A polite hello if they passed in the store?

Ugh. This was so stupid. She kicked at a tiny mound of sand in protest. Was Dean spending any time thinking about this stuff? Not likely. And the funny thing was, his behavior made it seem like *he* was mad at her. She knew why *she* was so angry; after what he'd done, she had every right to be. But he should simply be ashamed, or at least a little embarrassed. It made no sense.

Fueled by resentment, she picked up her pace. She was almost there, and she cut her gaze left without moving her head.

The deck was empty, save a pair of Adirondack chairs similar to her own, a wooden dining set, and a lounge chair. She needed to get the rest of her own outdoor furniture out of the garage when someone was available to help her. It had been difficult enough hauling the heavy chairs out of the garage and through the yard. Then, to get them up to the deck, she'd had to hoist each chair over her head and, bent at the waist, wobble up the stairs like some sort of mutant turtle.

Maybe Julia's boyfriend could help her wrestle the big circular table up there at some point. Apparently he spent a lot of time lifting weights. Or was that too much to ask someone she hadn't even met yet?

She supposed it wasn't exactly a priority, seeing as how she didn't have any upcoming plans to be entertaining out on the deck. Still, it would be nice.

A wave slipped over her foot, and her heart seized. She jumped sideways, sucking in a breath. *You're okay.* Steeling herself, she plowed forward, allowing the water to lap at her skin as it rolled onto the sand. She could handle that much. It was the thought of being submerged that caused her throat to close and her blood to chill.

She'd almost told Dean about her fear of water once, right here on this very stretch of beach, in front of the house she'd just passed. She could even remember the exact day—Labor Day, the Monday before senior year began. The unofficial end of summer. She'd been allowed to transition from lifeguarding back to her old job behind the snack counter, and she'd been let off work early as the lounge chairs around the pool emptied of all but the year-round members or the diehard seasonal residents determined to eke out the final hours of vacation. Julia had shot her a jealous scowl from her perch atop a lifeguard stand as Malorie playfully sashayed away.

Walking home along the beach, she found Dean and his brother, Matt, battling each other in a game which involved tossing bean bags into holes cut into slanted wooden platforms. She hurried back to her house to change into her bikini and grab a towel, and made it back in time to watch Dean take the win. Matt cursed, kicking at one of the bags on the sand before stomping off.

"He's not a very good loser," Dean pointed out, gulping water from a plastic bottle. "You'd think a 14-year-old would have better anger management skills." Capping the bottle, he dropped it in the sand beside his shirt.

She pulled her gaze away from the hard planes of his abdomen, her face growing warm. What was the matter with her? She worked around shirtless guys all summer. Eric had been fit enough, in a stocky, football player way. But Dean was taller and leaner than Eric, and a year older. His muscles rippled in defined curves and rigid angles with his every move.

Turning toward Matt's disappearing figure, she grasped for some appropriate words while trying to hide her flushed cheeks. "Aww. I'm sure he's dealing with a lot of guilt, after the fire. Even though it was an accident," she added hurriedly. That was what she had heard, anyway.

Dean shrugged. "He drank a few stolen beers and then fell asleep with a lit cigarette. It landed on the carpet. So, yes, it was an accident, but there was a fairly large dose of stupidity involved."

"That's awful. He's lucky to be alive."

"He's lucky our smoke detector went off."

Despite his sharp words, she could read the love he had for his brother in his expression. What must it be like, to have a sibling? Someone who shared your blood and experiences. A brother or sister to guide and protect when you were the stronger one, and to lean on when you needed support. A heavy emptiness seeped into her chest. She wished she had someone whose eyes flashed like that, with fierce loyalty and protectiveness, when they spoke about her.

No. Not just someone. *Dean.* It was Dean she wanted that kind of connection with. And, she realized with a start, not just as a friend or "like a sister". She was falling for him. Hard.

Which was absurd. She'd known him less than two weeks. She was coming off a break-up. Her father would flip out if he knew she was even hanging out with Dean.

Not to mention, she couldn't picture a world where Dean would want to be with someone like her. Guys like him surely preferred someone interesting and unpredictable. Someone whose fate was still open to exciting possibilities and unknown adventures.

"I shouldn't be too hard on him, though," Dean continued, his green eyes still dark with emotion. "I've never been an angel. And he's got even more reason to be messed up…his dad went to jail last year." Bending down, he snagged his crumpled towel and snapped the sand from it.

"*His* dad?"

He laid the wide striped towel out, motioning for her to sit. "Yeah. My dad died shortly after I was born. Brain aneurysm."

"Oh, God. I'm sorry." She lowered herself onto the towel, her pulse fluttering as he dropped down beside her.

"Thanks," he said, his voice distant as he leaned back on his palms. "It sucks, but I don't remember him at all." A moment of silence stretched between them as he stared out at the water. "My mom married Roy pretty quickly afterward. I think it was sort of a desperation thing, although she's never said it out loud."

She swallowed. "Money?"

He nodded, sitting forward and plucking a smooth rock from the sand. "I don't think she would have made it alone. And Roy adopted me. I know it's a weird thing to say, but he's really not a bad guy. Maybe not the sharpest tool in the shed, but he was decent at first." Dean tossed the rock to the side and closed one hand over his fist, hollow pops clicking as he pressed at his knuckles. "He worked construction, and he hurt his back real bad. He went on disability, and pain pills, and then he got hooked. Oxy led to heroin, and he started dealing it to support his habit. When they busted him, he was in a school zone, so that was that."

God, what was she supposed to say to that? Her heart ached for him, for his family, for everything they'd been through. It nearly rivaled her own tragic story. "That's so sad," she finally murmured. It was horribly inadequate, considering the depth of the connection she was beginning to feel toward him. But life threw crappy things at people, and sometimes the only thing you could do was acknowledge that fact.

"Yeah. On a positive note, though, I've decided to never get addicted to opioids. Hell, I even quit smoking pot."

He grinned at her, and she chuckled along with him, happy to follow his lead into lighter territory. "Silver lining," she agreed as she leaned into him a little, brushing against his bare shoulder. The contact sent a warm thrill down her arm, and suddenly her world narrowed to the feel of his skin against hers. She chastised herself internally. Here he was sharing his secrets with her, and all she could focus on was the contact between their bodies. She was in trouble.

A tiny part of her wanted to reciprocate, to reveal the skeletons in her own closet. But her father had drilled his expectations into her—she was not to discuss the accident. Hell, he'd moved them to a new town in an attempt to escape the taint of the truth.

And everyone here already knew about Dean's dad being in jail. He was only explaining the details. Still, telling her these things implied a certain level of trust, and her heart swelled with an unfamiliar ache.

He slipped his hand around the curve of her waist, and all coherent thought fled from her mind. Shivers danced up her spine as his rough palm settled against her skin.

"Let's go in," he said, his arm tightening to help propel her up. "It's so hot."

It took her a moment to process the meaning of his words. In. The water. Her lungs seized up as her throat turned to dust. Tension fired through her muscles. *Breathe.*

What now? She fought back the rising panic as she searched for the right way to handle this.

He'd gone swimming in the ocean at least a half dozen times when they'd been together, of course. Sometimes, she pretended to be dozing when he stirred from his own nap or set down his phone on the towel with a restless sigh. The two times it had been obvious she was awake, he'd simply told her he was going in the water, and accepted her nod and 'okay, I'm just going to hang out here' response.

Now he was outright inviting her to come with him, complete with the intimacy of a physical connection. Rejecting that felt like rejecting *him*, and oh, she did not want to do that. Part of her wanted to say yes, to let him lead her into the ocean, to stand beside him in the buoyant seawater, moving with the currents until their bodies touched.

But the terrifying images kept racing through her head like flashing sirens, obliterating everything else. The last thing she wanted to do was to have a panic attack in front of him. Nor did she want to experience the crushing fear that threatened to break her completely if she gave it a foothold.

Say something. The truth was not an option. Not now, when she barely knew him.

"You go ahead," she said as she leaned back, resisting his forward momentum. As his arm slipped away, she grabbed his hand and gave it a quick squeeze. "I'm not really feeling very well," she added, releasing his hand. It was an uncharacteristically bold move for her, but she didn't want him to have any doubts about how his touch made her feel.

His brow furrowed beneath a tangle of dark hair. "Are you okay?"

No. "Yeah, I just didn't sleep very well last night. I feel a little dizzy." The last part was true, anyway. She pulled in another deep breath, praying the galloping thud of her heartbeat was only audible to her.

He stood, bending to brush the sand off the towel. "Here, lie down," he instructed, motioning to the space he'd vacated.

Now she'd done it. Guilt stabbed at her as she lowered her upper body onto the towel. "I'm okay, really. Go swim. I'll watch."

"Maybe you're hungry. Should I get you something to eat?"

"I had a slice of pizza at the snack bar before I left work. I'm just going to close my eyes for a sec. See if a power nap will help."

"You sure?"

"Positive. And after that, I'm going to kick your ass in the beanbag game." She waved her hand toward the wooden platforms resting on the sand.

"Yeah, okay," he said, his voice threaded with laughter. "I've seen your range, remember? That bracelet didn't go nearly as far as you initially thought."

She stifled a giggle, shielding her eyes against the sun with her forearm. How could he calm her down so easily? And he likely had no idea what he'd done. Her pulse jumped again, but this time it was due more to his concern for her welfare than her frightening memories.

After a final check on her, he'd turned and jogged toward the ocean, never breaking stride as he plowed through the small waves and dove in. She had rolled onto her side to watch him, burrowing into his scent on the warm towel.

The growl of a motorboat broke the silence, pulling her from her ruminations. She'd reached the Club's property line, where a sign planted in the sand greeted them with the message "Members Only". Beneath that read "No Dogs Allowed". Brady sniffed at the sign post buried in the sand, then lifted his leg and peed on it.

Her face warmed even as she swallowed a chuckle, and she yanked him back toward her. "That's one way to show them how you feel," she murmured, casting a furtive glance toward the employees milling around. But no one was paying her any attention. The lifeguards were setting up for the day, dragging the tall white chairs closer to the water and wedging orange rescue boards in the sand. Other teens set up umbrellas and chairs and picked up trash washed ashore overnight.

The beach bar remained shuttered this early in the morning, but it wouldn't be long until the stools were filled with retirees and vacationers indulging in mimosas and daiquiris. Behind the bar, a stairway led up to the pool deck, where slatted lounge chairs still towered in stacks along the railing. Although it wasn't visible from her vantage point, Malorie assumed the snack bar was still over by the front entrance, opposite the locker rooms.

Maybe she'd go over to the pool one of these days, just to see what it looked like now. It wouldn't kill her to be social, either, if there was anyone there she recognized. She sighed inwardly and pulled on Brady's leash. "Come on, buddy," she called as she turned them back toward the house.

She walked faster on the way home, nodding to a fisherman casting a line into the surf. Farther down the beach, an older woman in a large hat crouched down, raking her fingers through the rocks and shells to find something worthy of the collection in the plastic cup she carried. They encountered one other dog walker, and Brady's entire rear end wagged enthusiastically as he and the golden retriever exchanged canine greetings.

After climbing the stairs to her deck, she sat on a chair and dusted her feet off, wishing she'd left a towel out to clean the damp sand off Brady's paws. She contemplated tying him up to the railing while she went inside to find one, then decided she didn't care. Once she had a permanent tie-out set up, things would be a lot easier. She'd find a pet store this morning and get one. Hopefully, they'd have one of those machines that engraved tags on the spot as well.

Crossing into the kitchen, she retrieved her phone from the island and glanced at the screen. After yesterday, she probably should have brought it with her. But one of her new goals was to find pleasure in exercise and nature without the distraction of technology. She associated her phone with her old life, which included the expectation of availability at any hour of the day. That rule no longer applied. Keeping her phone with her at all times was a stubborn habit, but she was determined to break it. So far, it hadn't been very hard over here, really—only Julia called or texted her these days.

Sure enough, the one message waiting for her was from Julia. Pouring a glass of orange juice, Malorie thumbed the image to call her back.

"Hey. I was on a walk." She headed toward the back staircase, then paused and turned back to the pantry to grab the plastic jar of peanut butter-filled pretzels. Why had she bought these things? They were her biggest weakness, and resisting them had been another one of the goals of her fresh start. But then she'd seen them at the store yesterday, and the lure of her favorite snack had been too strong.

"Wow." Julia's sleepy voice was tinged with admiration. "You've got me beat. All I've done today is lie in bed and play games on my phone." She yawned dramatically. "God, I love summer vacation."

Malorie laughed. "I think you're entitled to enjoy a few lazy mornings. It hasn't even been a week since school let out. Plus, I've been up since dawn, so I had a head start."

A murmur of agreement came across the line along with the sounds of Julia climbing out of bed. "I haven't looked at the news this morning, unless you count a quick scroll through Facebook. I didn't see anything about yesterday though. Did you hear anything? Like who the victim was?"

She shook her head into the phone as she reached the top of the stairs. "No. The cops gave me their cards and took my number, but I don't think they're obligated to keep me up to date or anything." Flipping on the light in the master bath, she assessed her reflection. Good enough to run errands? Maybe she should fix her messy hair knot.

"Yeah, you're probably right. I forgot to ask you if it was a secret or anything. Like, sometimes they withhold stuff from the press or whatever."

"They didn't say it was a secret." What they had said was that she herself wasn't entitled to any privacy, as one of the two people who had found the body. Her name was likely to show up in any news stories, along with Dean's. Great. Her lips twitched into a smile as she thought of her father's reaction to that article.

"Okay. I wasn't sure, so I didn't tell anyone last night."

Clamping the jar of pretzels between her knees, she unscrewed the blue lid and set it on the long marbled vanity. "It probably wouldn't have made the best dinner conversation during the anniversary celebration," she pointed out before popping a handful of the salty nuggets in her mouth.

Julia let out a low, one-syllable laugh. "Truth."

"How was it, anyway?" she asked around her mouthful of pretzels. "Sorry, I'm starving," she added after she swallowed. She filled a glass sitting by the sink with water and gulped it down as she listened.

"It was okay. I was kind of tired after our little happy hour, so I drove myself there and left as soon as I decided I could get away and still be polite. I said I had to get up early, which wasn't exactly true. They're all right in small doses, but Dr. and Mrs. Butler like to make little passive-aggressive digs at their kids. Apparently no one is living up to his or her potential. I didn't want to stick around to see if they'd get started on me."

"Ugh." Malorie grimaced with a mixture of sympathy and pain as she tugged the tangled hair tie from her scalp. "Owning a gym isn't good enough?"

"I guess not. I think they view it as more of a strange hobby rather than a legitimate career. They prefer his older brother's medical degree, even if he chose dermatology over orthopedics. I did try to point out how hard he's been working, though." The sound of running water hummed in the background. "Pete's there like 24/7 these days. He was headed back over after dinner, in fact."

"At night?"

"Yeah. He just made the gym a 24-hour facility a few weeks ago, and he's still a bit worried about the whole idea of members being there alone with no employees. I mean, he has cameras, and he can view the feeds on his phone, but he still shows up a lot at night just to make sure things are okay."

"That's understandable." Digging through her makeup bag, Malorie found a blush brush and swept the residue across her cheeks. Good enough for the pet store. She reached for another handful of pretzels. "So, when do I get to meet this guy who stole your heart?"

"I'm not sure I'd go that far. Living with someone is certainly a wake-up call. I'd definitely never marry someone without living with them first, that's for sure. It's one thing I've learned."

Things I'll never have to worry about, Malorie thought to herself. Out loud, she said, "Is everything okay between you two?" Guilt pricked at her as she realized she really hadn't asked about Julia's relationship during their time together yesterday. Nice.

"Yeah, yeah, it's fine. I think the excitement is just wearing off a bit, you know? Honeymoon's over and all that. It happens, I guess. Once you meet him, you can give me your opinion."

"Oh, great. No pressure." She snatched up the hair tie and worked it around her wrist. Now she just needed to locate her purse. Wandering around the master bedroom, she paused to admire the views of the ocean and the woodlands through the rear and side windows.

"Speaking of meeting, I have an idea."

"Yeah?" There. Her purse lay on the floor, beneath the nightstand next to the bed. She bent down and rifled through it for a moment, checking for her phone before realizing it was the device she was currently using to talk to Julia. Good Lord.

"How about a get-together at The Boat House on Saturday night? It could be like a little reunion. I'll put stuff out on social media, just like an open invite for anyone who's around."

"Oh." A thread of apprehension wormed its way through her. She hadn't seen these people in six years, and her final appearance hadn't exactly been graceful. Oh, well. She was bound to run into the ones who were still around sooner or later, so what harm could a planned event do? "Yeah, that sounds like fun. But let me check my calendar first," she quipped.

Julia chuckled with her. "It's not like I get out that much either these days. It'll be fun to see everyone. And it won't be packed with tourists yet, either."

"Great." Truthfully, she had no reference point on the crowds at The Boat House, or any other local drinking establishment, for that matter—she'd left before she'd been of legal age. Their partying had been relegated to unsupervised homes, deserted beaches, or bonfires in the woods.

And once she and Dean had become a couple, she'd preferred to spend weekend nights with him—when he wasn't working—curled up together on the couch, watching movies on the surprisingly small TV in Mrs. Walters' grand house. Or, if they were seeking privacy and the weather permitted, exploring each other's bodies on top of a blanket in the clearing in the woods, the moonlight painting a silver glow on their skin.

Stop. Pushing the images from her mind, she descended the stairs carefully, favoring her right ankle. Hopefully the ugly scratches crisscrossing her legs would be mostly healed by Saturday.

"Okay, then," said Julia, her words taking on the distinctive tone that indicated she was going to make something happen. "It's a plan. Now, I need to get my butt in gear and look over some of this paperwork for the farm. Maybe you could come by later to go through some of this stuff with me?"

"Sure. I'll text you later." Brady materialized in the front hallway, his dark eyes shining hopefully.

Were dogs allowed in pet stores around here? She wasn't sure. And if they weren't, it was too warm out to leave him in the car. "Sorry, buddy," she murmured to Brady, rotating the phone's receiver away from her mouth. She said goodbye to Julia and then to her dog, pulling the front door closed behind her.

Chapter Nine

The tension in Dean's body receded slightly as he watched the dark blue sedan drive by. It was the rental car he'd noticed in Malorie's driveway, and it slowed at the corner, turning onto the main road out of Sandalwood. *Good*. He'd been hoping she'd be gone when they got to her house. Or, if that wasn't possible, that she would at least stay inside and just let them get their work done. He turned from the flower bed he was edging to check on his brother's progress. Matt was with him today, and they usually worked quickly together. As long as there were no unforeseen problems, they should be finished with this property in the next fifteen minutes. Also good. Resuming his task, he guided the edger along its path, creating a fresh division between the mulch and grass.

The Montgomery property was next on their route, and during the six years he'd been working for Mr. Firenze, the house had been empty during the majority of their visits. Once Malorie and her father had moved overseas, the only person who had used the house had been Kay Montgomery, but then she had stopped coming as well. According to the grapevine, all her time spent at the beach bar had paid off, eventually resulting in marriage to a shy widower visiting friends in Sandalwood one summer. Dean had no idea where she was now. Nor did it matter. Regardless of occupancy, the grounds had to be kept up in order to comply with Sandalwood's HOA guidelines. Someone paid the invoices Firenze Landscaping sent out, and that was all that really mattered to his boss.

He sighed, grinding his teeth in frustration. Why was Malorie's sudden reappearance affecting him like this? They'd only been together for nine months, six years ago. He'd certainly been in longer relationships. Hell, he'd dated Nicole for almost two years before they'd called it quits, and running into her around town didn't bother him a bit.

There was just something different about Malorie. Part of it was the way things had ended, of course. His grip on the edger handle tightened, and he forced his fingers to relax. No use rehashing the past. They'd been kids, enamored with their defiant relationship, fueled by lust, devastated by the thought of their eventual separation. The usual teenage stuff.

He frowned. Now he was lying to himself. Despite how things had turned out, what they'd had wasn't typical. Malorie had changed him. And not because she'd tried to change him—she never had. Just being with her made him want to be a better version of himself. She'd made him believe he could have a future different from what the rest of the world envisioned for him. She'd made him believe he was worth more than what others saw.

Malorie possessed both kindness and class, not unlike the generous woman who'd opened her expensive home to his family without thinking twice. She preferred to avoid conflict, if she could, but she never hesitated to stand up for herself, or for others, if necessary. And while she led a life of privilege, she never once behaved like she was better than him. If anything, she often seemed in awe of him, which was mind-boggling. Him. A guy who grew up in a trailer park. Who failed the ninth grade. Whose stepfather was in jail for dealing heroin.

Enough. He'd made a decent life for himself so far, and he'd made good on his promise to his mother to watch out for Matt. He cut his gaze over to his brother, who was steering a stand-on lawnmower across the emerald grass in long, even rows. Two more passes and he'd be done with the front.

Cutting the power to the edger, Dean stood back and surveyed his work. The trench around the beds looked clean and sharp again. He'd already trimmed, and now this last area just needed a pass with the mower. The flower beds they'd planted last month were filling in nicely. By the 4th of July, everything should look perfect. Wiping an arm across his forehead, he crossed the yard to load the tool back into their trailer. Once the mowing was done, they just had to blow the clippings, and then they could move on to the Montgomery property.

Twenty minutes later, they were parked in front of 7 Beach Plum Drive, unloading the equipment. This was usually a quick job, since at this point the yard no longer contained any elaborate features. Trim, re-edge, mow, and blow. Hopefully, they'd be long gone before Malorie got home from work, or her appointment, or wherever she was.

His luck didn't hold out very long. He was only starting the trimming when the dark blue car rounded the little cul-de-sac in front of the house and pulled into the driveway. The dog's furry face appeared in the windows flanking the front door, the sound of his excited barks muffled by Dean's earplugs and the whine of the trimmer.

Damn it. His shoulders tightened as he cut his gaze over to the driveway. The brake lights went dark, and Malorie emerged from the car, keys in her hand. She cocked her head for a moment as she took in their presence on her property, her eyes hidden behind sunglasses. After yelling something in Brady's direction, she turned and retrieved her bags from the backseat.

Pulling in a deep breath, he returned his focus to the long blades around the mailbox post. The scent of fresh-cut grass and gasoline filled his nostrils. *Maybe she'll just go inside.* But when he lifted his gaze to check, she was walking back down the driveway toward him.

With a sigh, he switched off the string trimmer's power and removed his ear protection, settling the band around his neck. "Hey," he said, trying to keep his voice neutral. But this was exactly what he hadn't wanted to happen. The initial shock of her being back was still rattling through him, and now here she was again, only a few feet away. Close enough to touch. Close enough for him to see the little round birthmark above the arch of her right eyebrow. The faint dusting of freckles on the bridge of her nose. The seductive depression in the center of her full lower lip. A mix of emotions he couldn't even identify churned in his gut.

She lifted her sunglasses, met his eyes. "Why are you here?"

It seemed pretty self-explanatory. He waved a hand around the yard. "Because we come here every Monday. And I haven't figured out yet how to do my job telepathically." The words escaped before he could stop them, and he pressed his lips together to avoid saying anything else bordering on sarcastic or rude. He had no right to speak to a client that way, no matter who she was, or what she had done to him personally in the past.

She narrowed her eyes. "I don't know what that's supposed to mean."

"Sorry," he said, running a hand through his damp hair. He slid a glance toward Matt, who had moved closer to them, pretending not to eavesdrop as he picked up debris off the lawn. "I was just making a joke. We're here every week to keep up the yard."

"Wait. You're the landscaper my father uses?" Her brows lifted. "I find that a bit hard to believe." A fresh round of high-pitched barks emerged from the house, and she turned and called out, "Quiet! It's okay!" Brady had secured a better vantage point in one of the larger windows by climbing on some piece of furniture. His dark head poked out between white drapes like he was checking on an audience from the backstage of a play.

"Firenze Landscaping has had this account for years. Your dad was a client well before I started working here." He shot a warning look in Matt's direction.

"Hmm." Malorie's hazel eyes took on a calculating glint. But beneath the anger hardening her beautiful features, he could also see the hurt. *What was going on here?* His version of the events that summer did not seem to be lining up with her emotions, and a splinter of doubt stabbed at his chest. He needed to get to the bottom of this once and for all.

But not now, on company time. He had a schedule to keep. And he could not afford to lose this account because of personal reasons. Before he could stop himself, he reached for Malorie's arm to guide her further out of range of Matt's hearing. The moment his fingers touched her skin, a familiar jolt of chemistry burned through his blood.

He dropped his hand away as soon as he'd steered her closer to the deserted street. The flush rising on her cheeks told him she'd felt it too. Or, he was being an idiot, and it was simply the strengthening sun, beating down on their heads. God knew he was sweating.

"Look, Malorie," he said softly, lowering his head towards hers. "Your dad has no idea I work for Firenze, and whatever happened between us, it doesn't affect my job performance here. So I'm asking you not to mention it to him if you think he's still holding on to his…resentment…toward me."

She cringed slightly, as though his words were physical blows.

A string of curses floated through his mind as he processed her reaction, and guilt flickered through him. He didn't want to bring up painful topics, or put her into the awkward position of choosing sides. But he *had* to make her understand how serious this was for him. Clearing his throat, he scrubbed at his jaw with his free hand. "I'll be straight with you. Mr. Firenze has been talking about retiring, and he's considering selling the business to me. I can't lose an account we've had for twenty years right now. And if you don't care what happens to me, there's my brother to consider." He gestured toward Matt. "His girlfriend is pregnant, and they're getting married." That had been a hell of an argument in and of itself, but there was no way Dean was going to let Matt shirk his responsibilities yet again, especially after the promise he made to their mom. His nephew was going to at least get a shot at a stable life with both parents. "He needs this job," he finished.

A pained expression flashed across her face. "I never said I didn't care what happens to you, Dean. It's just...complicated."

Something inside him tightened at the sound of his name on her lips. "I know," he said, nodding in agreement. 'Complicated' was the right word. As if to prove this statement, his body took over before his mind could intercede, and his gaze swept over her, lingering on the scratches marring her otherwise-perfect legs. "How are you doing?" he asked, his tone softening. "You look rough."

"Thanks."

"No, I mean—hell." He shook his head, grimacing. "You look great. Exactly the same." The dangerous words slipped out before he could reel them back in.

Color bloomed on her cheeks again. "Thanks." This time the reply was free of sarcasm. "So do you," she added.

"What I meant was—you have a lot of scratches on your legs. It looks painful."

"Yeah. Don't you?" she asked, tipping her chin toward his legs, which were clad in khaki uniform pants as a layer of protection against flying debris.

A sudden pulse of desire settled in his groin, and he shifted his stance. Seriously, what was going on? "Yeah. I think you got the worst of it, though, chasing Brady." He gestured toward the dog's face in the window in a lame attempt to take her attention away from his lower body.

She glanced toward the house quickly, then met his eyes again, her bottom lip caught beneath her teeth. Warm air stirred between them for a few beats before she spoke again. "Well, I guess we'll both heal."

He nodded, understanding the double meaning of her words. Taking a step back, he tilted his head toward the lawn. "Okay, I should get back to work here. It shouldn't take us long at all—it's just regular maintenance." He paused. "Unless…there's anything else you want us to take care of?"

Her mouth curved in a surprised, grateful smile. "No. But thanks. I'm sure whatever you do is fine. As long as the Sandalwood yard police don't come after me, I'll be happy."

"We're on it," he said with mock gravity, offering her a crisp nod. He blew out a breath as he added, "I think we've both had our fill of police this week."

"You've got that right." She adjusted the straps of her purse, rolling her shoulder back. "Do you guys…need anything? A drink?"

Her movements pulled her shirt tight across her breasts, and he chastised himself inwardly for noticing. Forcing his gaze back to her face, he shook his head. "No, thanks, we have plenty in the truck." He jabbed a thumb toward the company vehicle parked on the street. Matt was unloading the mower, looking at him impatiently.

"Okay." She backed away toward the house. "I'll, um, see you later." She turned, striding up the driveway, her shadow following her on the cobblestones.

"You finished?" asked Matt. "We need to get going."

"Yes. I think we're finished." Something inside him sank. He switched on the trimmer power, ignoring his brother's irritated scowl.

Chapter Ten

Tonight he'd have some luck.

And if he didn't, he'd damn well create his own luck. Lately his excursions hadn't paid off, and the frustration was building. He felt like a bomb demanding to be detonated.

So he wasn't going to be patient. He was done leaving things to fate, waiting for a strung-out addict to come along. Where was the challenge in that, anyway? They willingly got into his vehicle. Sometimes, they didn't even fight during the sex if they really still thought at that point he was actually going to give them drugs when he was finished. Like it was some sort of trade.

That last girl had fought, though. Even after he'd started to choke her, she'd fought, which only made him squeeze harder. That's what she got, though. Her fault, really.

But resistance made it all the more satisfying—he had to admit that. Excitement hummed in his veins as he replayed the images from that night once again.

Turning into the deserted lot, he drove to the far end and parked near the woods. No cameras in this parking lot—or lights, for that matter. It was basically a dirt clearing in the woods that served as an entrance point to the Shining Sea Bike Path, a nearly 11-mile-long trail originating in Woods Hole and ending in North Falmouth. While stretches of the path offered spectacular views of marshes, ponds, and beaches, the majority of it cut through wooded areas. During the day, it was heavily populated with cyclists, walkers, and joggers. But right now, it was 4:00 in the morning. Completely empty.

The idea had hit him yesterday, when he'd noticed a smoking hot girl jogging. Sometimes people got their workouts in early. Ridiculously early. He knew that all too well. And in the summer, the likelihood of some over-achiever with a false sense of security hitting the trail for a pre-dawn jog was high. She'd probably be attractive, too, if exercise was that important to her. Attractive and strong.

Not stronger than him, though. Certainly not stronger than a stun gun and zip ties. He popped the glove box to get his tools, debating for a moment on the ski mask. Whether or not he needed to protect his identity depended on whether she lived or died. And that was something that would be decided in the moment. Pulling it out, he snapped the glove box closed and took a deep breath. The tang of his perspiration filled his nostrils.

He slipped out into the darkness, congratulating himself again on his plan. Even if no woman was brave enough to strap on a headlamp and start her run early, someone would come by in the early gray light of dawn, and things would still work out, as long as he was in an isolated enough spot. Stun her into silence, drag her back into the woods, and silence her again with threats. Or a fist in her face and a handkerchief in her mouth if she refused to obey.

The door shut with a click and he scanned the shadows. A small creature loped across the empty lot, its eyes glowing in the moonlight. It disappeared into the dark woods without a sound.

With a final glance around, he did the same.

Chapter Eleven

"There he is," said Julia, as a muscular man in cargo shorts and a white collared shirt wove through the clusters of people fighting for space on The Boat House deck. Julia took a step back, revealing a sliver of dark ocean beyond the railing as she made room in their circle. "Pete, this is Malorie."

Pete Butler extended a beefy hand along with an apology. "Sorry, I was on a call." He slid a cellphone into the pocket of his shorts with his other hand. "It's nice to finally meet you, Malorie. So, you're the financial wiz who's going to help Julia with her project?" He smiled broadly, revealing blindingly white teeth, but his tone seemed to carry a hint of condescension.

She bristled internally, masking her thoughts with her own smile. *He makes it sound like we're redecorating a room.* A competing inner voice reminded her to give him a break. She'd never even met the guy—how would she know if he was being patronizing? The stress of this whole reunion thing was making her extra-sensitive. She needed to relax. She intended to start a new life here, and renewing old friendships—and making new ones—was an essential part of that.

Out loud, she said, "I don't know about 'wiz', but I'm excited to help out any way I can. It's a huge undertaking," she added for good measure, pulling her fingers from his strong grip. For the most part, Pete resembled the pictures she'd seen—thick neck, square jaw, and dark blond hair, shaved in a buzz cut that highlighted his wide forehead. Full lips. In comparison to the rest of his features, his nose appeared slightly too small for his face.

His voice, however, was not the deep rumble she would have expected to emerge from his barrel chest. And tiny webs of wrinkles revealed the five years he had on them, age-wise. The photos had also failed to capture the penetrating gleam of his steel-gray eyes.

She shifted, sipping her wine as his gaze crawled over her. Was he checking her out…in front of Julia, no less? Or was she imagining things? Maybe she'd just been away from American men too long to remember social norms. Although she did have some male ex-pat friends in London who had never seemed to focus prolonged attention on her legs or breasts.

"You look familiar," Pete said, his brows drawing together. "Did you ever go to Harbor Rehab? I used to work there, years ago."

Her muscles tensed. She *had* gone to Harbor Rehab, back when her father had moved her here before senior year. The accident had occurred in the middle of March; she'd never gone back to school in Connecticut. The cast had come off her ankle before they arrived on the Cape in May, but she'd had to finish up her physical therapy sessions here. Other than Julia, she'd thought no one here knew about that. It was not a subject she wanted to discuss here, in a circle of people who had no knowledge of her past.

Julia's mouth dropped open. She appeared to be trying to come up with something to redirect the conversation, but Malorie was faster. "Oh, yes, I did go there a few times, for rehab on a broken ankle. Were you a PT?" If she'd learned one thing over the years, it was that people usually preferred to talk about themselves, if given a chance.

A muscle in his jaw twitched. "PT Assistant. I did it a few years, to see if I wanted to go for a doctorate, but physical therapy wasn't really for me." He lifted a shoulder. "At my gym, I still get to work with people trying to improve their physical fitness, and I get to be my own boss."

Malorie nodded. "Julia says you've been putting in a lot of hours."

"It's always something when you own a business." He tipped his head toward Julia. "I keep telling her to come workout so we can spend some time together, but she always has an excuse."

Julia rolled her eyes. "Yeah, I guess I don't see me flailing on the treadmill while you do paperwork as quality together time." She bumped up against him as he chuckled. "Besides, I still like horseback riding. That's my idea of fun exercise. Now that school's out, I'm hoping to get back into it," she explained to the rest of the group.

A monotonous buzz broke into their chatter, and Pete plucked his phone from his pocket. "Christ," he muttered, checking the screen. "I've got to take this. We're having AC issues." Turning away, he lifted the phone to his ear as he worked his way toward the exit to the parking lot.

Someone brushed against her, slipping an arm around her waist. Malorie turned slightly as Eric, the Sandalwood lifeguard she'd once dated, returned after making his social rounds.

"I know I said it before, but this was a great idea, Julia," he said, lifting an amber beer bottle in a toast. "We should do this every week."

Eric Hightower had changed a bit since high school. He was still good-looking in a clean-cut, preppy way, with reddish blond hair, blue eyes, and an easy smile. But his skin had taken on a ruddy cast, visible even in the dim light cast by the outdoor lights. And he'd gained a good thirty pounds.

His hand dropped down to her hip. "Let's get you a refill," he said, motioning to her wineglass. The bitter smell of hops accompanied his words. "What are you drinking?"

Angling her body away from his embrace, Malorie caught Julia's attention and rolled her eyes. Then she forced a small smile onto her face and shook her head. "I'm fine, right now, but thank you." As additional proof, she swirled the tiny pool of white wine left in her glass.

"Aww, it's a reunion! We have to celebrate." His voice, pitched over the music in the bar and amplified by alcohol, reverberated in her ear.

Had he always been such an overbearing drunk? It was hard for her to remember—she'd been partying right along with him that summer. Extricating herself from his grasp, she pretended to laugh at the conversation going on to her other side. It definitely was a reunion, he was right about that. Leave it to

Julia. The Boat House deck was packed with people they'd worked with at Sandalwood, people they'd gone to high school with, and their significant others.

That was part of the problem, at least when it came to Eric's behavior. According to the grapevine, his divorce had recently been finalized, and he was apparently either reveling in his newly single status or seeking affection to soothe his damaged ego. Or some combination of both. Either way, he was coming on a little too strong; he seemed to think their brief relationship gave them some sort of special connection. The snarky part of her wanted to ask him how Ashley, the girl he'd essentially dumped her for all those years ago, was doing, but she couldn't quite bring herself to be mean. Besides, like he'd said, this was supposed to be a celebration. She just needed to keep dodging any of his advances.

"Hey, Thompson!" Eric called to one of his former football teammates. "Come help me grab some shots! I'm buying!" A few cheers of approval went up from the various clusters comprising their large group.

She had to laugh at the enthusiasm, even as she shook her head. A large number of people were going to feel like hell tomorrow. She didn't intend to be one of them. In fact, she didn't intend to be around when Eric and Alec Thompson returned with a tray of shots. There were plenty of other people here she wanted to talk to who wouldn't make her feel like a killjoy for refusing a free shot. She caught Julia's eye and mouthed, "Bathroom?"

Julia nodded, excusing herself and following Malorie. They fought their way through the throngs of bodies on the wooden deck toward the indoor area of the waterfront bar. The night air cooled as they moved away from the crowd, the musk of cologne and alcohol giving way to the swampy scent of low tide. Next door to The Boat House, the piers of an actual marina glowed with dim safety lights. The boats nestled in their slips, masts reaching for the stars.

Inside the building, they wove through high-top tables toward the large bar forming a square against the back wall. Shelves of liquor were decorated with nautical accents, and fishing nets strung with tiny white lights draped from the ceiling.

"Oh, no," murmured Julia as they veered left toward the restrooms.

Her stomach clenched. *Bloody hell.* Dean was here.

Chapter Twelve

Of course he was here. Bloody small town. He stood by the bar, his fingers curled around a beer bottle resting on the scarred mahogany surface. A few people clustered around him, chatting.

She recognized his brother, Matt, laughing with a skimpily-dressed blonde. From a stool at the bar, another woman stared at them, her face clearly registering a mix of irritation and boredom. Judging from both her expression and her protruding belly, this was the pregnant girlfriend.

"I didn't know they'd be here," muttered Julia, touching her arm. Julia's other hand drifted higher to twist a lock of hair.

"It's fine," she answered through gritted teeth. "I see him all the time. Fate finds it hilarious, I guess." Without breaking stride, she added a fake laugh to make it look as though they were sharing a joke as they approached Dean's group.

It *was* fine, or at least it should have been. But she suddenly realized, as they closed the distance, who the woman standing next to Dean was.

Cherry.

The one person who had hated her relationship with Dean possibly as much as her father had. Cherry had resented Malorie from the start, for taking what she had believed to be hers. Never mind the fact that Dean had never had a romantic interest in Cherry—or at least, that's what he'd always told Malorie. Then, of course, he'd ditched Malorie on prom night in order to hook up with Cherry, so all those earnest claims he'd made about Cherry being "like a sister" were actually a fat lot of impressive lies.

She was still attractive, in her bold, over-the-top way. Her sleek curtain of hair gradually turned from nearly black at the crown to dark red at the ends as it fell beyond her shoulders. Heavy makeup lined her eyes and lips, and her long nails gleamed with dark plum shellac. Tiered earrings dangled from her ears, a choker with a heart pendant circled her neck, and rows of beaded bracelets and a cuff watch decorated her wrists. Her outfit—a tight denim skirt and a sleeveless black top— exposed skin glistening with a shimmery powder.

Malorie glanced at her own outfit: tailored white shorts that hit mid-thigh and a light-weight burgundy blouse. If she were to stand next to Cherry, she'd look like the no-nonsense assistant to an edgy rock star.

Thankfully, she would not be standing next to Cherry. Julia hustled them toward the bathroom, babbling something about their non-existent plans tomorrow. "Hey, guys," Julia called out as they approached, her voice upbeat and casual.

The crowd was thinner back here, so pretending not to notice them was not an option. Malorie pasted on a smile and offered a weak greeting of her own, sweeping her gaze in their direction for the barest second in an attempt to appear friendly—and unruffled—without actually making eye contact with anyone.

But Dean's eyes snagged hers, and he nodded as she passed. Some emotion she couldn't read played across his face, sending a lone butterfly flitting around her stomach. Was it regret? Longing?

She blew out a shaky breath. *Now you're really imagining things.* With a forceful yank, she pulled open the restroom door and followed Julia in.

Two hours later, Malorie had spoken to just about everyone she knew, with the obvious exception of Dean and his friends. She'd even met someone who also taught at Cape Cod Community College—the wife of a former classmate—and they'd exchanged information. She'd been forced to relate the story of finding the body more times than she would have preferred, but most people had seen her name in the paper, or heard about it from someone, and she understood the morbid curiosity surrounding such a gruesome discovery. Of course, this meant Dean's name kept coming up as well, and more than once, she had to respond that yes, she knew he was here tonight, too.

She'd nursed a second glass of wine, switched to club soda, and shared a plate of fried clam strips. When Eric came by with another round of shots, she'd fended him off, explaining she was driving. He'd slurred something about Uber before giving up and pushing the remaining glass on someone else.

Now, she was engaged in a table-top shuffleboard tournament, and she and her partner—a guy named Mason she'd worked with at the Club, who was just as hilarious as she remembered—were on a winning streak. Much to her surprise, she was having a really good time.

Julia appeared as Mason and one of their opponents began their turn from the opposite side of the table. "Pete really wants to leave," she said, watching the first two metal weights glide across the wood. "Which color are you?"

"Red." The second blue puck slid down, knocking one of theirs into the alley, and she frowned.

"Anyway, he's exhausted. He gets like zero sleep lately." Julia glanced back toward the entrance to the deck, where Pete was standing, scrolling through his phone. "Do you want to walk out with us?"

"I'll pretend I didn't hear that," said Mason from his end of the table, his tone filled with mock indignation. "We're in the middle of an epic battle here." He leaned forward, surveying his options. "One I noticed you haven't been spectating, by the way."

Julia gave him a playful smirk. "We couldn't get tickets." The clatter of a tumbling beer bottle traveled from the other side of the bar, followed by a burst of laughter.

A red puck whizzed by and tumbled off the table, into the alley. Overshot. "Cricky," Mal muttered. Turning toward Julia, she added, "Um, I think I'll stay. We're going to 21, and we only just started."

The corner of Julia's mouth scrunched up in apparent displeasure with this decision. She swept her gaze over the remainder of their group. "Make sure someone walks you out, then."

A surge of gratitude warmed her chest, even as she rolled her eyes at Julia's overprotectiveness. "I think I'll be okay."

Julia folded her arms across her chest. "There's a psycho running around killing women and dumping their bodies in the woods, remember?" One fair brow lifted, punctuating her argument.

"We don't know that," Malorie pointed out as she reached for her club soda. "It could have been an isolated incident." The final red puck settled in the two-point area, giving her team the score for that round. She lifted her glass in a victory toast. "Nice, Mason!"

Julia was not going to be deterred. "Well, a jogger disappeared in Falmouth on Wednesday, so I think we should err on the side of caution."

She *had* read about that in the news. A middle-aged woman had apparently vanished somewhere along the Shining Sea Bike Path. But no connections were being made to the victim she and Dean had found. That young woman had been identified as Jessica Cole, a 20-year-old heroin addict with no permanent address. The jogger had a steady job and no substance abuse issues, but she was apparently having the kind of marital and financial issues that occasionally prompted people to simply disappear on their own accord.

Malorie opened her mouth to note the differences, then changed her mind. Arguing with Julia—however playfully— wouldn't affect whether the two cases were related or not. It was just that she desperately needed to feel safe here. She'd left her life in the city for a fresh start in this sleepy little sanctuary. As a single woman, living alone, she was bound to be in many situations where she'd have to fend for herself. That was her reality. A destiny that could not be changed.

But just because she was prepared to be self-reliant didn't mean she couldn't accept help when it was offered. And like Julia had said, better safe than sorry. She played with the straw in her drink, nodding. "You're right. I'll make sure I leave with someone."

"She can leave with me," Eric said with a wink as he materialized by her side. His hand grazed the small of her back.

Julia leaned around Malorie to shoot him a look. "I'm trying to make sure she makes *good* choices, here, Eric."

He held up his palms in a gesture of innocence, widening his eyes for effect. "I meant, I'll walk her to her car."

"I'm sure." Julia shook her head as she pulled Malorie into a hug. "Maybe try to find someone who could actually do something in the event of an attack," she murmured in her ear.

She laughed, inhaling Julia's floral scent against the sour air of the bar. "Probably a good idea." With a final squeeze, she released Julia and clapped her hands together. "Okay, I'm up."

Julia dipped her chin toward the table in a crisp nod. "Go kick some ass." Flicking a glance in Eric's direction, she lowered her voice and added, "And don't do anything I wouldn't do."

Suppressing a giggle, she followed Julia's gaze. Eric was turned away, his head bouncing to the beat of the music as he watched two scantily clad girls dancing together. She wrinkled her nose. "Yeah, don't worry." Returning to the table, she corralled her four red weights and nodded for her opponent to take the first shot.

While the score remained close throughout the game, Malorie clinched the tournament for them with her last turn.

She let out a whoop as she rushed over to high-five Mason. She had no idea why she seemed to have a knack for this game—it wasn't like she'd hung out in the pubs in London, practicing. Maybe it was just the universe's way of balancing things out, of imbuing her with random skill at some unimportant thing to make up for her general shoddy choices and bad luck.

Or maybe she was just the most sober.

And on that note, it was probably time to go. Two glasses over four hours hadn't made her tipsy, but it had made her tired. Plus, Brady was home alone. Normally, that wouldn't be a big deal, but it was still a new house for him.

Plucking her phone from the nearby table, she checked the time. Almost midnight. "All right, guys," she said to the group. "Time for me to head out."

A few groans of protest went up, and she smiled, pleased, even if their objections were probably more about losing one more in their party than her in particular. But it *had* been a fun night. "No, I really do need to get going. We should do this again soon, though." Looping the small purse she'd brought over her shoulder, she tucked her phone in beside her wallet and keys.

Eric drained the beer in his hand and tipped the empty bottle in her direction before setting it on a table. "As promised, I'll walk you to your car." His fist covered his mouth as something between a cough and a belch escaped his chest.

She hesitated, then shrugged. Inebriated Eric would probably not make even the first cut if she were hiring a bodyguard, but all she really needed in this situation was the presence of another person. That in and of itself would be enough to deter any potential attackers, in the very unlikely scenario a serial rapist and killer really was on the loose, and was in fact currently lurking in the parking lot of The Boat House, looking for his next victim. "Okay. Thanks."

He cupped her elbow with a clammy hand as she called out her last goodbyes and propelled her across the room, toward the deck.

The outdoor area was beginning to clear out as well, and without all the bodies, the chill off the water found her easily, surrounding her like a restless spirit. Goosebumps prickled along her skin, and she shuddered.

"Cold?" Eric wrapped an arm around her as they approached the exit.

Bloody hell. She should have anticipated that. "I'm fine," she assured him. Fortunately, a set of wooden steps led down from the deck, and she was able to easily maneuver away from him in order to descend the stairs single-file.

A paved, sloping hill flanked the side of the bar and led up to the parking lot. Eric caught up with her to walk by her side again, but he kept his hands to himself. To their right, the coastal land returned to untouched wilderness, and the dark wall of woods angled down toward a small, crescent-shaped beach. Overturned rowboats dotted the sand like the shells of some prehistoric mollusks. Some were chained to the spindly trees sheltering the little cove, their exposed roots gripping the ledge of sandy soil for dear life. A public boat ramp stretched out into the dark water, and a murky, oily smell hung in the air.

Faint music drifted through the walls of the bar, competing with the crickets serenading from the woods. Eric cleared his throat as they neared the back end of the building. "I know I said it before, but you look great, Malorie. Really hot."

Her muscles tensed. "Thanks." She didn't feel she could return the sentiment, so she left it at that. The pitch of the slope grew slightly steeper as they approached the top, and her calves burned from the effort of walking uphill in wedge sandals with rigid soles.

His arm brushed against hers. "I'm glad you're home."

She made a noncommittal sound as she mulled over the last part of his statement. Was this her home? Apart from summers, she'd only lived here one year. But she guessed at this point, that was as close to a "home" as she had.

"You know, I've always thought of you as the one that got away."

Oh, no. Alarm bells jangled in the back of her head, drowning out the peaceful melody of the crickets and frogs. She didn't like where this was heading. How to respond? If she simply offered a dismissive laugh, he might take that as flirtation, especially in his emboldened state. Instead, she went with the simple truth, delivered with a teasing tone that hopefully underscored the ridiculousness of this conversation. "If I recall correctly, you didn't do a whole lot to keep me."

His head fell forward as he shook it. "I was stupid." He slowed as they reached the top of the hill. "But now we could have another chance."

Now a laugh did slip out. "I think that ship has sailed, Eric." Gesturing with her chin, she quickly added, "I'm over there." Her car sat in a row of mostly empty spaces, far from the one weak light of the parking lot. Despite Eric's nonsense, she was glad she wasn't completely alone up here. Gripping the strap of her purse, she continued toward her rental. God, she couldn't wait to get home.

Eric caught up with her in two long strides, turning to face her. "We were so good together. We could try again." His voice held a sharp edge that made the statements sound more like demands than requests.

Her pulse accelerated. She angled away from him, picking up her pace. "Eric, I know you've had a rough time lately, but this isn't a good time to talk about this." And there never would be a good time to talk about it, as far as she was concerned. She was banking on the hope he wouldn't even remember this. "Right now, I just want to get home."

They'd arrived at her car. "I could come with you," he suggested, taking another step toward her.

Unease rippled through her. She was trapped, her back pressed against the locked car door. "I'm really tired." Pulling her purse across her body, she hugged it to her stomach like some sort of flimsy shield as she fumbled with the zipper. Why hadn't she dug her keys out earlier?

"Oh, I think I can wake you up." He leaned over her, bracing his arms against the car, caging her in. A sharp, bitter mix of alcohol and cologne rolled off of him.

Panic rose in her chest. They were nowhere near the water, yet she could feel icy fingers licking her ankles. Trapped. Her throat constricted, refusing to let her protests out. *No!* She twisted her head to the side as his mouth sought hers.

He pinned her with his body, his hips grinding into hers, his lips sliding over her neck. "I promise you won't regret it," he murmured, his breath hot on her skin.

Her voice finally broke through the barrier. "Eric, stop. Please!"

He flew back suddenly, the crushing weight of his body disappearing like smoke. "Get the fuck off her," the figure behind him growled.

Chapter Thirteen

Her knees turned to liquid, and she slumped against the cool metal of the car. *Breathe.* Clutching her chest, she fought against the panic as her mind struggled to process the scene in front of her.

Dean had appeared out of nowhere, hauling Eric off of her with enough force to cause him to stumble backwards. Eric landed hard on the pavement, his loud grunt echoing through the darkness.

Dean spun toward her, his hands shooting out to grip her upper arms. "Are you all right?"

Despite the mix of terror and relief surging through her, her mind registered the heat of his fingertips against her chilled skin. A new tremor that had nothing to do with fear traveled along her arms. Swallowing hard, she managed a shaky, "Yes." She felt like a ragdoll, held up only by the strength in his hands. *Please don't let go.*

But he did, as a string of muttered curses accompanied Eric's awkward struggle to return to his feet. Dean released her, keeping his body in front of hers as he turned away.

"What the fuck is your problem, Slater?" Eric spat out, clenching his fists by his sides.

"You are my problem. She said 'stop', and you didn't. So I stopped you."

Eric's lips curled into a sneer of disbelief. He peered around Dean to try to catch her eyes as he made a scoffing sound. "Malorie, tell this asshole to crawl back into the hole he came from."

Dean's wide shoulders tensed beneath his navy T-shirt, and he shifted slightly to block Eric's view of her. "I'm going to give you one chance to go back inside. One."

Her heart skittered. Dean absolutely hated Eric. Years ago, as she and Dean had grown closer, she had told him why Eric broke up with her. She could still picture the rage glittering in his sea-green eyes as she relayed the reason their relationship had ended. And Eric had no love for Dean either, after what had happened on prom night, although Mal had later wondered whether Eric's anger truly stemmed from concern for her feelings, or if her humiliation was just a convenient excuse.

Testosterone hung in the air as the silence stretched out, and Malorie held her breath, staring at Dean's back. The muscles along his arms tightened and bunched. She really didn't want them to fight—especially over her. "Eric, you're drunk," she called out. "Just go back to the bar."

With a shrug, he dusted off the back of his shorts. "Gladly. You two are a joke." Swaying slightly, he turned and made his way back across the parking lot.

Dean muttered something under his breath, then turned toward her. A few hollow pops drifted upwards as he cracked his knuckles, the sound stirring memories of the habits she once knew so well. "So...are you really okay?" he asked.

"Yes," she said automatically, pulling a shaky hand through her hair. "Thank you." But was she okay? Her mind was spinning.

He nodded. "I'm just glad I saw you leaving."

Wait. What? Had he come out here purposely, out of concern for her safety? Once upon a time, he would have done anything to protect her. A flash of desire joined the tangle of emotions swirling through her, and suddenly, irrationally, all she wanted was his hands on her body again. Which was ridiculous. Madness. What he'd done to her back then was worse than what Eric had done. At least Eric had been up front about his intentions: no sex, no future for their relationship. Dean, on the other hand, had strung her along for months, gaining her trust, until she had slept with him. Then he had abandoned her in the most public way possible, standing her up on prom night in order to hook up with Cherry instead.

The jagged shards of betrayal that lurked inside her reawakened to stab at her heart, and she folded her arms across her chest as if she could shield herself from the pain. Her defensive wall had broken down, with everything that had just happened. She needed to shore it up, right away, before it— and she—crumbled entirely.

She met his cool gaze, lifting an eyebrow. "Not to sound ungrateful, but are you following me now?"

His features remained unchanged, but his eyes narrowed slightly. "Not as a rule, no. But after seeing the way that guy was acting all night, I just had a bad feeling when you two left together."

"So you…what?" She tilted her head, hugging herself tighter. "Hid in the shadows?"

Now his jaw hardened. "I just came out here as a precaution. For all I knew, you wanted to be with him. God knows I've seen that act before."

"What?" She chewed her lip, trying to make sense of his last sentence. Either she was too shaken up to process it, or he was making things up. Either way, this was veering out of control. All she wanted to do was go home and climb into bed, with Brady's comforting weight draped over her legs. "I don't even know what that means."

His laugh was devoid of any humor. "Right," he said, his voice glacial.

She shook her head, dropping her arms and swinging them out in exasperation. "Okay, well, if you're just going to stand there and say cryptic things, I'll be on my way." After a moment's hesitation, she added, "Shouldn't you be getting back to Cherry, anyway?"

Even in the weak glow of the sparse parking lot lights, the rigid tendons of his neck stood out. "Cherry and I aren't together. We never have been." The words came out slowly and deliberately, like stones dropping.

She huffed out a breath. "Right. I can see the way she looks at you, even from across the room."

"Maybe she feels that way about me, but that's not something I can control. She knows where I stand. Where I've always stood. We're friends."

His voice held so much conviction, she almost wanted to believe him. She searched his face in the shadows, replaying what had happened that night. She'd been ready, almost breathless in anticipation of his arrival. Her beautiful new dress hugged her body, and her heels clicked against the wood floors as she went to check her makeup in the bathroom mirror while she waited.

He'd been late. And then the texts arrived, telling her he had some emergency that he couldn't reveal. He'd told her to go on ahead to the dinner and dance with her friends, said he'd meet her there as soon as he could.

He never had. She shuddered as the memories assaulted her.

"You're cold. Let's get in the car."

Her mouth dropped open. "What?"

"You're cold. And it's late. And I think we need to talk. Do you mind giving me a ride home?"

Was he worried she couldn't make it home safely? She bristled slightly. Yes, she was still shaken, and she wasn't looking forward to the short walk from her car to the front door, but she was used to taking care of herself. Despite what had happened tonight, she didn't need his protection. Or his pity. "You don't have to make sure I get home," she assured him. "I'll be okay."

"I know, Malorie. But with everything going on, I'd feel a lot better if I see you get into the house safely. It's late, and our neighborhood is still pretty deserted."

It was true. And she couldn't pull the car into the garage, since there was a large table and a set of chairs currently parked inside. "But...what about your friends? And your car?"

He shrugged. "I see them all the time. I can just text them to let them know I've left. As for the truck, Matt and I share it, and his girlfriend Sharon has the keys at the moment. She's always the designated driver these days."

A small smile tugged at her lips. "Lucky her."

"Yeah, I'm sure she loves it." Chuckling along with her, he gestured toward the car. "So?"

What was the harm? She'd certainly be safe with him—she couldn't imagine Dean ever forcing himself on someone. Besides, he had no interest in her romantically. She nodded. "Sure, okay. But I'm driving," she added, pulling the keys from her purse and hitting the unlock button. A chirp rang out as the lights flashed.

He leaned over the driver's seat as she slid in, shooting her a skeptical look. "You *will* remember which side of the road we drive on here, right?"

She rolled her eyes. "Yes. I rarely drove over there. Didn't need to."

"I'm trusting you," he warned.

His arms were braced on the driver's side door and the car's roof, pulling the material of his shirt across his muscled chest. She dropped her gaze, tipping her chin toward the passenger seat as she pulled at the door handle. "Yeah, yeah. Just get in. Like you said, it's cold."

The engine hummed to life, and she reversed out of the space, anxiety suddenly returning as the interior lights dimmed and returned them to darkness. The quiet, enclosed space felt somehow intimate, and the distance between their bodies seemed to shrink with each passing second. How had she wound up in this position? Thankfully, the drive home would only take ten minutes.

And hadn't he said he wanted to talk? She slid a glance in his direction, trying to ignore the pulse of heat in her belly triggered by his handsome profile. *Oh, no.*

"I want to believe what you said about Cherry," she said carefully. Maybe bringing up their history wasn't the best idea, but she needed the distraction. "But...I saw you there that night. Prom. I know you were at Cherry's."

He looked at her sharply. "How do you know that?"

"My father wasn't about to let me just drive off alone, so I asked a group of people to pick me up. And one of them said they'd seen your car turning into the mobile home park. So we drove through on the way, just so I could check with my own eyes. Your car was there, right in front of Cherry's trailer."

"I see."

Her fingers tightened on the wheel. "That's all you have to say?"

"Maybe you shouldn't have been playing detective."

"Seriously?" Her voice rose, shrill in the confines of the car. She drew in a breath. "Back then, we told each other pretty much everything. Then, on the biggest night of senior year, the night that was supposed to be our special night, you go missing, and just send mysterious texts saying you can't tell me why. And then I find your car at her house. What was I supposed to think?"

"That I had my reasons, and that I would get to the dance as soon as I could."

She flipped off her high beams as they left the windy back road behind, turning onto Route 28. "And what were those reasons?"

A muscle in his jaw twitched. "I couldn't...it wasn't my place to tell you that."

"So what was I supposed to do?" She shook her head in frustration as they approached the small rotary in the center of town. Small American flags were planted in the grass around the inside of the traffic circle in preparation for the upcoming holiday. "Just be okay with that?"

He lifted a shoulder. "I guess you were supposed to trust me."

She flinched. "Yeah, well, I have trust issues, okay?"

For a long moment, only the sound of their breathing filled the car. Dean stared straight ahead, out into the darkness beyond the windshield. "I was always truthful with you, Mal. Always."

She shook her head hard enough to make her neck twinge. "I'm not putting that on you. The stuff I'm talking about happened before I even met you. Before I moved here."

"What happened?" He turned toward her, studying her profile as she slowed to allow the car in front of them to turn left.

Damn it. How was this happening? How did a simple night out turn so complicated? "I...I don't want to talk about it. It doesn't matter anymore." She pressed down on the accelerator, wishing she wasn't back on a dark, winding road with a 30-mile-per-hour speed limit. This was the longest drive in eternity.

He scrubbed at his jaw. "I thought we told each other everything, back then," he said, echoing her earlier words.

I said 'pretty much everything', she corrected internally. Out loud, she heaved a sigh. "Look, it's not something I talked about with anyone." A bolt of shame flared through her. That was a lie. She'd told Julia. But she'd just never quite trusted Dean to still love her if she told him.

"I guess we both have our secrets."

"Will you tell me now? Why you went to Cherry's instead of taking me to prom?"

He sighed. "I can't. It's still not my place to tell you." Pausing, he cracked his knuckles. "I did come to the dance, though. It was late, but I was there. I saw you leave."

Oh, no. "What do you mean you saw me leave?" She couldn't remember much about leaving the dance; only a handful of confusing images appeared when she tried. Vomiting in the ladies' room. Julia and two other girls, picking her up off the hard, cold tile of the floor. A pair of strong arms holding her upright, then hustling her outside before any of the chaperones caught on. Her father's expression when she'd stumbled in the door, makeup smeared, hair sticking to her tear-stained face.

She didn't remember the drive home at all, but she found out later who it was who had volunteered to leave the dance to take her home: Eric.

"I mean I got there in time to see you clinging to Eric. Getting into his car. And leaving with him. You couldn't even give me until ten o'clock before going home with your ex."

Bloody hell. "Dean, I was wasted. Really, really drunk. After I saw your car, before we even went into the dance, I downed a whole lot of shots of Fireball. Someone smuggled some into the dance, too. And I couldn't eat a thing, which made things worse. I was so angry and devastated, Dean. It hit me hard and before long I couldn't even walk straight. If I'd been caught, I wouldn't have graduated. Eric managed to get me out the door and drove me home."

"You were...drunk?"

"Almost unconscious, really. Some of this I heard about later. And of course my dad was home that week, for once in his life, and he found out. He grounded me and took my phone. And then a few days later, we left for London." Slowing, she flicked on her blinker and turned into the main entrance to Sandalwood. *Finally.*

"I came by that next day...to talk to you. Even though I was angry as hell at what you'd done. What I thought you'd done. Your dad told me you didn't want to see me ever again, and that you were leaving the country for good anyway. Then he reminded me how I was not, never had been, and never would be good enough for you, and explained how you'd finally seen it for yourself."

Oh, God. No. She sucked in a breath. "And you believed him?"

He shrugged, shifting in his seat. "I saw you with Eric. And you never tried to get in touch with me. You wouldn't even look in my direction at the graduation ceremony."

"Like I said, I had no phone. I was grounded. And all I could think about was how stupid I'd been."

"Stupid to drink so much?"

"Well, yes. But I meant…stupid to think you wanted anything more from me. After…well, you know."

He shook his head. "I really don't."

"It wasn't that hard to figure out. We had sex a few days before prom, and that was enough for you." Flames engulfed her face, and she was grateful for the darkness.

"Is that really what you thought of us? What you thought of me?" His voice was filled with infinite sadness.

She swallowed past the dust and the misery clogging her throat. "I guess it's what I thought of myself."

He didn't reply as she drove up the main street and made the final turn onto Beach Plum, swinging wide over to the opposite side of the deserted road and slowing to a stop in front of his house. Pale moths fluttered in the beams of the headlights, and he stared out at them, lost in thought, his mouth pressed into a hard line.

Shifting the car into park, she searched for the right words, for some sentence to break the tension, some statement to ease their stunned pain. *He had come for her that night.* At least now she understood why he had seemed so angry with her since she'd returned. And not only that, he had come to the house to talk to her, even after seeing what he thought to be her own betrayal of him. Of course her father had never told her about that.

Guilt seared her insides, and she blinked back the sting of tears. Had their disastrous breakup been all her fault, too? Had her assumption that those who loved her would eventually abandon her—helped along by her father's determination to maintain the elite Montgomery image—caused their pain?

No, she wouldn't take the blame for all of it. He was the one who had stood her up in the first place, with no explanation beyond a vague text. And he still refused to tell her what had been so important, even after all this time.

It was all just too much. And it didn't really matter, anyway, except from the standpoint that maybe they could be civil to each other in the future. No matter what the circumstances, they would have had to end things eventually. Her situation dictated that, even if she hadn't been mature enough to realize it then.

The tick of the engine as it idled brought her back to the present. Finding her voice, she managed, "Um…we're here."

He pulled his gaze from the dark pavement as if suddenly aware of their surroundings. Turning toward her, he furrowed his brow. "Why are we at my house?"

"What do you mean?" Where else did he want to be? Home with her? Treacherous, unbidden images leapt into her mind: Dean, following her through her front door, pressing her against it as they shut out the world along with the night air. Dean leading her up the stairs and into the bedroom, pulling her down into her cream-colored sheets.

"I wanted to make sure you got into your house safely, remember? I can't exactly do that if you drop me off here. I'll walk from your place."

Warmth crept up her neck. "Oh…right. Sorry." She shifted back into drive and eased the car down the road toward the little cul-de-sac. "I guess I was…distracted…by our conversation."

"Yeah," he agreed with a sigh.

She drove around the circle, a small shiver passing through her as the headlights swept over the thick black wall of woods. What had happened to that poor girl in there? Pulling into her driveway, she noted the unwelcoming darkness of her house— she'd forgotten to leave lights on when she'd left earlier in the summer twilight—and slid a grateful gaze in Dean's direction. "Thank you for making sure I got home okay."

"No problem," he said as he climbed from the car. He came around and joined her, walking beside her along the neat cobblestone walkway he and his company maintained.

She opened her mouth to tell him that she would be okay from here, that he needn't accompany her to the door. But the harsh truth was that she wanted him with her. A traitorous part of her body wanted him to stay, despite still refusing to divulge whatever secret he held with Cherry.

Her pulse skittered as they climbed the three steps up the porch. Cold metal dug into her damp palm as she clutched the keys. Inhaling, she turned to face him. "I want to say…I'm sorry for my part in what happened that night. I'm sorry I didn't believe you were coming."

He nodded, his expression cloaked in the shadows. "I'm sorry, too, for jumping to the wrong conclusion when I saw you leave with Eric."

Her hair fell forward as she looked down at the smooth wood planks of the porch. "I guess maybe we set ourselves up, putting such high expectations on a single night. One change in how things were supposed to go was enough to snowball into both of us suspecting the worst. It sounds like we both let our fear of separation and doubts about how the other person felt take control."

"Agreed."

He raised his hand slowly, and she stilled, her breath catching. His fingers hovered beneath her chin for an agonizing moment before their skin connected. Warmth spread along her jaw as he gently lifted her face upwards, forcing her to meet his gaze.

"Just so you know, Mal. Sleeping with you would never have been something I would have chosen to do only once."

Her lips parted as their eyes held, every nerve in her body longing for him. For Dean, the man she'd spent the last six years hating.

But his hand fell away, brushing her own as he gestured toward the keys clutched in her fist. "Night, then," he said, his voice low.

She didn't trust herself to speak, so she nodded, slipping the key into the lock with trembling fingers. The click of Brady's paws scrabbled down the stairs as he came to greet her, and Dean's footsteps retreated into the night.

Chapter Fourteen

She lay in the darkness, the small ribbon of light reaching through the cracked bathroom door turning her furniture into bulky shadows. The distant rhythm of waves drifted through the open windows; aside from that, the absence of noise was an eerie reminder of her isolation. Eventually, she supposed, she would get used to it—maybe even appreciate it—but for now, the silence was such a change from the 24-hour bustle of Mayfair that it registered as a distraction, like some sort of echo chamber, amplifying the violent storm of thoughts and emotions spinning through her mind.

She was never going to sleep. So many revelations had come out tonight, turning everything she'd believed for the last six years upside-down. Everything except that initial betrayal: choosing Cherry over her on prom night for some secret reason. And now, based on the combination of sincerity and sadness she'd detected in Dean tonight—in his actions, in his voice, in his touch—she was starting to develop the sinking feeling that he had a good excuse for his deception. Which would make her exactly what he thought she was: an impulsive, faithless fool, incapable of real love and trust. Incapable of being loved or trusted.

No. She had Julia. Julia knew everything about her, everything that had happened, and she still loved her, trusted her. And Malorie returned those feelings, hopefully adequately. Their friendship defied the rules fate had placed on her life.

It's not the same thing, a condescending inner voice pointed out. Sighing, she twisted beneath the sheets, flipping to the opposite side. As much as she wanted to deny it, it was true. Friendship—even one as special as they shared—was different. Julia would never have to depend on Malorie for things she might not be able to deliver. Julia wasn't considering pledging her life to Malorie, in sickness and in health, till death do them part. Julia wasn't hoping to someday leave her in charge of a successful company she'd built from nothing. If the worst happened, Julia only stood to lose a best friend.

Not that she was discounting her friendship with Julia; she was lucky to have it. And Julia was giving her the opportunity to make a real difference in the lives of children and families…a rewarding prospect that also meant her own life would have meaning. Those things were enough. They'd have to be.

Unfortunately, her body didn't seem to agree. Her skin tingled where Dean had touched her, and ached where he hadn't. Desire pulsed through her as his words repeatedly drifted through her mind: *Sleeping with you would never have been something I would have chosen to do only once.*

He hadn't been finished with her after one time, hadn't been disappointed with her performance. He hadn't conquered the rich girl's virginity, found it underwhelming, and moved on to something better.

For years, she'd tried to block out the memory of that magical night, to avoid the pain that accompanied it when she invariably searched for some clue that Dean's experience hadn't matched her own. She could only conclude that she'd been so filled with love, passion, excitement, that she'd only imagined Dean's emotions paralleled hers.

Now the memory was forcing its way back up to the surface, playing out against the backs of her eyelids as she tossed and turned. This time the pain it brought was different, bittersweet. She could remember now what it was like to make love with Dean without the accompanying taint of regret and humiliation. But she'd also have to accept that it would remain just a memory—that they could never be together, like that, again.

It had been a Wednesday in June. Three days before prom. Less than a week until their Monday graduation. From there, she'd have at most two full months with Dean before she had to leave for college in a foreign country she'd only visited once. She was still negotiating with her father on the timing of her departure—he, of course, wanted to move her there immediately. Get her acclimated, he said. She was going to push for staying put until the very last minute, even if it meant dealing with Aunt Kay all summer. It would be worth it to delay the impending devastation of their separation.

Dean had told her he had something to show her in their clearing, so she'd met him at the entrance to the trails. The sun was beginning its descent, washing the sky in brilliant gold and rose as they made their way through the woods.

"What could you possibly have to show me in the clearing?" she asked, squeezing his fingers. "Did you get me a unicorn?"

His brow creased. "Do you want a unicorn? This is the first I'm hearing of it."

She pretended to consider. "Actually, if Julia's horse is any indication, it might be a lot of work." Every time she accompanied Julia to the stable where her horse was boarded, she relearned that lesson. Usually she ended up playing with the barn cats while Julia picked the dirt from Pirate's hooves and combed tangles from his mane.

"I think they take care of themselves, really. More like a wild animal."

She nodded. "Plus, they're magic. That probably helps."

"I'm sure. They could easily conjure up some food if their caretaker forgets. But it's not a unicorn, so don't get your hopes up."

"Can you give me a clue?" She was honestly stumped; they'd been to the clearing together hundreds of times, and she couldn't imagine what he had to show her there that he couldn't show her on the beach or at his house. Anticipation hummed through her veins.

A hint of uncertainty flickered across his face as he glanced at her. "Yeah, okay. But you have to promise to tell me if you hate it."

She frowned. "I doubt I'll hate it. The only thing I hate is when you force me to run with you." Extended bouts of cardio had never been a big part of her gymnastics training, and she always felt like she was fighting to keep up when they jogged together. She got her chance to show off when they did their crunches, though. Biting her lip, she ventured another guess. "Oh, God…it's not a pair of treadmills, is it?"

Laughing, he shook his head. "Definitely not. Still…you promise?"

"Yes. Of course."

Now he looked downright uncomfortable. He released her hand as they veered off the path and began picking their way through the brambles and toppled trees. "So…you know what you decided, about prom night? What we decided, I mean."

"Yes." She knew exactly what he was talking about, and the anxiety radiating from him mingled with her own. Had something happened to change his mind?

She'd been shocked, initially, when he'd asked her to prom two months ago. It had never occurred to her that he would want to go, given his general lack of enthusiasm about school-related events. But it was a rite of passage, he'd said, and he wasn't about to let her miss it because of him. When she'd jokingly suggested she could find someone else to go with, if that was his only concern, his green eyes had flashed with jealousy and he'd kissed her hard. "You're mine. You're not going with anyone else. And I'd have to be crazy to miss a chance to see you in a hot dress and heels."

Most of his friends had decided if Dean was going, they could bring themselves to attend as well. Ontoquas was a small school, and despite the wide spectrum of income levels beyond the walls of the building, most of the students had been together on a daily basis for thirteen years. One last night to celebrate the bonds they shared wouldn't kill anybody.

As the weeks rolled by, she became increasingly sure she was ready. She knew by now what she felt for Dean was real love, not some teenage infatuation. The fact that he felt so strongly about her not missing prom only made her even more sure he felt the same. When she told him she wanted prom night to be her first time—their first time—she made it very clear it wasn't some sort of quid-pro-quo situation, and thankfully, he knew her well enough to chastise her for even suggesting he might think that. It was just that she wanted the fairytale…a magical night of beginnings and endings, an enduring celebration of being in love, being alive, and balanced on the cusp between youth and adulthood. Lace, cufflinks, flowers, dancing: it would all serve as a romantic prelude for what was to come later, when they were finally alone.

"Well, I said I'd look into a hotel room for us…take care of everything."

Ah. She *had* mentioned she didn't want her first time to be in a car. Or on Mrs. Walters' couch, with Dean's mom and brother somewhere upstairs. So maybe this was a location issue.

"Is nothing available?" she asked, gingerly stepping over a tangle of bull briar. "I could help make some calls." Ontoquas itself had only two small, single-story motels, both of which had seen better days. In a town that didn't allow fast food chains, high-rise hotels were certainly not welcome. But she had assumed they could find something suitable in a neighboring town, especially in early June, before the season officially began.

"No, it's not that. I mean, there are rooms we could get. It's just that none of them are all that nice."

"I don't need anything fancy. Just privacy."

"I know. But I was thinking about it, and the thing is…if we have to drive to Falmouth or Hyannis after the dance, and then drive back, because obviously your dad is going to expect you home, we won't have much time together."

That was true. Her father was at the Sandalwood house this week, and there was no way he would accept an 'I'm spending the night at Julia's' alibi on prom night without checking directly with Mrs. Pearson beforehand. The most she could hope for would be an extension of her curfew. He might be willing to give her an extra hour, given the special circumstances of the night. Then again, he might not, given who her prom date was.

"So, basically," he continued, "we'd be spending a lot of money on a crappy room that we'd only get to stay in for a few hours, max."

She opened her mouth to reiterate that she'd pay for it, but quickly snapped it closed. They'd had this conversation already. And she understood his insistence—the spending money she'd earned working over the summer was long gone by now. Any money that came from her would actually come from her father, and Dean had drawn a very firm line at the idea of using Russ Montgomery's money to take his daughter to a hotel. He had his own money from his restaurant job, he pointed out. But Malorie also knew he contributed quite a bit of it to help pay the bills.

They would just have to figure something else out. Her fairytale shouldn't send the Slater family to collections.

Suddenly she realized the purpose of this walk, and her heart rebounded from its slow downward spiral. How could she be so obtuse? Just because she'd pictured something a certain way in her head didn't mean that was how it had to happen, and obviously Dean had already come up with a new plan. He wanted them to come here, to their special spot, and he'd likely done something to make it even more special.

She searched the woods ahead, and sure enough, a few tiny pinpricks of light peeked through branches like sparks from the fading sun. What had he done? She picked up her pace, ignoring the thorny brambles that slapped against the bare skin of her legs. Her Keds sank into the soft earth as she stepped over a rotting log.

Clearly he knew she'd figured it out. He caught up with her, facing her as he turned to walk backwards. "If you don't like it, I can still make reservations. It's just an idea."

"I love it already," she said firmly, her voice cracking with emotion. "I'm just mad I didn't think of it first."

"Well, in your defense, we'll be dressed up. You'll be in a dress and heels. It doesn't make a trek through the woods an obvious choice."

"Turn around before you hit a tree," she instructed, rolling her eyes. "We'll work around it. I can stash some shoes by the rocks. And my dress is pretty short, so there's that." She flashed him a wicked smile.

The corners of his mouth lifted along with his brows as he made an appreciative noise. Turning back to face forward, he led them to the clearing.

It was beautiful. Hundreds of tiny white fairy lights glittered from the branches like curtains of stars. Two champagne glasses rested on a cooler topped with a white cloth. In the middle of the circle of trees, where they'd often lain on the rustic cushion of moss and pine needles, layers of feathery quilts formed a more traditional bed. Her pulse skittered at the thought about what they'd do in the soft, inviting haven he'd created.

She blinked at him, her hand pressing against the heady thumping of her heart. "How did you do this?"

"I found the lights in Mrs. Walters' shed. Must have been for a party or something...I didn't think she'd mind."

"No, I'm sure she wouldn't."

"And I borrowed the battery pack from a neighbor at the park," he added, gesturing toward a black plastic box tucked away by the base of a tree. The strings of lights culminated in a single outlet on the side.

"The blankets are from the house, too. I found them in storage—I guess maybe in case someone came during the winter." He paused, a soft pop emerging as he pressed his knuckles. "I'll set it all back up on Saturday. And get a hold of some champagne. But I'll leave the lights—those took a long time."

"I'm sure it did." Literally dozens of interconnected cords were wrapped around tree trunks and woven into branches. She shook her head slowly. "I can't believe you did this."

"I checked the forecast for the next few days, too. It's supposed to stay nice. No rain."

A ruddy tinge colored his cheeks, making the faint scar beneath his left eye stand out like a tiny crescent moon. He was worried that his efforts weren't enough, or embarrassed that it was the best he could do. Her chest tightened painfully as she searched for the right words to reassure him.

Maybe words weren't the answer. She launched herself at him, laughing as he caught her with a grunt. He held her aloft for a moment, his strong arms supporting her weight. Then he eased her down, sliding her body against his with delicious deliberation.

Nuzzling his neck, she breathed, "It's perfect." His hands traveled lower, cupping her bottom as he pulled her hips even closer. She tipped her chin up and he seized her mouth with a hungry kiss.

She clung to him, her arms wrapped around his neck, as desire flooded her system. The rush of her blood echoed in her ears, drowning out the sounds of the woods. Her legs trembled as heat grew between them, and she squeezed her thighs together. "It's perfect," she sighed as his lips moved across the curve of her jaw. "I can't wait."

"I can't either." His hands moved back up, beneath the thin cotton of her shirt, his warm palms searing the skin of her back.

I can't wait, she repeated silently, the words drifting through her hazy mind. *I can't wait one more second. I don't want to.*

Her eyelids fluttered as she glanced at the makeshift bed set up in the clearing, surrounded by tiny diamonds of light glowing in the twilight. This was the fairytale, right here, right now. She couldn't imagine a more perfect moment, and her body was demanding release. Even though she was technically a virgin, she knew exactly what his fingers could do to her...and what hers could do to him. Over the past few months, she had spent many exquisite, shuddering moments lying in his arms, under the cover of trees here in the clearing, and under the cover of a blanket on his couch, her moans pressed into his chest. And she'd eagerly explored his body in similar fashion, reveling in her ability to give him such pleasure with her hands or mouth.

She couldn't think of a single reason to wait any longer, and very soon, she was going to be beyond thinking of anything at all. They would be safe—she'd gotten herself on birth control, with Julia's help, over a month and a half ago. She had spent too much time being the responsible adult to ignore something so important, and even fairytales required some practicality. Dean already knew this, and he'd swore to her that he'd always used condoms in the past. She believed him; he would never take that kind of risk, out of respect for both the girl and for his mother. An unusually heavy burden of responsibility was something they'd both had placed on their shoulders at an early age.

His thumb grazed her nipple, and all coherent thoughts fled. A sound somewhere between a gasp and a groan escaped her lips. "Let's not wait, then," she murmured urgently. "I can't wait. One. More. Second."

He pulled his head away, breaking the kiss. "Wait. What?" Confusion flickered in his heavy-lidded eyes. "What about prom night?"

"Prom night can be our second time. Or our tenth," she added with a suggestive smile.

Moaning, he gripped her tighter, and the hard swell of his erection pressed into her belly. "You're killing me here, Mal. Are you sure?" He levered his hips back and touched his forehead to hers. Their breath mingled as their chests heaved in unison. "We've waited this long, we can wait a few more days."

"I can't. I want to be with you right now. Be with you completely. I love you. And I'm sure."

"I love you, too." The rough pads of his fingertips slid across her skin as he fanned his hands around her ribcage. He cleared his throat. "But I didn't bring you here to push you into anything…"

"I would never think that. I want to come here on prom night, too…and it will still be special. Because it's *us*. But right now, this is what I want. I want *you*." She slipped her arms from around his neck and held them over her head, keeping her gaze locked with his.

He licked his lips and nodded, watching her face as his fingers drifted to the hem of her shirt. Slowly, he lifted it up and off, dropping it to the forest floor. Then he reached back and pulled his own shirt over his head. It joined hers with a soft rustle of pine needles.

He was so beautiful. Ridges of muscles formed hard planes across his chest; his shoulders and arms were equally rounded and chiseled. No fancy gym equipment had helped sculpt his physique—there was no money in the tight family budget for that. Instead, he managed to stay in shape with simple exercises that required nothing but willpower and a little bit of space and creativity: sit-ups, pull-ups, and push-ups, sometimes with her lying on his back to add more weight. And running; he loved to run. It was something he'd always done, a means to escape the stress of his life…and all the hours and miles had paid off not just mentally, but physically as well.

Her fingers curled around the waistband of his shorts, and he stilled, his stomach tightening. As she worked at the button, he plunged his hands into her hair, holding her head and kissing her deeply. He walked her backwards, toward the blankets, his lips never leaving hers. The woods were silent, as though time had stopped in reverence for the enormity of what they were about to do. Tiny tremors crackled through her nerves as they sank down onto the fluffy comforter.

"Are you okay?" he whispered, caressing her back as they kneeled across from each other.

She nodded, wrapping her arms around his neck. He could tell she was nervous, and she didn't want him to think it had anything to do with sudden doubts. It was only a slight fear of the unknown; anxiety over finally taking this step. That she wanted it to be with Dean, right now, was a certainty.

Relax. Although she had no basis for comparison, to her it seemed everything they'd done up to this point was just as intimate as what they were about to do. But the wild horses galloping through her chest told her otherwise. This was different. This was joining together, experiencing everything at the same time. Giving and receiving pleasure simultaneously, rather than taking turns.

Would she measure up? That was the greater fear, the one that lurked deep inside, waiting for any opportunity to unsheathe its claws and tear into her soul.

"I'm okay," she assured him, nuzzling his ear. "I just don't want to…disappoint you. You know, as a first timer and all." She lifted her shoulders in a small shrug, keeping her gaze averted.

"Hey." He gathered her hair in one fist and tugged gently, forcing her to lift her head. "You could never disappointment me. Not ever. You're perfect."

Hardly. But joy mixed with another surge of desire at his words. "So are you," she murmured, trailing kisses along his jaw. She shivered with anticipation as he unhooked her bra and pulled it from her shoulders.

The remainder of their clothes were torn off with renewed urgency, and she lay beneath him on the blankets, reveling in the solid weight of his body anchoring her to the earth. She was aching with need, and she moaned into his neck as his fingers worked their magic.

He was teasing her, now, bringing her close to that shuddering moment of release, then slowing down to caress her gently. It was exquisite torture, and she couldn't bear it for one more second.

"Please," she managed, bucking her hips. One of her legs was restrained, pinned down under his, inhibiting her movements. Every muscle shook. "Please. I want you so badly."

He brushed his nose against hers. "You're sure? I'm so afraid of hurting you." His voice was rough, and she couldn't imagine how he was maintaining control.

"You won't," she promised, although she had no idea if he would or wouldn't. And at this point, she didn't care.

"Okay." He paused, kissed her tenderly. "I just want you to know…in a way, this is sort of a first time for me too. First time with someone I love."

Her throat swelled with emotion, and she clung to him, her heart thudding against his own. He pushed himself into her slowly, watching her face with his dark green eyes. When the pain came, she winced slightly, but it vanished almost instantly, replaced by indescribable pleasure. *This* was what it felt like to truly be one with the person you loved.

He rocked inside her, and she dug her nails into his back, moving with his rhythm. She wanted this to last forever, yet she knew instinctively they were both close to the edge. Waves of pressure built, deep and demanding, until the final crescendo caused her to cry out. He followed her, groaning into her hair as his body tensed and stilled.

The powerful sensations eventually subsided, and she dragged her eyes open with a soft sigh. The fairy lights danced in the edges of her vision. "That was…incredible."

"Yeah," he agreed, shifting slightly to his side and pulling her with him.

They remained joined, locked together in an embrace, their hearts beating in unison, as the light drained from the sky and the shadows fell around them.

Chapter Fifteen

Dean woke Sunday morning with the echo of a headache and the vague, restless tug of unfinished business. Malorie's image popped into his mind, and he sighed, scrubbing his face. What a bizarre night. Stretching, he turned towards the clock. Almost nine a.m. Well, that was something, at least. He couldn't remember the last time he'd slept so late. It was probably a ploy by his subconscious, a stealth attempt to avoid thinking about what he'd learned last night.

Because it changed the narrative of the story he'd told himself for the past six years. Malorie hadn't given up on him when he didn't show immediately. She hadn't left for a tryst with the ex who had once discarded her like an old toy. The guy who Dean hated with every cell in his body.

Guilt knotted his stomach, and he reminded himself that he had tried, back then. Despite what he'd seen, despite the jagged cracks in his heart, he'd tried to call—and text—her. When that resulted in radio silence, he'd tucked away his pride and gone over to her house.

He'd knocked on her front door that afternoon, knowing full well he'd likely be greeted by Malorie's father, a man who had made his distaste for Dean clear in their few encounters. Luckily, he was often away on business trips, and Dean spent almost no time at the Montgomery house. But this time there was no choice; he had to see her, had to straighten this out.

Mr. Montgomery's face was already twisted into a scowl when he opened the door. "Yes?"

The clipped, one-word greeting, intoned in a voice dripping with cool dismissiveness, made Dean feel like a door-to-door salesman who'd blatantly ignored a "no solicitation" sign. Despite whatever had happened last night, he deserved the respect due to someone who had been an important part of his daughter's life for nine months now. Squaring his shoulders, he meet Mr. Montgomery's steely gaze. "Hi, Mr. Montgomery. I was hoping to talk to Malorie."

"Were you?" His eyes narrowed. The gold-green shade of his irises had been passed down to Malorie, but while her hazel eyes shone with warmth and humor, his were cold and hard.

He kept his hand on the doorknob as he studied Dean, blocking the entryway. "Let me get this straight. You failed to pick my daughter up last night, refusing to come to the door and escort her to her senior prom like a gentleman. It's my understanding you then failed to show up at all, after inviting her as your date several months ago. And now you want to talk to her?"

A mix of anger and guilt burned through Dean, and he fought to remain outwardly calm. This man had no idea what he'd been through last night. Relaxing his clenched fists, he nodded. "Yes. Please."

A flicker of disbelief passed over the older man's strong features. "I'm sorry to disappoint you," he finally responded, not sounding sorry at all. "But she doesn't want to speak with you. Not today, and not in the future. Let me be clear. You are not, have never been, and never will be a suitable companion for her. Romantic or otherwise. The sooner you come to terms with that, the better, because she certainly has. We'll be leaving for London soon, and she has a lot to do to get ready, so we'd both appreciate it if you'd leave us to it."

Then he'd shut the door in Dean's face.

Grimacing at the memory, Dean climbed out of bed. He'd been so willing to believe those words, back then, because he'd known in his heart that they were true. Malorie was going places, literally: to Europe, to college. He was going nowhere. What right did he have to try to hold on to her? Those dark realities, combined with Malorie's actions and her father's lecture, had been enough to convince him that he had no choice but to let go.

But if Malorie was telling the truth now, she hadn't decided her father was right about their relationship. And she'd never even known Dean had come to the house to look for her. Hell, her father had probably even deleted all his texts and calls from her phone before he returned it—or purchased an entirely new phone, with a new number, once they'd arrived in London.

Thoughts ricocheted through his head like a hailstorm, adding to the dull ache in his temples. In the bathroom, he cranked the shower faucet as hot as it would go and stepped under the scalding spray, turning so the heat pulsed down onto the back of his neck.

What now? He just kept picturing Malorie, standing on the porch last night, appearing both fragile and fierce in the surrounding shadows. And beautiful. So, so beautiful...just as she'd always been. He'd wanted to kiss her.

And that was a problem, because despite all the revelations, nothing had really changed. Even if they did somehow find their way back to each other, even if she could decide to trust him again...he still would never be good enough for her. What did he have to offer? The last name of a convicted felon. A level of formal education far below her own. A job that would never provide the kind of wealth she was used to, even if he did manage to buy the business. A house that someone had handed to him, with property taxes he could barely pay. A moody younger brother who Dean was now responsible for—a brother who now resented Dean for pushing him to do the right thing and offer to marry Sharon when she decided to have the baby. It appeared they'd all be living here, together, once the ceremony took place, and Dean fully expected to do his share of childcare once his nephew arrived. He'd promised his mother he'd take care of the family, and that's what he intended to do.

Then, of course, there was Malorie's own family. He couldn't even imagine the rage her father would go into if they got back together. He'd probably disown her.

Jesus Christ, what was wrong with him? There was no indication Malorie had any interest in him; for all he knew, she had someone back in London. Here he was deliberating a future with her when they were only barely back on speaking terms. Just because he'd wanted to kiss her, to hustle her upstairs and reacquaint himself with every inch of her, did not mean she felt the same. Snatching up the shampoo, he squeezed some into his palm.

And what if he had kissed her, and she'd reciprocated? What if they had ended up in bed together? Or if they did, sometime in the future? Those things happened between consenting adults, and it didn't have to mean anything. So why was he even dwelling on what he could—and couldn't—offer her in some imaginary future relationship? God, his thought process was seriously messed up. But not entirely surprising, either, because this was how it was when it came to Malorie. She had a hold on him. He knew, without a doubt, that if they started down that road, he'd never be able to get enough of her. The idea that she could have thought, after they'd had sex, that he'd felt it lacking and decided to move on…it tore at his heart.

He scrubbed his scalp, as though he might be able to rid his brain of this whole subject if he used enough force. It was his day off, and he needed to focus on all the crap he needed to get done. He'd run later, after this headache had hopefully faded and the cooler air forecasted this evening arrived. In the meantime, he had to get the food shopping for the week done, and change the oil in the truck. It could probably stand to be washed, too.

When he got downstairs, he was pleasantly surprised to find coffee already brewed. As he poured a cup, he heard movement in the living room, and he carried his cup around the corner and into the large space that, like in many of the beachfront houses, stretched the full length of the back of the house to provide an uninterrupted view of the water.

Sharon was lying on one of the couches, one hand on her swollen belly. Her short, dark hair stood out at awkward angles, highlighting the pallor of her face. Dean had no idea what time she and Matt had returned home last night, but apparently she had spent the night. Hopefully not on the couch.

"Morning," he said, sitting down across from her. His brows tightened as he watched her grimace. "You okay?"

She closed her eyes and drew in a slow breath. "I think so," she replied weakly, turning her head toward him. "Cramps."

His pulse accelerated and he leaned forward, the coffee sloshing dangerously in his mug. He quickly did the calculations in his head. Seven months…way too early. "How bad?"

She exhaled, a combination of a moan and a sigh. "I'm sure it's just some Braxton Hicks contractions. But it's making me feel kind of nauseous."

"You want me to call the doctor?" *Where the hell was Matt?* He should be down here, attending to the mother of his child. A ripple of anger coursed through him.

"No, no. I just need to…rest for a sec."

The doorbell rang, and they exchanged frowns as Dean stood. "Are you expecting anyone?" he asked.

She shook her head wordlessly, returning her focus to whatever was going on beneath her baggy maternity shirt.

Malorie. He strode down the hall, struggling against the tide of conflicting emotions accompanying this assumption. Good Lord, he'd managed to keep her off his mind for less than five minutes since he'd woken up, even with Sharon lying on his couch with Braxton whatever contractions. He rolled his eyes in disgust. He needed help.

It probably wasn't even her. And yet, a tiny part of him was forced to admit he *wanted* it to be. And that was pure self-torture, because he'd already been through the reasons this morning why they couldn't be anything to each other but neighbors.

But what if she was here because something was wrong? His heartrate spiked again, and he flung open the front door without even looking through the side windows.

Not Malorie. The woman standing on the porch was older, although her lax, nicotine-stained skin made it difficult to guess her precise age. She had kind but weary eyes, and her dishwater-colored curls clung tightly to her scalp.

He was quite sure he'd never seen her before. "Um…can I help you?"

She shifted uncomfortably. "I'm sorry to bother you. I'm looking for…Dean Slater?"

He automatically went on the defensive, even though he was quite sure he hadn't done anything illegal lately. Old habits died hard. *Relax.* "You've found him," he said, scanning the front yard. A beat-up compact was parked on the street. The smell of cigarette smoke drifted into the house along with the heat.

"I'm Ruth Cole." She paused a beat, then added, "Jessica Cole's mother."

It took him a second more, and then the recognition slammed into him. *The dead girl's mother.* What on earth was she doing here? He suddenly pictured his nearly full mug of coffee, sitting on the table by Sharon. Too much was happening this morning before he'd even put some caffeine into his system. Not to mention food.

"Oh," he managed. Brilliant.

She drew in a shaky breath. "I know I shouldn't have just shown up, but your name was in the paper as having...found Jess, and I just wanted to talk to you about it. To you and, um, Malorie Montgomery."

"Malorie's not here," he said stupidly. *God.*

"Oh, I know...I looked up her address too." She offered a scrap of paper in her hand as evidence. "She lives at number seven?" Her thin eyebrows went up, looking for confirmation.

A surge of protectiveness rushed through him. He did not want this woman confronting Mal while she was alone. Ruth Cole looked harmless enough, but grief made people do strange things. Did she think they had something to do with it? And, really, he had no proof this woman was who she said she was. For all he knew, she could be some crime junkie, seeking attention.

If she was, she was a good actress. Tears now glistened in her pale blue eyes. "I only want a minute of your time. Really. Please," she added, twisting the paper in her hands. "She was my daughter." Her voice broke on the last sentence.

Shit. He turned back and looked down the hall, even though he couldn't see much of the great room from his viewpoint. But Sharon was probably still on the couch, feeling sick and in pain, and she didn't need this stress. Nor did he want to kick her out of the room while she was resting.

And he didn't want this woman taking Malorie by surprise, either. Knowing how kind Mal was, she'd let her in immediately, most likely. He made a snap decision.

"Okay, Ms.—ah—Cole. I can try to answer any questions you have, but my…sister-in-law…is pregnant and not feeling well, so I'd prefer not to disturb her any further. If you don't mind waiting out here for a moment, I'll check on her, and then we can go over to Malorie's. Together." That would work. And whatever this woman wanted, it would save her time, too, talking to both of them at the same time. Kill two birds with one stone. *God.* Poor choice of words, even for an internal dialog. He grimaced inwardly as he waited for her response.

Ms. Cole nodded, taking a step back as her gaze dropped to her feet.

A pang of guilt pricked at him as he shut the door on her and checked the lock on the knob, but his family's safety came first. And as soon as he checked on Sharon, he was going upstairs to wake Matt the hell up.

He rushed back to Sharon, cracking his knuckles savagely on his way down the hall. She was still on the couch, but now she had a plastic food storage bowl perched on her chest. *Uh oh.* "How are you doing?" he asked softly.

Her eyes fluttered open. "Okay. I just…I got up to go to the bathroom, and there was…a little blood. Sorry to be graphic." She closed her eyes again. "It just made me worried. And dizzy. I brought this just in case I have to throw up," she added, tipping her chin toward the bowl.

He was completely out of his league. "Is any of this…normal?"

"I think it is, yes. I'm probably overreacting, but it's hard when you don't know what to expect. Scary."

"I'm sure it is. I still think you should maybe call the doctor, if only for peace of mind. Or at least have Matt look this stuff up. I have to run out, so I'm going to go get him."

She chewed her lip. "Oh, no…that's okay. I'll be fine. It's his only day to sleep in."

"Too bad," said Dean, already headed for the stairs.

He'd given over the master bedroom to Matt when Sharon got pregnant, even though she hadn't officially moved in yet. Dean had no reason to believe they were going to live anywhere else but here. Sharon worked as a waitress, and her maternity leave would be unpaid. Once the baby was born, of course, it was going to become even more difficult for her to take on shifts. And Matt's wages from Firenze were not going to be enough to support all three of them and pay for their own place. Babies needed lots of things.

So Dean had resigned himself to their future living situation already, and it really didn't bother him. He could count the things he knew about babies on one hand, but he was willing to learn. He'd need to know this stuff someday, for his own family. He just wished their own mother hadn't been cheated out of meeting her grandchildren. It had been her biggest source of anguish at the end.

Dean pounded on the master bedroom door twice with the bottom of his fist, then opened the door before waiting for an answer. "Get up."

The air in the room was heavy with beer and perspiration, and Matt lay in the middle of the bed with the sheets pulled up to his waist. With a groan, he flipped away from the door and buried his face in his pillow. "Fuck off," came his muffled reply.

Anger flared, and Dean fought to control the impulse to grab the keyring off the dresser and hurl it at his brother's head. Matt seemed to be turning into a bigger asshole by the day, but Dean was trying to cut him some slack. He knew his brother was not ready for the responsibilities coming his way. But, that was life, and Matt had made his own bed, so to speak.

"Get up now," he reiterated in a firm voice, his fingernails digging into his palms. "Your girlfriend isn't feeling well."

"What am I supposed to do about it?" he grumbled. But he was getting up. He dragged his hands through his messy hair, muttering curses.

"Hurry up. I have to go out, I'll be back soon," he called over his shoulder as he hurtled back down the stairs.

Ruth Cole was wandering along the walkway, smoking a cigarette. Her floral shirt and shapeless shorts were both too large, as though she had lost an alarming amount of weight in the last week. She looked broken, swallowed by grief. And yet she'd forced herself to come. A wave of pity tugged at him. He couldn't imagine what it must be like for a parent to lose a child.

A flicker of motion caught his attention, and he sighed. His nosy neighbor was at it again, peering through the curtains. Great.

Ruth startled and turned as the door swung shut. "Sorry," she said, glancing down at the cigarette in her hand.

He dismissed her apology with a wave. "No problem." Shooting a glare at his neighbor that she most likely couldn't see, he joined Ruth on the walkway. The sky was overcast yet somehow still bright, the thin blanket of clouds holding the humidity in like the lid of a steaming pot. Glancing down the street, he nodded his chin toward the wooded circle at the end. "Malorie's house is only a short walk, if you're okay with that."

She drew in a lungful of smoke and nodded. "That'd be fine," she said, exhaling a gray stream into the heavy air.

Dean pulled his phone from the pocket of his gym shorts as they walked in silence. He wished he could give Mal some notice they were on their way over, but he didn't have her number. With an inward sigh, he put it away. There wasn't much else he could do. Ruth Cole had been planning on showing up at Malorie's door unexpectedly, with or without him. At least this way, he'd be there to support her through whatever was coming.

Chapter Sixteen

Two thumps rapped on the door, sending Brady scrabbling down the hall and her handful of peanut butter pretzels flying into the air. Bloody hell. Was it normal to be this startled by a simple knock on the door? Her heart hammered as she jumped off the couch, her book and blanket sliding to the floor.

"Coming!" she called out, doubtful her voice could be heard over Brady's barking. She tossed everything back on the couch and plucked the pretzel nuggets she could see off the floor. Brady would find the rest. Hesitating for one second with her hands full, she shrugged and dumped the retrieved snacks back into the big plastic jug. Her floor was clean enough.

She hurried down the hallway, glancing in the mirror hanging on the wall along the way. Good Lord. Her hair was an enormous mess of tangled waves that could potentially hide a flock of small birds. Oh well, nothing to be done about it now. It was probably Julia anyway, stopping by for an impromptu visit. Maybe with a fancy caffeinated drink that more closely resembled a sundae than a coffee. That would go nicely with what she'd had for breakfast so far.

"All right, all right," she said, pushing Brady out of the way with her knee. She peered out the window and her pulse accelerated again.   Dean.   With some woman she didn't recognize.

This was…unexpected. She dodged out of view, dragging her hands through her hair and settling its weight behind her shoulders. That was the best she was going to be able to do without forcing her visitors to wait any longer. Then she sucked in a steadying breath, latched on to Brady's collar, and opened the door.

"Hi. Sorry." She nodded toward Brady, who was straining to greet their guests. "Um, come in, if you don't mind him. He's friendly," she added, searching the woman's face for signs of fear.

The woman appeared slightly uncomfortable, but her expression seemed to indicate that was more about the unannounced visit than the prospect of encountering an excited canine. "I like dogs," she said, her gravelly voice not quite matching her gentle tone.

"This is Ruth Cole." Dean locked eyes with Malorie as he bent to stroke Brady's head. "Jessica Cole's mother."

Who? Then it came to her, and a bolt of shock shot through her, followed quickly by sympathy. "Oh! Please, come in." She stepped back, pulling Brady along with her. "I'm so sorry for your loss." *What on earth was the dead girl's mother doing here?* Her mind spun with possibilities and landed on several unsettling ones. She released Brady as Dean closed the door behind them, and her empty hands twisted together in front of her stomach, mimicking the similar turmoil churning inside.

He cleared his throat. "Ah…Ms. Cole wanted to ask us a few questions about finding her daughter. She stopped by and since she wanted to speak with both of us, I thought it would be easier for us to come over here together. So she doesn't have to...go through the discussion twice." He sent Malorie a meaningful look when Ms. Cole dropped her gaze.

She got it. He had come over not just to make things easier on Jessica's mother. Somehow they could still read each other's body language, and his silent message told her he was there for her too. To support her, or to protect her, or maybe a combination of both. Her chest tightened even as her other muscles relaxed under the wave of gratitude.

"Of course," she managed, swallowing hard. "Why don't we go into the great room?"

Dean touched the back of her arm as she turned, just a small, steadying gesture that was over in a second. Still, it imbued her with a sense of reassurance she desperately needed. The fact that her nerve endings continued to spark where their skin had briefly touched was slightly concerning, but she pushed that out of her mind as she led them down the hallway. Clearly, she couldn't control how her body reacted to him, but she *could* force herself to focus on what was important here.

On that note, she wished she were wearing something more appropriate, but in her defense, all her day had consisted of so far was a walk on the beach and reading on the couch. No plausible scenario for her morning had included anyone dropping by for a somber conversation. She tugged her tiny yoga shorts a little farther down her thighs and briefly considered running upstairs to grab a sweatshirt to cover the equally tight tank top she had on. But that would only draw more attention to her outfit.

She'd opened the windows to allow some fresh air in before it got too hot, and the briny scent of the ocean filled the room. Thank God. She breathed it in, clearing her nose of the stale smoke clinging to Ruth Cole's clothes.

"Can I get anyone a glass of water?" she asked, guiding them toward the sitting area in the middle of the room. "Or I could make coffee or tea." As she moved the signs of her quiet leisure time to the end of the white couch, she caught Dean staring at the book. It was the most recent historical fiction novel by Dean's favorite author. Heat rose on her cheeks.

Maybe it wasn't even his favorite author anymore, she reminded herself quickly. That had been six years ago. When they were seniors, they'd had to read the same novel for a class they were in together, and they spent a lot of time discussing the book in the early stages of their relationship. After that, they'd continued trying to read the same book at the same time, taking turns choosing a title. Dean gravitated toward historical fiction, and when he'd picked Pillars of the Earth, they'd both become Ken Follett junkies.

So what if she still was? It had nothing to do with Dean and everything to do with the author's talent. And now she finally had the time to catch up on reading.

"Some water would be nice."

Ms. Cole's request snapped Malorie out of her spiraling thoughts. She blinked and nodded. "Sure. Nothing else?"

"No, thank you. I don't want to take up much of your time."

Dean shook his head silently when she looked in his direction, so she quickly carried her empty glass and the tub of pretzels into the kitchen and pulled out a clean glass for Ms. Cole. After she filled them both, she returned to find them both standing by the windows, looking out at the ocean, Dean scratching Brady's ear absent-mindedly.

A twinge of jealousy pricked at her as she noted her dog's new-found affinity for Dean. Seriously, they'd only met once, and that had been just a week ago. Dean wasn't even plying him with food. Jeez, where was the loyalty? She scowled to herself before making a small sound to avoid sneaking up on them.

"Here you are, Ms. Cole," she said, handing her the glass. "Do you want to sit down?" She waved her arm toward the couch and chairs.

"Please, you can call me Ruth." She followed Malorie back toward the sitting area and settled herself tentatively in one of the striped chairs, gripping her glass of water as though terrified to spill it. With her free hand, she pulled her battered purse across her stomach like a shield. "Like I said, I don't want to take up your time. I just…well, I needed to ask something. I promised my daughter I would."

"Your…daughter?" Malorie asked, trading a look with Dean.

"My other daughter, I mean. Jessica's younger sister—her name's Jocelynn. She's fifteen. This has been real tough on her."

Malorie nodded sympathetically. "I'm sure it has."

"The whole thing's been tough on her. Jessie was always a good girl, but she got in with the drugs, and she's been fighting this addiction for years now. Made her a different person a lot of the time. She'd do anything to get her drugs. Come over and beg me for money. Beg her little sister. Steal our stuff to sell it." Ruth paused, carefully lifting her water glass to her lips.

Malorie looked away for a moment in order to give the woman a chance to compose herself. The story was certainly tragic, but so far she hadn't heard an actual question posed for her or Dean to answer. Maybe Ruth Cole just needed to speak to the people who found her daughter to gain some type of closure. People handled grief differently—she could certainly attest to that. Crossing her legs, she laced her fingers over her knees. Traces of the scratches from the day they found Jessica's body still marred her skin. Her stomach lurched as the image of that gray, motionless foot surfaced in her mind.

Ruth set the glass down and stifled a cough. "Before all that, she and Jocey were real close, even though they were five years apart. One year, Jocey bought Jessica a necklace for her birthday—it had the letter J on it. She was real proud of it. And Jessie loved it. Once she put it on, she never took it off. It was one thing she never sold, even when she was desperate.

"I'm not foolish enough to believe that she wouldn't have tried if it was worth something…but it wasn't. It was just cheap, fake gold. But it meant something to her. She didn't live with us—I couldn't have that around us anymore." Ruth's mouth formed a grim line as a combination of guilt and defensiveness passed across her weathered face. "I had to look out for Jocey, you know?"

She and Dean nodded in unison, and Malorie added a soft, "Of course."

"But when I did see her, when she came by, she was still wearing it. Always."

Where was this going? All the nodding was starting to make her feel like a toy someone would put on a car dashboard, so she kept still and just offered a small smile of encouragement.

Ruth licked her dry lips but ignored her water glass. "It's the one thing Jocey wanted back to remember her by," she continued, her voice breaking. "They're keeping the clothes for evidence, and that's fine. But they're saying, the detectives, that there was no necklace."

Her head drooped, her shoulders heaving as she suppressed a sob. A long moment passed, then she lifted her chin and drew in a shuddering breath. Her fingers fluttered, clearly seeking the solace of a cigarette, but she brought her hand to the base of her throat instead.

"I don't know how to ask this without it sounding like I'm accusing either of you of something, but that's not how I mean it. I just wanted to know if...you saw the necklace on her, when you found her." The words spilled out quickly now as she leaned forward, her watery eyes pleading. "Maybe if she still had it on, I can go back to the police and ask them to look again. Maybe it got misplaced somehow. Or maybe someone took it for some reason, and I can explain how it's not worth much except sentimental value. Or it could be whoever did this to her took it, and maybe that's a clue to finding him." She lifted her brows hopefully as she looked at them in turn.

Malorie cringed, and Dean jumped in immediately. "It's understandable you'd want to recover such a sentimental article, Ruth, and we certainly don't feel you're accusing us of taking it ourselves." He gestured toward the couch, his jaw working as he searched for the right words. "Malorie only saw a small part of the scene—Jessica's...ah...foot. Of course that shocked her, and I responded to her calls for help. I did check everything out, to make sure...um, to make sure there was nothing we could do. And so we could accurately report everything to the police.

"I did notice the bruising around her neck, and unfortunately there was no necklace that I could see. I'm so sorry," he finished with a small shake of his head.

Malorie's chest tightened as she watched the hope drain from Ruth's face. "There were a lot of leaves," she pointed out, grasping for some way to help this poor woman. Her voice sounded unnaturally high. "Maybe it fell off and the police just didn't find it?"

Dean's forehead furrowed as he rubbed his knuckles. "My guess would be they scoured the area. And if the—if Jessica—was moved, it could be anywhere."

"She was moved to the woods," Ruth confirmed, pulling a trembling hand through her gray-brown curls. "After. That's what the detectives said."

After. After someone had raped and murdered her, according to the papers. A pause unspooled as Malorie cast about for the right thing to say. Nothing came to mind, so she finally offered, "I'm so sorry we couldn't help you."

She sighed, her entire body sagging in resignation. "I knew it was a long shot. But I had to try. And before I saw these houses, I thought...well, I thought maybe whoever found her took it to sell." Her sallow cheeks flushed with color. "Some people will pay a lot for things connected to crimes, you know? But I don't think that's something you all would need to do. Or want to do. You seem like nice people, and I'm sorry I bothered you with this." She stood, hitching the straps of her bag over her shoulder.

Malorie jumped up from the couch. "It's no bother, really," she said as Ruth started toward the hallway. She followed, chewing on her lip, with Dean and Brady behind her, a strange little parade. By the time they made it to the front door, Ruth was already fishing in her bag for her cigarettes. She pulled out a crumpled pack and a green disposable lighter, stepping to the side to allow Malorie to open the door.

A wall of humidity pushed its way in, the force of it nearly equal to the obvious waves of nicotine craving rolling off of Ruth. She fidgeted, a cigarette already perched between her fingers. "Thank you both again for talking to me. I have to be getting back now." With a sad smile, she stepped out onto the porch and sparked the lighter. She didn't look back as she trudged down the steps to the walkway.

Malorie had expected Dean to leave with her, since they'd arrived together, but he hung back with her by the door. "Do you mind if I hang out for a minute?" he asked. His eyes held an unsettling intensity as he studied her face.

Her pulse, which had almost returned to normal, resumed its racing staccato rhythm. "Oh. Sure."

"I just wanted to talk to you for a sec."

She swallowed, stepping back and shutting the door against the heat. "Is there something you didn't tell her?" she asked, her voice a hoarse whisper despite the distance and the solid wood separating them from Ruth. There was no way she could possibly overhear them and yet still, the situation seemed to call for it.

"No, nothing like that. I just...wanted to make sure you're okay. I know you're strong, but after last week, then last night, and now this...it's a lot."

He thought she was strong? An ache seeped through her chest as her heart contracted. It was nice to hear, even if it wasn't really true. But then, he didn't have all the information. Dragging a hand through her mass of tangles, she blew out a shaky breath. "It's definitely been a lot. But I'm okay." But her muscles disagreed, and she leaned her back against the door for support. "And, actually, I'm not even sure if I said thank you for last night. It was nice of you to come and make sure I was all right...especially since at that point you still didn't know what really happened on prom night."

He took a step closer, eliminating the small distance between them. "I wasn't about to let him hurt you." He paused, his strained expression revealing an internal struggle. Clenching his jaw, he closed his eyes for a moment. When he opened them, their green depths flashed with something like defiance, and he cursed under his breath. "The thing is," he finally continued, his tone rough with barely harnessed emotion, "I still feel...protective of you. I want to keep you safe."

Her lungs stopped working. Alarm bells jangled in a distant part of her mind as he leaned over her. This was dangerous. *She* was dangerous. Swallowing past the knot in her throat, she forced the words out. "You don't need to feel that way."

His hands gripped her shoulders, setting her skin on fire. He lowered his head, bringing his lips inches from hers. "I don't think I can control it."

She couldn't move. She simply didn't have the willpower— or the desire—to stop this from happening. Every cell in her body was clamoring with need for him; it was a force of its own. All coherent thought fled as the moment stretched out in an agonizing slide toward the inevitable.

His mouth seized hers, and time sped up, fueled by urgency. She was trapped between the door and his body, and she wanted to stay there forever, lost in the bruising kiss. The last six years melted away as their lips and tongues clashed. She was nothing now but heat and nerves.

Closer. There was no space between them, but she still needed to be closer. Her shoulder blades ground against the wood of the door as she fought to wrap her arms around his neck. She clung to him, her fingers knotting in his hair as though she could hold them together forever by this connection alone.

"Mal," he groaned, cupping her face with his hands, holding her in a grip that felt both tender and possessive. The calloused pads of his thumbs swept across her cheekbones, trailing sparks as they scraped against her skin. God, being kissed like this was like being consumed...like she was some essential element he'd been deprived of for far too long.

Her need for him ran just as deep; she couldn't get enough of his taste, his touch. She gasped as he tilted her head back further to ravage her neck. *Oh, God.* A fresh surge of desire rocked through her, and every muscle trembled in response. His hand slid down her side, hooking beneath her thigh and hiking her leg up to wrap around the outside of his own.

Closer.

Suddenly a series of thumps rang out directly behind her head as someone knocked on the door, and her eyes flew open.

Chapter Seventeen

She jumped forward instinctively, but the solid mass of his chest stopped her momentum, and she wobbled as she tried to balance on the one foot actually connected to the floor. With a sharp bark, Brady scrambled out from his spot beneath a narrow table in the hallway, sending a picture frame clattering to the floor.

Dean groaned, cursing softly as he brought his forehead to hers. "Just stay quiet and they'll go away," he murmured. Their breath mingled in hot bursts as they stood frozen in place. Beside them, Brady raised himself onto his hind legs to peer out the column of windows flanking the door. His feathery tail brushed against the skin of her leg, which was still hoisted up near Dean's hip.

Keeping still, she glanced over at Brady as he whined, then locked eyes with Dean again. He shook his head silently, but she raised her brows. "It's probably Ruth. And she knows we're here," she whispered. Her heart slammed against her ribcage as though she were hiding from a deranged killer instead of a harmless, grief-stricken woman. This was ridiculous. She pressed her leg down until Dean released his grip on the back of her thigh with a frustrated sigh.

She eased over to the other side of the door to peer out the windows currently unoccupied by Brady. Eric stood on the porch, his elbow crooked as he massaged the back of his neck with one hand. His head snapped toward her, and he smiled sheepishly as their eyes met. He lifted his hand from his neck and gave a small wave.

"It's Eric," she said, in a hushed, urgent tone that would have been more suited to the deranged killer scenario. She slipped back between Dean's body and the door.

He shrugged, rolling his eyes. "Then definitely ignore." Leaning down, he brushed his lips against her ear.

"Stop," she hissed, ducking away. "He saw me." She pressed her palm into his muscled chest and turned her back on his dark look. "I have to answer the door." Louder, she called out, "Hang on a sec! My dog got a little excited!"

She pulled in a calming breath, tugging her shorts down and hitching a fallen strap back over her shoulder. She felt like a criminal caught in the act, and in a way she was. What on earth was she doing, kissing Dean? How did she let that happen? *Hormones*, she decided as she attempted to smooth her tousled hair. Thank God they'd been interrupted before things had gone further.

"Seriously?" he grumbled from behind her in one final protest. But he stepped back to allow her room to open the door.

She latched on to Brady's collar and pulled him back, then cracked the door just wide enough to fit her body in the opening and block a potential escape by the dog. This arrangement served the dual purpose of hiding Dean's presence here, but he immediately stepped directly behind her. *Oh, hell.* This was not going to be good. What had happened to her relaxing Sunday morning? "Hi, Eric," she managed, fighting to keep her voice steady. What was he doing here?

He cleared his throat. "Hey, Malorie." A thin sheen of sweat glistened on his forehead, and his cheeks were red from the heat, or a hangover, or both. The faint tang of alcohol still clung to him, despite his freshly showered appearance. His puffy features hardened as his gaze moved from Malorie to Dean. "Oh." His blue eyes returned to her face, lingering on her swollen lips. "Am I interrupting something?"

She hurried to speak before Dean could say anything. "No. But I do actually have a lot of work to get done today, so…" She let the words hang, lifting her brows expectantly.

He nodded. "This won't take long. But, ah, could we talk in private for a moment?" he asked, flicking a glance over her head.

"After last night?" Dean nearly growled. "I don't think so."

She frowned at Dean speaking for her, but she had to agree. She wasn't exactly afraid to be alone with Eric, but she didn't feel the need to invite him in and grant him a private audience, either, especially after his behavior last night. Her head had been spinning since Dean and Ruth had arrived, and she really *did* have work to do today—both for her upcoming class and Friendship Farm. "I don't think that's necessary. If you have something to say to me, I'm sure it's fine for Dean to hear it too."

His mouth scrunched with displeasure, but he nodded. "Okay," he began, wiping his meaty hands on his blue-and-white-striped seersucker shorts. "Well, it's about last night, actually. I just wanted to, um, apologize. I don't really remember everything—and I know that's no excuse—but I do know I came on to you way too strong, and I'm sorry about that."

She exhaled, fighting the instinct to tell him it was okay, because it wasn't okay. Chewing on her tender bottom lip, she took a moment to compose her response. "I appreciate your coming over to apologize. It was a really unpleasant ending to the evening, but I do realize you were very drunk." *There.* She hadn't exactly accepted his apology or excused his actions, but hopefully it was enough to get him to leave. She could literally feel Dean's anger crashing against her back in hot, red waves, and every second that ticked by ratcheted up the tension between the two former rivals. Plus, the hopeful light in Eric's light blue eyes had her worried he might do something incredibly stupid and offer to take her out to 'make up for it' or something. Seriously, how could this be happening? If these two men had any idea what a ticking time bomb she was, they'd both run in the opposite direction so fast it would resemble an Olympic track event.

"So, I do need to get back to work now," she said hurriedly when he opened his mouth again. "Was there something else?"

His eyes narrowed, a line forming between his sandy brows. He studied them both for a moment, then squared his thick shoulders. "No. That's it. Sorry to disturb you." Shaking his head, he huffed out a derisive laugh, devoid of actual humor. "I didn't realize you guys were together again." The corners of his lips curved into a mocking half-smile.

She knew he was fishing, and that she didn't owe him an explanation or even a response. Still, she needed to say it, and for Dean to hear it too. "We're just friends," she said firmly, wincing internally. She couldn't bear to turn around to gauge Dean's expression. Hopefully, it was one of complete indifference. They'd simply been caught up in the moment. Strange things happened when death crept near—even if the deceased was someone they hadn't known personally. It was natural to seek out more pleasurable activities after such a depressing conversation. Sort of a reaffirmation of life. That their momentary escape involved making out in the hallway was just a product of their old relationship. *And the hormone thing.*

"Thanks for coming by," she added hurriedly. That was okay—after all, he didn't *have* to come by and apologize, so the fact that he did was something. But she could have done without his attitude. Although she did understand his reaction, since he was still under the impression Dean had stood her up that night. Still, it was none of his business or concern what she did, and with whom.

God. She shouldn't be doing anything with anyone...especially not with Dean. Jagged nerves coiled like barbed wire in her belly as she glanced up at him. His green eyes were shuttered, his expression neutral. A twitching muscle in his jaw was the only outward sign of what he was feeling.

But she knew him. He was confused at the very least; angry and hurt as well at worst. *It's for his own good.* And hers. She had to guard her heart. Unfortunately, the rest of her traitorous anatomy was still aching for his touch. She had to get him out of here.

Shutting the door on Eric, she leaned back against it and blew out a breath. "Well, it's been an interesting morning." Then she realized she was right back in the position she'd been in when she and Dean had been kissing less than ten minutes ago, and she rotated to the side and bent down to stroke Brady's ruffled mane. Dean certainly didn't look like he wanted to kiss her now, but it was better to be safe and all that.

An electronic trill rang out, and her pulse leapt again before she identified the harmless sound. Just Dean's cell phone. Bloody hell, she needed to calm down.

His forehead furrowed as he pulled the phone from his pocket and checked the screen. "Hey," he answered, concern flickering over his face. "Is everything okay?"

Who was it? She pictured Cherry on the other end of the line, and a shard of jealousy stabbed at her chest. *Stop it*, she ordered herself. It was none of her business who was calling him.

"I didn't see your text," he continued, an impatient edge to his voice. "Just—" There was a beat of silence as he listened. "Yeah, that's fine, I'll be right there." He thumbed the screen and lowered the phone to his side.

He was leaving. Relief sluiced through her, but there was a flicker of something else beneath it. Something that felt a lot like disappointment. Gritting her teeth, she inhaled through her nose as she straightened. She swallowed back the impulse to ask who had been on the phone in favor of a more innocuous question. "All okay?" she asked, lifting her brows. Hopefully she'd managed the right degree of casual concern. Pretending she thought of him as a friend shouldn't be this hard.

He snapped out of his inner thoughts. "Yeah. I mean, I think so. Sharon's been feeling sick all morning."

She cocked her head, chewing on her bottom lip. Tiny sparks of pain flared as her teeth worried the still-tender flesh. "Sharon?" Her muscles tensed as though in preparation for a physical blow.

"My brother's girlfriend. She's seven months pregnant, and Matt wants to use the truck to go pick up a few things for her. So I should probably go home, so she's not alone while he's gone. I'm sure she's fine, but still." He shrugged.

"Oh, yes, Sharon," she said, nodding with probably too much enthusiasm, considering the circumstances. For God's sake, there was a pregnant woman in distress, and here she was, just happy Sharon wasn't the girl Dean was currently dating. She had to get over these possessive feelings, and quick. *Say something appropriate.* "Um...she's at your place, then?" Not brilliant, but acceptable.

"Yeah, she pretty much lives with us at this point, although it won't be exactly official until they're married. I'd like to say that will be soon, but Matt's a big fan of procrastination." Rolling his eyes, he tucked his phone in his pocket.

She blinked at him for a long moment as she processed this new information. "Wow. You're going to have a newborn in the house?"

He raked a hand through his hair. "Yeah, crazy, isn't it?" The coppery waves fell back into place as the corner of his mouth quirked up in a smile that hinted at both wonder and disbelief. "I'm sure it will take some getting used to, but I'm trying to view it as a learning experience. I'll be ahead of the curve in terms of knowing how to change a diaper or prepare a bottle if I ever have my own kids."

Her heart contracted painfully. "You want kids?" she asked, fighting to keep the tremor from her voice. She shouldn't be asking. It didn't matter. But the likely answer would serve to strengthen her resolve.

He lifted a shoulder. "Sure. I mean, someday. I guess I've always pictured myself having kids, since my mom always hoped for a lot of grandchildren. But who knows. I'd have to find the right person, first." He stared at her for an agonizing moment before looking away.

She flushed. Once upon a time, they'd pledged to spend their lives together. A nervous laugh escaped as she studied the pale pink nail polish on her toes. "Yeah," she managed, turning to open the door. "Well, you should go make sure Sharon's okay. Let me know if you need any help." She couldn't imagine what kind of help she could offer—her only experience with pregnancy consisted of directing polite questions toward her father's new wife when she was carrying the twins. And an awkward baby shower. Still, Malorie could probably be useful enough to stay with the mom-to-be and call the doctor or an ambulance if something went wrong.

He nodded, reaching a tanned arm down to scratch Brady's ear as he passed.

"Thanks for coming over to make sure I didn't have to have that conversation with Jessica's mother alone," she called to his back. The air outside shimmered with heat.

He turned and walked backwards for a moment, squinting in the bright sunlight. "Sure. I guess I'll see you around,

Malorie." His chin dipped in a quick nod before he turned back around and strode away.

With a sigh, she closed the door and leaned her forehead against the warm wood. What a morning. Brady rubbed against her leg and she dangled her hand toward his head. The shock of his cold, wet nose against her skin made her flinch, but she didn't move from her positon against the door. Was it possible to fall asleep like this, propped up in the front hallway? Her body seemed to be begging her to at least try. Her muscles had been replaced by liquid, and she pictured herself melting into a puddle on the hardwood floor. Maybe Brady would be willing to serve as a pillow.

But she really did need to get some work done today. Groaning inwardly, she considered her options.

The paperwork for Friendship Farm was spread out on the dining room table, awaiting her attention. The notes for her upcoming classes were stacked in the study beside her laptop, and so far, she'd only created one slide—the title page for "Intro to Business". There was a lot more to be done, on both projects.

She pushed herself away from the door in slow motion. Neither task seemed particularly appealing; in truth, the ability to concentrate on anything beyond walking in a straight line felt well beyond her at the moment. She was far too unsettled to focus. Maybe a real meal would help. And some herbal tea. Six years in London hadn't done much to enhance her appreciation for tea, but the soothing lemon chamomile blend one of her university flatmates had introduced her to during exams did tend to promote a sense of calm.

To the kitchen, then. She took a few dragging steps down the hall, stopping by the table where the frame that had tumbled lay face down on the floor. Bending, she picked it up. It was an old family picture: her mother, her father, and herself, posed in the backyard of the Connecticut house. The glass wasn't completely smashed, but jagged cracks now cut through their group like bolts of lightning. She pressed her lips together. If fate had been looking to create some appropriate symbolism, it had done a good job.

Her grip tightened on the whitewashed frame as she carried it with her to the kitchen. From beneath the glass, her mother's face stared back at her, and a tight lump formed in Malorie's throat as she studied Isabelle Montgomery's familiar features. They were so similar to her own, but in this picture, they were devoid of that wild spark that sometimes lit her from within.

Isabelle had been on her meds then. Even if Malorie hadn't remembered that detail from the time period—this was taken on a sunny day in the fall of her freshman year, to be used for a Christmas card—it was easy to tell from her mother's appearance in the photo. Isabelle's face was puffy from the weight gain. Her eyes were dull, her smile forced. There was only a faint echo of the stunning woman her mother once was, before her illness unsheathed its claws and dug in, ruthlessly and permanently. And unfortunately, the powerful but necessary medications also affected her mother's personality and crushed her creativity, which was why Isabelle often stopped taking her pills. The timing of the fallout varied, but the results were always the same: chaos.

As she set the frame down on the kitchen island, Malorie conjured up an image of the fourth person involved in the photo—the woman who had taken the picture. Martha. One of the "housekeepers" her father had hired over the years to make sure things stayed on track when he was away on business. Malorie credited these women with providing some sense of normalcy to her childhood. They did their best to make sure Malorie ate regular meals and got to where she needed to go when Isabelle was unable to function.

She'd liked Martha, and the kind older woman had lasted longer than most. But two weeks after this photograph was taken, Russ was in London and Martha was gone. Isabelle had gone off her meds, insisting once again they made her lethargic and confused, and that she was "cured". It was the cruel cycle of paranoid schizophrenia, a disease that affects the very organ directly responsible for interpreting reality and making judgements. Isabelle had finally been diagnosed with the devastating mental illness when she was 30 and Malorie was 10, but the symptoms had been growing in frequency and intensity in the years before the bizarre behavior was finally given a name.

Once Isabelle began flushing her pills down the toilet that autumn, it didn't take long for her to accuse Martha of spying on the family for a shadowy organization with ties to the government. At least Martha, aware of the situation, had called Russ to let him know she'd been let go and told in no uncertain terms to stay away from the Montgomery house. He was able to return home and get Isabelle back to the doctor, but not before she'd pulled all the cable and phone wires from the walls to prevent further infiltration.

After that episode, Isabelle learned to get sneakier when she was off her meds. In order to keep her valuable secrets safe, she knew she had to pretend not to know her imagined enemies were watching her. Listening to her. Even reading her mind, if she wasn't careful. The first hints would come only once she was far enough gone to corner Malorie in the bathroom, turn the water on, and warn her of the danger in a paranoid whisper.

Malorie shuddered at the memories, her appetite suddenly waning. But she needed to eat. And then maybe a walk with Brady. Stress was her enemy—there was some evidence it could trigger paranoid schizophrenia in those with a predisposition to the mental illness.

But it could also strike for no reason at all, simply because of her genetic makeup. While researchers still didn't know the exact cause of schizophrenia, the familial link was conclusive. Having a parent with the disease significantly increased her odds of developing it as well. And in women, symptoms often began later, usually in the late 20s. If she ended up following her mother's path, she had about two more years before the delusions and hallucinations began turning her life into a nightmare.

Her father had actually been worried her colossal mistake at work—forgetting to make a trade that cost a client hundreds of thousands of dollars—was a sign the disease was beginning to manifest. Even when it became clear her error was unrelated to any break with reality, Russ decided the stress of the job was too much for her. She knew on some level he was concerned for her health, but she also knew his decision was based on more than that. Over the years, he'd gone to great lengths to keep their family tragedy a secret. The company he'd built relied on personal reputation and trust, and he did not want his wealthy clients or his business partners to associate the Montgomery name with paranoid schizophrenia. And now that Russ had two healthy twin boys, he no longer had to rely on Malorie as the only possible heir to the business he'd spent his life building. It hurt, but she understood. A person who might suddenly suffer delusions and hallucinations could not have access to so many people's sensitive information and bank accounts.

Her father had also been the one to suggest she remain on birth control at all times, just in case. No need to risk spreading the tragic mental illness inadvertently. That awkward conversation had taken place before she started college, but it had been no less painful than her dismissal from Montgomery Wealth Management.

Really, it was all for the best. She'd rather be here, near her best friend, and doing something more altruistic with her life than making wealthy people wealthier. Especially if she only had a few years left until her life instead became about managing a debilitating mental illness. And Julia was here to serve as her warning system. Aside from her father and his wife, Julia was the only other person who knew about her mother. Long ago, Julia had read up on the initial signs of schizophrenia, at Malorie's request, and she'd promised to get Malorie to a doctor immediately if she started displaying symptoms.

Thank God for Julia. She turned from the island, glancing at the papers for Friendship Farm, scattered on the dining table. That's what she'd dedicate the day to, once she'd eaten a proper meal and maybe taken a walk. If they stayed near the water, the heat might not be so bad. Okay, now she had a plan, anyway. Opening the fridge and scanning its contents, she pulled out the makings for a turkey sandwich.

Chapter Eighteen

Sharon was feeling better by the time Matt arrived home with antacids, ginger ale, a loaf of bread for toast, and a handful of tabloid magazines with glossy, star-studded covers. As they gathered in the kitchen, Dean relayed the details of his odd morning at Malorie's, leaving out Eric's visit and, of course, the kiss. But he himself couldn't stop thinking about it.

Only hours ago, he'd been reminding himself not much had changed—he still had little to offer her, even if she were interested in resuming their former relationship. But then, he'd kissed her, and she'd kissed him back, and now everything had changed. There was no question in his mind that their connection was still alive, the spark between them still strong. He'd *felt* her desire for him in every nerve in his body, just as sure as he'd felt his own hunger for her.

And then that bastard Eric had shown up. *Damn him*, Dean's inner voice growled as his muscles went rigid. The interruption had caused Malorie to throw her barriers back up, and he could only think of one reason why—he hadn't told her Cherry's secret, hadn't explained why he hadn't shown up for Malorie on prom night. Even after all these years, the betrayal surely still stung, especially since she'd considered Cherry her rival, despite his assurances to the contrary. But even he could admit his case didn't appear very strong when he refused to give Malorie any real answers about what had happened that night.

He was going to fix that. If things were to go any further between them, Mal had to trust him. So now, as he prepared to go back out to the store to get the rest of the week's groceries, he texted Cherry to see if she was home. They needed to talk.

A half hour later, he was turning into the trailer park at the edge of town, where Cherry still lived with her ailing mother. Where he had lived for most of his life. The memories assaulted him as he drove along the curving main road, glancing at the mobile homes lining both sides. Not a lot had changed. Many of the trailers fit the negative stereotype in most people's minds: tired, neglected shacks with chipped paint and sagging features, squatting on concrete blocks in an unkempt lot. But others appeared well cared for, boasting quaint, if tiny, outdoor decks, wooden lattice around the frames, bright curtains in the windows, and potted plants. Most fell somewhere in between, much like a typical neighborhood anywhere. Except Sandalwood.

At the thought of his new house in the exclusive community—and how little he'd done to deserve it—a pang of guilt twisted through him, spiraling deeper as he approached their old lot. The mobile home they'd lived in after the fire was still there, inhabited by new residents with small children, judging from the colorful plastic sandbox in the side yard. Laundry hung on a line strung across two thin trees, the damp clothing limp and motionless in the still air. A tiger cat slunk around the corner of the house and disappeared into the woods.

The 24 x 60 foot double-wide he'd grown up in had been a total loss after the fire, but that was the interior he still pictured as he gazed at the newer trailer sitting among the familiar surroundings. While he couldn't remember his father, the photographs and the stories his mother had told him painted a picture of a happy, loving family, despite their financial constraints. Even after Roy moved in and Matt was born, things were generally calm and stable, until Dean grew into a rebellious teen with a knack for finding trouble, and Roy hurt his back and began his downward descent into addiction. Matt followed in Dean's defiant footsteps, eventually surpassing him as the most screwed-up brother with a level of destructive behavior that sometimes made Dean wonder if Matt thought it was some sort of competition.

Things continued to escalate after Roy Slater went to prison, and then Matt set the fire that burned down their trailer, leaving the three of them homeless. Cherry's mother, their mother's best friend, offered to take them in, but there was barely enough room for their own family in their single-wide mobile home down the street. Donations from the community funded their stay in a motel for those first few surreal days, until Mrs. Walters heard the news. Suddenly they'd relocated again, from a dingy pair of connected rooms to a lavish oceanfront house.

Investigations and insurance claims had followed, and it had taken nearly nine months to get everything settled. But eventually the new trailer was delivered, and one week after Malorie left for England, they were back in the mobile home park. It was like the charmed life he'd lived for nearly a year—

a beautiful house, a backyard beach, and an amazing girlfriend he loved more than he could have ever imagined—had been merely a fantasy, a dream he'd conjured up that had vanished in the harsh light of reality.

Now, thanks to Mrs. Walters' generosity and her friendship with his mother, he had the house again.

But not the girl.

And it was becoming increasingly—and painfully— apparent that she was what he needed most. Despite the legitimate arguments his mind presented, his heart told him something else entirely. They had unfinished business, that was certain. And maybe, just maybe, they still had a chance to be together.

His jaw tightened as he cut the engine in front of Cherry's trailer. That was why he was here, after all. To get Cherry's permission to share her secret from that night, so he and Malorie could put the past behind them and hopefully move forward. A cause that Cherry wasn't likely to embrace. *What if she refuses?*

She won't, he decided as he strode past the car in the driveway and climbed the wooden steps leading to the entrance on the right side of the trailer. But doubt gnawed at his gut, biting deeper with each of his raps against the flimsy door. Cherry was...complicated. They'd known each other forever, connected through their mothers' friendship like cousins—but at some point, her feelings had evolved beyond family and friendship, despite his consistent efforts to make it clear he did not feel the same. It hadn't always been easy, either. Cherry was fun, sexy, and, when it came to him, not shy about making it known she was always willing…a combination that was sometimes almost too much to ask a horny teenager to resist. But resist he had, out of love and respect for her. Fooling around with Cherry when he knew how she felt would have not only been cruel, it would have likely ended their friendship. Even his own mother had given him a few subtle warnings about the potential hazards, once she noticed Cherry's flirtatious behavior around him.

"Hey," she said in a cool voice as she pulled the door open. Her normally warm brown eyes flashed with irritation. "Where did you disappear to last night?" She stepped back and motioned him in, turning slightly to plug her phone into the cord resting on a small table beside a stack of mail. The front half of the trailer served as both the kitchen and the sitting area, and an ancient air conditioner rattled in one of the windows, wheezing cold air into the main room. On the television, a sitcom was playing out with the volume muted. Cherry dropped onto a worn dark blue couch across from the screen and leaned into the armrest, curling her legs up beside her on the cushion.

Here we go. He lowered himself into a chair upholstered in textured tan fabric and white cat hair. "I had to talk to Malorie."

She wrinkled her nose as she reached for the can of diet soda on the end table. "Why would you want to do that?" she asked, looking into the can like it might have the answer. She swirled the contents around before lifting it toward her pursed lips. "Sounds like a good way to ruin a perfectly good Saturday night to me."

"Because we had some things to straighten out." He paused, pressing his knuckles into his other palm. "And as it turns out, we both made some assumptions about…that night…that were wrong." His pulse quickened as he waited for her reaction. There was no question she wouldn't understand exactly what night he was referring to.

For a long moment, only the rattle of the air conditioning unit filled the room. His phone vibrated, and he glanced at the screen. Matt, adding more items to the grocery list. He turned it off and slid it between his leg and the armrest as he looked back up at Cherry.

Frowning, she drained the rest of her soda and stood up. "Want one?" she asked, flipping her two-toned hair behind her shoulder. Her hips swayed beneath cut-off denim shorts as she crossed the narrow room to the kitchen area. "Or anything?" She pulled open the fridge door.

"I'm all set." He watched her study the contents of the refrigerator, her posture radiating a forced casualness. This wasn't a conversation she wanted to have, and he didn't blame her. It wasn't one he wanted to have either. He cleared his throat and plowed forward. "So, yeah, about that night. Malorie didn't exactly leave willingly with Eric. Apparently she found out I was over here and then got smashed. Eric carried her out before the chaperones could find out and drove her home. I saw them leaving together, from a distance, and I figured something else was going on. But it was innocent."

She sank back into her spot on the couch, cocking an eyebrow at him skeptically. "You believe that?" Outside, a car passed by, its speakers blasting a thunderous bass. The sound vibrated through the walls, competing with the air conditioner.

He nodded, leaning forward and clasping his hands between his knees. "I do. She would have been devastated once she found out I was here. And Eric, well, as much as I despise him, I know he still cared about her. They were still friends. She wouldn't have graduated if she got caught." That was motivation enough for Eric to have helped her, but Dean could think of a few more reasons why her ex ended up being the one to rescue her, and his jaw clenched as he considered each one again. The bastard had probably still felt guilty over dumping her the way he did. Beyond making up for that, Eric likely saw an opportunity to play the hero and maybe get her back. Or, it was like he'd just told Cherry, and he was simply being a friend. They would have needed a strong guy to get her out, and at that point, he probably would have been the obvious choice.

She fixed her gaze on the silent TV, where a group of actors bantered around a table in a brightly-colored kitchen. "Huh," she finally said. Her shoulders twitched in a small shrug. "Well, that's a different story than what you thought happened."

"Yeah. It is. And I was glad to finally know the truth." He inhaled carefully. "But *she* doesn't know the truth, yet, about why I was here that night."

Her eyes hardened. "And that matters to you?"

He held her gaze. "Yeah."

She looked away, blinking rapidly as she surveyed the ceiling. Her fingers twisted nervously in her lap, and her ever-present stacks of bracelets clinked against each other. One hand slid protectively around the opposite wrist as her head dropped forward.

He steeled himself as she examined her scars, fighting to keep the memories of that night at bay. But an echo of the overwhelming panic he'd felt back then surfaced along with the horrifying images: the locked bathroom door...the pink water...Cherry's pale, still form, lying in the tub.

Cherry had always been prone to vicious mood swings, but that week was something different. Her father, who'd left them years ago, failed to acknowledge her 18th birthday with even a phone call. Her mother had begun dating a younger man, and suddenly *she* was behaving like the teenager—going to bars, staying out all night, and returning home reeking of sweat and booze and complaining of headaches.

He certainly hadn't been emotionally available for his friend, as preoccupied as he was with Malorie and the ticking clock marking the time they had left together. His sudden desire to attend the school's prom had taken most of his friends by surprise—hell, it had even taken *him* by surprise at first—but once he'd embraced the traditional rite of passage, some of the group had followed suit and purchased tickets. But no one had expressly asked Cherry, and she had maintained her conviction that the whole thing was stupid, anyway. A lame event, not to mention a ridiculous waste of money.

But her sense of abandonment sank to dangerous depths by that Saturday. First came the disturbing text, hinting at what she was going to do. His replies received no responses, his calls went to her voicemail. His initial attempts to reach her mother, with the help of his own mother, failed, and finally, although it was nearly time for him to pick up Malorie, he raced over to the trailer park to check on Cherry.

He'd pushed their old car to its limits during the fifteen minute ride, his heart accelerating along with the engine as the seconds ticked by. He barreled through changing lights, cold sweat dampening the crisp white material of his rented tux shirt. His mind reeled with the panic of being too late, and also with the realization that Malorie was waiting for him, along with her father. Mr. Montgomery had been adamant that Dean pick his daughter up for prom at the house, no doubt more out of a desire to make Dean uncomfortable than any sentimental tendencies. For Malorie, Dean was glad to do it—but now, he had no idea if he'd even show up. What if one of his oldest friends had killed herself? Why hadn't he realized how bad things had gotten? Dread clawed at his chest as he slammed on the brakes in front of the Jones' trailer.

The door had been unlocked, and he'd banged into the living room, calling Cherry's name. Now, his eyes followed the path he had taken six years ago, and he could almost hear the echo of his stiff, shiny dress shoes, thudding down the hall in time with his pulse.

The scene he'd found in the bathroom would be forever seared in his brain, and he closed his eyes against the vivid flashbacks. Somehow, he'd managed to do what needed to be done; he'd bound her wrists with tight strips of a ripped T-shirt and awoken her from a drugged sleep. The shallow, horizontal cuts had stopped leaking blood almost immediately, and thankfully, Cherry's mother had arrived moments later, having finally answered his own mother's calls. Together, they had dressed Cherry and loaded her into the Jones' car. It was a compromise—despite her groggy physical condition, Cherry had argued against going to the hospital at all, and her despair had escalated into hysteria at the idea of an ambulance arriving in their neighborhood of crowded, close-set homes. She finally agreed to go in their own car, and Mrs. Jones allowed it not only because the bleeding had stopped, but also because of their sparse insurance coverage. He'd followed them in his own car and stayed until he knew Cherry was out of any physical danger. Then he'd rushed to the banquet hall, his mind struggling with how to explain his absence to Malorie when Cherry had begged him to tell no one what she'd done. He'd never come up with the solution, but, he'd never ended up needing it, either.

She sighed, the sound heavy with resignation. "So you want to tell her I took a bunch of pain pills and then slit my wrists to keep you from taking her to prom?"

He recognized her attempt at grim humor and played along. "Well, I wasn't going to word it exactly like that."

The corner of her mouth tipped up as she shrugged. "It's true."

"Hey," he said, leaning forward. "You were going through a lot then. You were feeling...alone. Abandoned."

She closed her eyes for a moment, her chest hitching as she pulled in a breath. "Yeah." Opening her eyes, she met his gaze and held it. Two pink splotches rose on her skin, one above each cheekbone. "And of course that wasn't all about you, but you're the one I hurt. I guess...I convinced myself that I needed you more than anyone else that night. I wanted you to be with *me* that night. Not her. I was feeling sorry for myself." She hung her head, spilling a curtain of hair forward.

His chest constricted. "You were hurting. Don't beat yourself up, Cher."

The crimson ends of her hair swung as she shook her head. "God. Why do you even still talk to me?" Rearing up suddenly, she grabbed her soda can as if it were the source of her anger. "What a mess I was," she mumbled into the can as she knocked it back.

"Because I care about you. We're friends, always. I'm just sorry I didn't realize how bad things had gotten."

She shook her head again, her lips set in a firm line. "No. Don't do that. Don't put any of it on yourself."

He lifted one shoulder in a dismissive shrug. "You can't tell me what to do." She rolled her eyes, masking a smile with a scowl, and he felt some of the tension in the room drain away. "Anyway, if the situation had been reversed, you would have still been there for me, right?"

Her expression turned serious. "You know I would. I always will be." She shifted her position on the couch, pulling her knees into her chest. "And...for the record, I'm sorry I was such a manipulative bitch. But in my defense, I knew she was leaving anyway."

"But now she's back," he said carefully. "And I want to tell her what actually happened that night."

She angled away from him, staring down the little hallway leading to the bedrooms. Her arms tightened around her shins as her fingers toyed with the bracelets layered along her wrists. The silence spun out, interrupted only by the wails of a child in a neighboring yard.

He waited, linking his hands to avoid popping his knuckles. The mantra that had accompanied him since he arrived repeated in his head. *What if she says no?* His muscles tightened with each passing second, until the tendons along his forearms stood out like cords. Finally, he couldn't stand it anymore. "So?"

She released a shuddering breath. "Fine. Whatever. Tell her."

Relief surged through him, numbing his limbs like a shot of whisky. He pushed away the accompanying pangs of guilt. The last thing he wanted was to hurt or embarrass Cherry—but it was time for the truth to come out.

"Thank you." He scrubbed at his jaw, still covered in stubble. He'd never even shaved this morning. Suddenly, the emotional toll of the day began adding up, and just the thought of finishing the things that had to get done drained his remaining energy. His hand moved to the knot at the back of his neck. "I know you've worked really hard to put all that behind you," he continued, weighing his words carefully. "But I think we can trust Malorie to keep it a secret. She's not the kind of person who'd tell anyone else."

Her mouth scrunched to the side as she uncurled her body from the protective pose. "Whatever," she said with forced nonchalance. She picked her soda can back up and fiddled with the tab. "What's so…" Her nose wrinkled as she trailed off, her gaze fixed on the little piece of aluminum she was twisting. She shook her head slightly and tried again. "What is it about her?"

He tensed again, his nerves vibrating like a small engine. It was a loaded question, and he was intuitive enough to understand the real information Cherry was seeking: Why Malorie, and not her?

Clearing his throat, he gathered his thoughts. Was there a right way to answer this question? "It's...hard to explain." Lame, but it was partly true. And it would only cause Cherry more pain if he sat here and tried to vocalize his feelings for Malorie. It wasn't just physical attraction, although that part had always been there—he was drawn to her face, her body, the graceful way she moved. But it was also her personality, her strength, her kindness, and her sense of humor. And then there was the way she made him feel...the way she'd once looked at him, like he was the most important person in the world. She'd never looked down on him or dismissed him as second class. The bottom line was that she'd claimed a piece of his heart, long ago, and their kiss today had reminded him how long he'd been living without it. Without her.

Cherry's forehead creased as she waited for him to elaborate, but then she waved her hand dismissively. "Never mind." She ran her fingers through her hair, pulling it off the back of her neck. "I probably don't want the gory details anyway."

He chuckled, his shoulders relaxing. He was off the hook. But, man, was he exhausted. So far today, he'd cycled through more emotions than was usual for an entire month.

She smiled with him, but pain still flickered in her eyes. Reaching for the remote, she gestured with it toward the door. "I'm guessing you want to hurry off and tell Malorie what a hot mess I am, so I'm going to get back to my busy day." Her light tone couldn't quite conceal the sadness beneath it.

"No, I need to hurry off and buy groceries for the week. Sharon was going to make a few meals tonight, but she was feeling bad this morning, so I don't know." He filled Cherry in on that part of his morning, relieved to have another subject to discuss, even if it did involve discomfort on his soon-to-be sister-in-law's part. He left out the incident with Jessica's grieving mother—no need to turn the conversation back to Malorie. As he made to leave, he collected his phone and retrieved Cherry's for her, planting a kiss on the top of her head as he said goodbye.

Back out in the heat, he pulled in a lungful of thick air and squinted against the glare bouncing off his truck. He'd left his sunglasses on the seat, and he reached for them as he eased himself into the stifling cab. Now what? Thoughts whirled in his mind like leaves caught in a wind storm, and he leaned his head back and closed his eyes against the onslaught.

Like Cherry had suggested, part of him did want to race right over to Mal's to present her with the truth. If there was a chance they could be together after all this time, he didn't want to wait one more second. But the heavy weight of doubt warred with his impulsive streak. What if the truth about what he was doing at Cherry's that night wasn't the reason she was holding back? What if she just had no interest in a guy with a blue-collar job who had never been outside of New England, with the exception of a childhood visit to Florida he could barely remember? That made the most sense. All the thoughts he'd awoken with cycled back to remind him of his shortcomings.

Jamming the gearshift into drive, he turned the truck around and headed back toward the entrance to the trailer park. His grip on the steering wheel loosened as he made his decision. He'd do the things that needed to get done, the mundane things that nevertheless were required to take care of his family. Hell, Malorie probably had things to get done too—she'd said as much this morning.

And there was no need for him to run back over there today like some desperate, lovesick kid. She needed room to breathe, to get comfortable back here. Malorie was not someone who liked to be rushed into things.

So...he would wait. At least a day or two. The way they'd been running into each other, an opportunity to talk again would probably present itself sooner rather than later. All he could do is hope that when that time came, this new information about Cherry would make a difference. His heart lurched with uncertainty. If it didn't, could he go through the pain of losing her again?

You don't even have her to lose her again, a disdainful inner voice reminded him. *Get a grip*. A dull ache flared along his jaw as he ground his teeth together. Enough. He had things to do. Glancing up, he watched the trailer park disappear in the rearview window.

Chapter Nineteen

The wind off the ocean whipped her hair across her face, and she used the strands as camouflage against her confusion. Was Dean really waving her over, toward the deck of his house? And should she go?

She narrowed her eyes against the evening sun, fighting to control her wild hair and her energetic dog, who seemed intent on climbing the rise of dunes to the Slater's home. Who could blame him? The scent of grilling beef drifted down from the deck, momentarily overpowering the sharp brine of the sea air. Her own empty stomach grumbled in response.

Dean hadn't been out there when she and Brady had passed earlier, on their way down the beach to the Club, and she'd berated herself for even searching the deserted deck. But it was impossible not to think of him, especially when his house was right there along the path she *had* to take if she wanted to stay on the beach instead of walking through the woods. And while she shouldn't want to see him—in fact, she should actively avoid him—she couldn't ignore the traitorous flutter in her chest at the sight of his familiar tall, muscular form, lifting a hand in her direction. She resisted the urge to look behind her, to make sure he wasn't gesturing to someone else. There was no one else anywhere near her on the beach. It was always quiet down here, away from the Club, where the stretch of sand began to narrow and coarsen as it gave way to the woods, even in the height of summer. Where the number of houses dwindled as the neighborhood approached the conservation area. And this early in the season, many of the homes were still unoccupied, even on a warm Friday evening in June.

A force beyond her control, stronger than Brady's enthusiastic tug, pulled her toward him, and she angled up toward the house—toward Dean—despite the warning bells clanging in her head.

Perplexed, she chewed on her lip as she neared the wooden steps up to the deck. Why would he even *want* to see her? She'd practically pushed him out the door the last time they'd been together. Right after they'd kissed. Her pulse skittered at the memory, and a corresponding surge of desire, warm and heady, simmered in her veins. *No. I can't have him.* She reminded herself of the other piece, the conversation after the kiss that had slammed reality back into focus. He wanted kids. She couldn't have them. Not even through adoption—the risk was too great. Cutting her eyes back toward the ocean, she suppressed a shudder. Dean deserved more than she could offer. He deserved a happy, healthy family. They were destined to lead different lives, and she needed to keep that in the forefront of her mind.

It would be hard, considering the effect his presence had on her. After what had happened between them Sunday, she'd gone out of her way on Monday to make herself scarce, knowing he'd be by at some point to do the weekly yardwork. Like a coward, she'd run over to Julia's, ostensibly to go over paperwork. But they'd accomplished little, the conversation turning to the troubles in Julia's and Pete's relationship. Malorie had been happy to serve as a sounding board, sympathizing with her friend while avoiding the topic of Dean. A pang of guilt stabbed at her. Julia would kill her, slowly and painfully, if she discovered Malorie was holding out on her. But the kiss had been a one-time thing, never to be repeated. Not worth mentioning. A mistake best forgotten.

Good luck with that. It was literally the only thing she could think of as he smiled down at her from his post in front of the grill. *Oh, God.* This was a mistake too. A dangerous one. She'd find out what he wanted and then leave, quickly. She steeled herself even as her heart soared at the sight of his handsome face.

"Hey," he said, reaching for the beer on the grill's side shelf. "Happy Friday." He lifted the bottle in a mock toast before taking a swig.

She pulled her gaze away from the ripple of muscles along his throat. How could he make such a simple movement sexy? Unfair. She mentally chastised herself again. Clearly, he'd awakened something long dormant inside her with that kiss. And she needed to put it back into permanent hibernation immediately.

"You too," she replied, searching for a distraction. She found one in Brady's tug against the leash as he struggled to reach Dean. "Oh, jeez. Sorry. Is it okay for him to come on your deck?"

The roll of his eyes was softened by his grin. "Course. Hi buddy." He extended his arm to allow Brady to sniff his hand.

An angry red scratch marred the tanned skin. "Work," he explained when he caught her staring at it.

"Oh!" The mention of work shook another safe subject loose from the jumble of traitorous thoughts crowding her mind. "I owe you a thank you."

His brows pinched together as he dragged a hand through his tousled hair. "For?"

"For setting up my deck furniture." She tilted her head toward the large rectangular table on his deck, as though the sentence needed visual aids. A bowl of creamy pasta salad and a platter of glistening sliced tomatoes currently sat in the center, along with a stack of napkins weighted down with a smooth stone. Her mouth watered, and she swallowed against the sight—and smell—of all the fresh food. So far, her cooking-for-one plan hadn't been as successful as she'd hoped. Frozen dinners and peanut butter-filled pretzels accounted for more of her meals than she cared to admit.

"I mean, I assume it was you," she continued, the fingers of her free hand toying with the frayed edges of her cut-off jeans shorts. It had actually freaked her out when she'd first returned from Julia's on Monday evening to find the heavy circular table in its place on her deck. She'd brought Brady with her to Julia's, since their plan for the day had included a walk along the bike path, but the house had been locked up, and nothing looked disturbed. What kind of burglar broke in to set up an outdoor table, anyway? Then she realized Dean and Matt probably had the code to the garage and had done it when they'd been there for the lawn.

"Oh, yeah. I hope that was okay. I noticed it when I went in to check the irrigation system panel. Figured you'd prefer it up on the deck, and now you can use the garage for your car." He turned and lifted the top of the grill to check the burgers, releasing another aromatic cloud of steam.

"Oh, no, it's fine." She watched him shut the grill and pick his beer back up. "I really appreciate the help." The same rush of warmth she'd felt on Monday after discovering the table swept through her again, heating her blood. Her hand clenched, her fingernails digging into her palm. Why did he have to be so thoughtful on top of being so hot? She needed to get out of there. Immediately. "So," she began, shifting her weight. "Did you...um...need me for something?"

He took another pull from his beer, considering. The hint of a grin tugged at his lips as his gaze raked over her, slow and deliberate. "That's an interesting question."

Flames licked at her cheeks. Damn, she'd walked right into that one. Every cell in her body longed to reciprocate—to return his wicked smile along with a suggestive response of her own. But that would be leading him on, giving him the impression they might continue where the other day's kiss left off.

And unfortunately, even if she were to allow herself to flirt back, she had to admit she was momentarily rendered speechless. Did she even remember how? It had been so long since a man had looked at her the way Dean was looking at her right now.

The moment was mercifully interrupted as the back door opened and Sharon emerged from the house, carrying an empty platter. Matt followed, a bag of rolls in one hand and a wire basket of condiments in the other. They both came to a sudden stop, taking in the unexpected presence of a neighbor and her dog on their deck.

Dean immediately stepped closer to her, as if protecting her from their scrutiny. "Sharon, this is Malorie Montgomery, an old friend. She lives a few houses down." He gestured down the beach with his chin. "She lives in the last house on Beach Plum."

"Hi," Malorie offered, trying to hide her discomfort. Just being on this deck, outside of this house, was bringing back memories she didn't want to encourage. Once upon a time, she'd found acceptance and love here. Now, she was just an intruder. She needed to make an escape, quickly.

"Matt, you remember Mal," Dean continued, seemingly intent on continuing the awkward situation. "Oh, and this is Brady," he added, ruffling the dog's ear.

"Oh!" Sharon's face lit up, either from an inherent kindness, or maybe just the presence of another female. "It's so nice to meet you. Will you join us?" She nodded toward the table. "We have plenty."

"Have you eaten yet?" asked Dean as he took the empty platter from Sharon. He lifted the cover of the grill and slid a long spatula under a burger.

She tore her eyes away from the food and shook her head. "Oh, I'm not hungry, thanks." But her stomach chose that moment to grumble in disagreement, the plaintive sound rising above the hiss of steam from the grill. Blood rushed to her cheeks as she wished for a giant hole to appear in their deck, large enough to swallow her whole.

Sharon's laugh was high and musical. "Have a seat. What do you want to drink?"

Her final argument was Brady, but Dean and Sharon quickly put that to rest, maneuvering a chaise lounge onto its side to block the stairs and setting a bowl filled with water by the deck railing. Their determination to include her tugged at her heart, and even though she knew she did not belong, and that she shouldn't pretend otherwise, it was wonderful to feel so thoroughly wanted and welcomed. *What was the harm in one meal with her neighbors?* Shoving her concerns aside, she set about helping with the final preparations.

Dinner was both delicious and pleasant; the conversation had flowed easily once the subject had turned to the baby. There was one awkward moment, when a marriage license was mentioned, but Brady managed to break the tension, lunging at a rogue seagull eyeing the extra rolls by the grill.

When they were finished, Malorie began clearing the table, insisting on doing her part. But once everything was inside and she announced her intention to do the dishes, Dean intervened.

"Matt can do it," Dean said, leveling a pointed gaze at his brother, who was lounging in an armchair, his long legs stretched nearly horizontal.

Matt pulled his attention away from the screen of his phone and shot Dean a dark look. But he pushed himself to standing with a heavy sigh, tucking his phone away as he made his way toward the kitchen.

Had Matt always been so sullen? It was hard for her to remember...six years ago, he'd spent the majority of his time either locked in his room upstairs, or back at the trailer park with his friends. But right now, at least tonight, he seemed to be simmering with barely disguised contempt. She hoped it wasn't due to her presence.

"Oh, no, I'm happy to do it," she said hurriedly. "It won't take long."

"Exactly. It won't take long." Dean nodded toward the small stack of serving dishes next to the sink. "It's his night anyway, and I need to talk to you," he added, his voice lowering as he turned toward her.

Her heart stilled. *Uh oh.* "Oh, well...I can help out while we—"

"No. I need to talk to you in private." He reached out, caught her hand in his.

Sharon's brows lifted, her eyes flicking from their linked hands back up to their faces. A small, knowing smile pulled at the corners of her mouth as she held up the remains of a hamburger. "Okay to give this to Brady?"

At the mention of his name, the dog scrambled to her side and sat down eagerly, his full attention on the half-eaten burger in Sharon's hand.

"Oh. Sure." The words came out breathless and raspy. Heat was creeping up her neck, flooding her cheeks. She swallowed, tried again. "He'll be your best friend."

"Great. Then Brady and I will both help clean up, and you and Dean can go...talk." The suggestive pause was short, but there. Pressing her lips together against another smile, she retreated to the kitchen with Brady by her side.

In private. The phrase spun through her mind as panic rose in her chest. She should not be alone with him. Not because of what he might do, but because of what she might do. She had to stay strong, protect him from becoming any more involved with her than he already was. But if he kissed her like that again...

Please, her inner voice sneered. *You're not that irresistible.* And it was true; she was probably being ridiculous. Talking could mean anything. Maybe it had to do with Jessica Cole. Or maybe he needed advice about buying the landscaping company. She was a business major, after all.

But as he led her toward the stairs, her pulse picked up, surging through her veins at an alarming rate by the time they reached the second floor. His fingers tightened around hers as they passed the door to the master bedroom and made their way down the hall to the room he'd slept in all those years ago. Her hand was damp inside his strong grip, and her thoughts were floundering. Time was contracting, the present melding with the past.

They crossed the threshold, and she pulled her hand from his as he shut the door behind them. Her eyes darted around the room. Similar, but not exactly the same as it was six years ago. Taking a few steps away from him, she took a deep breath and meet his gaze. "Is everything okay?"

"Yes. I mean, I hope it will be." Muffled cracks punctured the air as he pressed his knuckles into the palm of his other hand. "I talked to Cherry the other day. Because I want to tell you everything that happened that night."

Oh. She hadn't seen this coming. Her knees went weak as a wave of dizziness slipped over her. She should sit down. But the only option was the double bed, and that seemed like a bad idea. She'd stand. "You don't have to do that." Her voice sounded high and tinny.

"I want to. I need you to know why I didn't show up that night."

"Okay."

He scrubbed at his jaw. "She...tried to commit suicide that night, Mal. She cut her wrists."

"Oh my God." Her legs wobbled.

"Yeah. I got a text from her that sounded a lot like 'goodbye' shortly before I was supposed to pick you up. I knew she'd been depressed, and that she was home alone. And then she didn't answer any of my texts or calls. So I raced over and I found her...in the bathtub."

Oh, God. Nausea bubbled up in her stomach, and she gave up and sank onto the end of the bed as Dean related the horrifying details.

"That's awful," she said, once she found her voice. "I don't even know what to say. I never even imagined it was something like that."

"I know. How could you? And she was embarrassed and ashamed—she made me promise not to tell anyone. I'm not sure how I was going to keep that promise and explain why I was late to you, but...I never got the chance."

This was too much. Tears pricked at the back of her eyes as she fought to process what he was telling her. "I don't know what to say," she repeated, swallowing against the lump in her throat. "I'm so sorry."

He sat down beside her, the weight of his body bringing their shoulders together. "No, don't be sorry. I mean, not about anything you did. The whole night was a perfect storm of completely fucked-up events, and we were young."

She nodded, battling back the sob lodged in her chest. How could she have been so stupid?

"Mal, stop. I know what you're thinking. I didn't tell you to make you feel bad." He laced his fingers through hers again, resting their joined hands on the bare skin of her thigh. Sparks hummed along her nerves as the rough pad of his thumb stroked the top of her hand. "I told you because the idea that you thought I didn't want anything else from you, after we made love…" he paused, his voice growing rough. "It's ripping me apart."

Her chest hitched. "It was a long time ago," she whispered.

He angled toward her, reaching up to tuck a stray lock of hair behind her ear. "But all this—the truth—is fresh. We both made the wrong assumptions back then. But now we know." He cupped her face, wiped at the moisture beneath her eye. "It was a life-or-death situation. Nothing else in the world would have kept me away from you." His head lowered until his forehead rested against hers.

Warning sirens screamed through her, adding to the chaos of fierce emotions already at war.

"And now you're here again." His nose grazed her cheek as he murmured in her ear. "I can't believe you're here."

A delicious shiver rocked her as the scruff of his jaw scraped against her skin. *Oh, God.* He'd still wanted her, back then. He still wanted her, now. And she wanted him. Desire pooled in her belly, hot and demanding.

No. There would be serious consequences to sleeping with him. It would only bring them closer, when what she needed to do was keep her distance—for both their sakes. She had to be strong.

His lips brushed the corner of her mouth. She breathed in the scent of him, clean and male and still familiar. Time slowed. *Be strong.*

But it was all over. Her body was responding to her need for him on its own accord—she could no more stop it than she could stop her eyelids from blinking or her lungs from drawing breath. Lifting her chin, she brought her mouth to his, and heat shot through her as their lips met.

With a groan, he pressed his palm into the tender flesh of her inner thigh, his fingers slipping beneath the frayed hem of her jeans shorts. His kisses grew bruising, as if he were determined to consume her, and she responded with her own fierce longing. Her nerves smoldered with the need for his touch. For him. For release.

They tore at each other's clothes as they sank onto the bed, and once he had removed the last lacy scrap of fabric from her body, he stilled, holding himself above her, the muscles in his arms and chest bunching beneath his skin. She lay beneath him, trembling slightly as his gaze traveled over her. Hunger flared in his dark green eyes. "God, you're so beautiful." Something like reverence passed over his handsome features before he lowered his head, capturing her nipple in his mouth.

She gasped as the sensations burned across her flesh, and she clawed at his back, pulling him closer. His hands slipped between her legs as he trailed kisses up her chest and along her neck, and she bucked and moaned. Oh God oh God oh God. His fingers stroked and explored, and her muscles tensed. Exquisite agony. Unbearable pleasure. "Please," she whispered, her voice thick with need.

His weight pinned her down as he reached toward the nightstand beside the bed. "Condom."

"I'm on birth control. It's fine."

He locked eyes with her, smoothing the hair from her forehead. "You're sure?"

In answer, she pulled his head back down, seizing his lips in an urgent kiss as she lifted her hips. Her hands clutched at the hard muscles of his shoulders, her fingernails digging into the taut flesh.

He entered her slowly, and she relished the faint twinges of pain that accompanied the pleasure. It had been so long since she'd been with anyone. But beyond the physical, there was another, deeper ache inside her chest…the bittersweet joy of being reunited, wholly and completely, with this man, if only for a fleeting moment in time.

He stilled for a moment once he was completely inside her, and their shallow breaths filled the silence. With a groan, he thrust deeper, and she gasped, clinging to him. She met his rhythm, losing herself in the sensations. She was nothing now but trembling muscles and smoldering nerves. Heat and flesh, joined with his.

Spasms rocked her body as she came, and she cried out, wrapping her legs around him. His powerful climax sent another wave of shuddering contractions through her, turning her cries into whimpers.

His heart slammed against hers as he nuzzled her neck. "That was…intense."

She murmured in agreement, licking her swollen lips. Her throat felt raw from her moans and cries. Her eyes flew open. "What were we thinking? Matt and Sharon are right downstairs! Do you think they heard us?"

He kissed the tender spot beneath her ear. "Who cares?" With a slow grin, he added, "They should probably get used to it."

When she didn't return his smile, he furrowed his brow. "Come here," he said, rolling onto his back and gathering her into his arms. "It's fine, really. They can't hear us from downstairs."

But she was beyond caring about that anymore. His casual joke had invited reality back in. Pain and regret sliced through her. *They should probably get used to it.* Oh, God, what had she done?

Squeezing her eyes shut, she allowed herself one more moment of stolen happiness. *Please don't make this harder than it needs to be.* Steeling herself, she began wiggling away from him. The room was turning gray in the fading light.

"Hey," he said drowsily. He caught her wrist. "Will you stay?"

She pulled away, collecting her clothes before she climbed out of the bed. "I need to get Brady home." She kept her gaze on the window as she slipped into her underwear. Outside, the sky was a collage of purple and cobalt streaks.

"Brady's welcome, too. I can take him for a walk and bring him up here with us."

Her insides twisted. "Well, he might need more to eat," she lied. She'd fed him his dinner before their walk, and he'd had bonus leftovers here. "His food's at home." *Where were her shorts?*

"Oh, right. Well, we could stay at your place, then."

The vise around her heart tightened. This was a nightmare of her own creation. *Damn it, Mal.* She hid her expression, feigning utter absorption in buttoning her jeans shorts. "Um…I don't think that's a good idea."

"Oh. Okay." He swung his legs to the side of the bed and pulled on his shorts. "Well, I get off around four tomorrow, I could take you out to dinner."

Please, no. Her heart cracked, and despair flowed into the seams, burning like salt in a wound. She took a deep breath. She hadn't been strong before, so she needed to be strong now. For both their sakes. "Thanks, but I think it's best if we just…stay friends."

He stood slowly, turning toward her. "Friends."

"Yes."

His features hardened. A small muscle twitched in his jaw. "Is this something you do with all your friends?" he asked, sweeping his hand toward the rumpled bed.

She cringed inwardly as the shot hit its target. But she deserved it. Releasing a shaky breath, she shook her head. "Of course not. No. But it was a mistake."

"A mistake? You certainly seemed to be enjoying yourself."

Heat surged to her cheeks. She swallowed, trying to clear her scratchy throat. "I wasn't trying to say it wasn't...enjoyable." *Understatement of the century.* "Just that it shouldn't have happened."

His green eyes flashed as he took a step closer. "There's someone else, isn't there? In London?"

"No, no. There's no one. Not in London, not here. And I don't want there to be anyone. Please don't take it personally."

His bitter laugh was devoid of humor. "Why the fuck would I take it personally?" He stared pointedly at the bed for a beat before plucking his shirt from the tangled sheets and yanking it over his head. "Jesus Christ."

This was spinning out of control. The room slipped in and out of focus. She bit down on the inside of her cheek until the taste of copper filled her mouth. "What I meant was...this is about me. I can't be with anyone right now. So, it was a mistake to be...intimate...with you."

A heavy silence hung between them as he waited for more. But she didn't think she could get any more words out. Her throat was clogged with misery. She tried to force herself to meet his eyes, but it was too hard. She could feel his icy glare as she bent her head and studied the floor.

Finally, he exhaled, the sound laced with another incredulous laugh and punctuated by the fierce crack of his knuckles. "Great. Well, I'm glad we've cleared everything up." Sarcasm clung to each word like oil.

She nodded, motioning toward the door. "Well, I'll just go find Brady."

He stepped in front of her, yanking the door open. Then he followed her through the hallway toward the stairs.

"I can find my way out," she said as they descended the steps.

"It's dark out. And I'm going for a run anyway."

"Now?" she asked, glancing out the windows by the front door. The last purple streaks of twilight were fading rapidly to black.

He didn't reply.

Smoothing her tangled hair, she followed the sounds of the television to the great room. Sharon was laying on the couch, a stack of pillows under her feet. One hand rested on her protruding belly, and one hand scratched Brady's ear as he sat beside her.

"No wonder he's so quiet," Malorie said, fighting to keep her voice level. "Great food and extra attention."

"Oh," Sharon said, lifting her head. "Hey there." She pushed herself up with one arm.

"Please don't get up. I have to get going, I just wanted to say thanks so much for dinner."

"It was so great to have you. You're welcome anytime."

Malorie pasted a smile on her face as she winced internally, trying to picture Dean's current thoughts on that invitation. She cut her glance over to him, bracing herself for his thunderous expression, but he was retrieving running shoes from a closet.

"Okay, well, thanks again. Come on, Brady, it's time to go." She located his leash by the door to the deck, and Brady hurried over at the promise of a walk.

A half-moon hung in the sky, its reflection shimmering on the dark water. The lights of a few distant boats flickered on the horizon like fireflies. Something scuttled into the seagrass as they made their way down the crest toward the flat sand.

They turned toward her house and the woods, following Brady's lead. "It's so nice out," she finally said in a lame attempt to ease the awkwardness. He didn't respond, and she gave up. The walk was excruciating, even though it was only the length of five houses. It was an eerie echo of their strained trek through the woods on the first day she'd been back. In two weeks, they'd come full circle, and they were back to where they started. Actually, they were in a worse place now. How, how had she let this happen? Bloody hell. Damn her hormones. Damn his hotness. Damn his kind soul and his honorable intentions. Damn it all.

When they reached her house, she jerked her head toward the steps to her deck and stated the obvious. "Well, this is it." Thank God the darkness hid her flaming face. Pulling Brady up the hill, she debated what else to say. 'Thank you' might be interpreted with more scorn. She settled on, "I appreciate your making sure we got home safe."

"Sure," he said, his expression unreadable in the absence of light.

She hurried up the deck steps and opened the unlocked French doors, cutting her gaze to him without turning her head. The moment she was inside, he turned and broke into a jog, lengthening the distance between them with each stride until he disappeared into the night.

Chapter Twenty

"No!" she cried, the strangled syllable ripping her from the nightmare. Cold sweat dripped down her face as she thrashed in the sheets. Gasping, she pushed herself up against the headboard and blinked into the darkness. Brady's eyes glittered in the moonlight as he watched her with canine concern from the end of the bed.

"It's all right," she assured him, although it most certainly wasn't. Her blood was beating against the walls of her veins as though it were trying to escape, and nausea swam through her belly, slick and heavy. She checked the clock by the bed: 3:15 a.m. Ugh.

There was no way she could go right back to sleep after that. Drawing in a shuddering breath, she climbed out of bed. "Come on," she murmured to Brady.

She used the bathroom and splashed water on her face, then wrapped herself in a terry robe. Downstairs, she brewed a cup of the lemon chamomile tea and carried it outside. She clipped the long tie-out she'd bought to Brady's collar, and it slithered down the steps behind him as he went down into the sandy backyard.

Sinking into a chair, she clutched her warm mug and stared out at the water. A tremor ran through her, causing the tea to slosh with little waves. Maybe being out here was a bad idea, but she'd craved fresh air to clear her mind. Unfortunately, scenes from the dream continued to play out in her head, like a movie she couldn't look away from.

This nightmare was different from the ones that had been plaguing her recently. It certainly wasn't new—similar versions of it had tormented her for six years now. But lately, in the weeks since she'd returned to the Cape and she and Dean had made that gruesome discovery, the terrible dreams that woke her involved the cold, gray foot of the girl in the unmarked grave. This macabre scene usually melded into a frantic race through the woods in search of Dean. He was missing, and it was imperative she find him before something awful happened. An overwhelming panic tore at her, along with sinuous vines and skeletal branches, as she searched for Dean without ever finding him.

She sighed. It certainly didn't take a psychology degree to understand a selfish, secret part of her didn't want to lose Dean again. And after what had happened between them a few nights ago—and how she'd treated him—it wasn't surprising her subconscious was acting out in her sleep with increasing frequency and intensity.

But tonight had been a return to the nightmare that began right after the accident. True to form, it was really more of a flashback—an unbidden replay of the events of that March day, surprisingly devoid of embellishments from her imagination. Her mind apparently realized it was horrifying enough on its own.

It had been a Saturday morning, and Malorie had a gymnastics meet. Her car was in the shop, however, and so she'd planned on taking her mother's car. But as she gathered the last of her things, her mother had decided she wanted to go as well, in order to visit the art store near the high school hosting the meet and then watch some of the events. Isabelle Montgomery offered to drive.

In hindsight, Malorie should have been more suspicious. But Isabelle was free to drive when she was on her meds and emotionally stable, as she had been for the past six months. Granted, she didn't venture out very much, but there *was* a huge art supply store near Westgate High.

It would become clear later that Isabelle had been off her meds for at least three weeks at that point. She'd become so adept at hiding it—and so paranoid about the shadowy enemy factions monitoring her behavior—that the signs were difficult to spot. And Malorie was seventeen and distracted herself. She'd heard rumors today that Ryan Rose was going to ask her out, and she wasn't sure how she felt about that. He was cute, and sweet, but...dull.

So Malorie climbed into the passenger seat, grateful for the opportunity to continue texting with her friends about her dilemma. She didn't lift her attention from the screen until she noticed, out of the corner of her eye, trees and buildings whipping by outside the window. How did they even get on this road?

"Mom! You're going way too fast! And this isn't even the right road!" She recognized it now—a winding back road that cut through some horse farms and conservation land.

Isabelle's only answer was the tightening of her grip on the steering wheel. The tendons of her arms rose from her skin like wires as she stared out the windshield.

"Mom, slow down!" she yelled, panic rising in her chest as she studied her mother's profile. *Oh, no.* Isabelle's face was less bloated, her features sharp…and unusually animated. A muscle in her temple was twitching, and her jaw was set in a determined line.

"They said you'd say things like that." When she slid her gaze to Malorie, her eyes were cold and calculating.

Fear seized her, and all she could do for a moment was brace her arm against the dashboard and reflexively press her right foot into the floor, as if brakes might suddenly materialize on her side of the car. *Think.* Trying to deny the existence of the imagined enemies was pointless, and would only make matters worse. It would feed into the delusion.

"If we get into an accident, the cops will come." That might work. When in this state, Isabelle perceived the police as a threat. Part of the secret network.

Her mom laughed, a short, sharp, almost gleeful cackle. "They'll be too late."

Her blood turned to ice. She flicked her gaze back down to her phone. Should she call 911? What could they do? The car swerved around a bend in the road, and she gasped, dropping the phone as her shoulder banged against the door.

She put both hands back on the dashboard. Struggling to keep her voice calm, she tried again. "Why don't you pull over and let me drive, Mom?"

"I know who you are," her mother said, giving her a dark, knowing look. "I don't know how you got into my daughter, but I'm not a fool. I have informants too."

Oh, God. Her heart flailed against her ribcage. *What do I do?* Should she try to grab control of the steering wheel? No. That would certainly lead to an accident. The road here was lined with trees.

"I'm just Malorie. No one has gotten into me. I'm on your side," she added, her attempt at a soothing assertion turning into a high-pitched shriek. God, why wasn't there more traffic? Another car, someone in front of them to force her to slow down?

They swung around another bend, then miraculously, there was one. A white SUV, traveling at a normal speed as it descended a small hill. On the right, Laurel Lake came into view as the trees thinned.

"There's no passing on this road, Mom," she pointed out, removing her sweaty palm from the dash for a split second to gesture toward the double yellow lines. Her stomach lurched as they closed the distance between their sedan and the SUV.

In response, her mom punched the accelerator. "This is the only way. I bet none of you saw this coming!"

A scream tore from Malorie's throat as they sped toward the taillights of the SUV. Bracing for impact, she closed her eyes, but instead of a sickening crunch, she was suddenly flung sideways as the car swerved. Her eyes popped open and she screamed again. "No!"

They were off the paved road now, the car bouncing wildly as it careened toward the lake. Terror clawed at her, primal and all-consuming, cutting off her screams, stopping her heart.

The car sailed off the bank, time slowing as steel, glass, and rubber launched through the air. Then they hit the water, and the breath left her lungs in a whoosh as she was thrown forward against her seatbelt. A searing pain flared in her ankle. Water slapped against the windshield with a powerful splash.

They floated in stunned silence for a moment. Her mind was blank, her body frozen. *Think!* They'd gone over what to do in a situation like this in Driver's Ed. She just needed to calm down and remember. She knew she had only seconds to act.

Isabelle's eyes were closed, her lips moving in a silent internal conversation with the voices in her mind. Blood leaked from her nose. "It's done," she murmured, nodding her head.

The front of the car tipped forward, weighed down by the engine. *Get out!* Malorie's hand reached for the door handle instinctively, but that wasn't right. No. The window.

Her shaking fingers found the correct button. Would it still work, with the car partially submerged? If not, she'd have to find a way to break it. *Please, God,* she prayed as she tried.

The window slid down, but the sudden rush of water pouring in stole her breath and any sense of accomplishment. The lake forced its way into the car, soaking her legs, speeding up the vehicle's descent.

"Mom! We have to get out, right now, or we'll die!" she screamed, shaking her mother's arm.

Isabelle's eyes flew open. "Yes," she said, although whether it was to agree that they needed to escape or that they needed to die, Malorie wasn't sure.

"Open your window! Then you have to swim out!" Malorie tried to reach over further, to help her, and panic gripped her again as she realized she couldn't move. Her seatbelt! She plunged her hands into the water and managed to release it. The car was filling quickly. She had to get out.

"Mom, open your window and get your seatbelt off! We have to get out now!"

Shock and confusion seemed to be warring against her mother's former resignation. The cold water now covered their chests.

Malorie's survival instinct waged its own battle, every cell in her body screaming to escape. Now. There was nothing more she could do if her mother was determined to die, and if she stayed any longer, she would die too. At this point, the electric controls on the driver's side would no longer work. The only way out was the passenger side window, and water continued crashing in with terrifying force and speed.

She prepared to push herself out against the powerful surge. One last idea came to her, one final plea. "Mom, if you don't escape, they'll win. The good side needs you. You have to unbuckle your seatbelt and push yourself out through my window. Follow me. And then swim really hard, toward the surface! Now!"

Her heart was going to explode with fear and despair. How could she leave her mom here? But how could she stay and drown? And then her mother began following her directions.

Somehow, either her words—or the voices in her head—had changed her mind, or her own survival instinct was kicking in. She pulled the seatbelt from her shoulder and scrambled toward the open window.

Thank God. Malorie tilted her head upwards and gulped in a huge lungful of air. Fighting against the flow of water, she grabbed the window frame and forced her way out. She pushed off the car with her feet, and a dull stab of pain registered somewhere in the back of her mind. She clawed her way to the surface, praying her mother was behind her.

She was out. Splashing wildly, she spun around, looking for her mother. "Mom! Mom!" Someone else was yelling, too, and she turned toward the sound. The white SUV, the car they'd almost hit. They must have seen them plunge into the lake. A man was swimming toward her, and a woman was standing on the bank, a phone clutched to her ear.

"My mother's still inside," she screamed, but then, miraculously, Isabelle's head broke the surface. She flailed her arms, gasping and coughing.

"Is that her?" the man yelled. "Is there anyone else in the car?"

"No, we're both out!" she answered, relief flooding her veins as she realized it was true. They were both out. Just in time. The rear of the car slipped beneath the surface and disappeared.

She was suddenly thrust back into the present as her mug slipped from her hands, crashing onto the deck and splashing hot tea on her bare feet. "Oh!" she cried, jumping up from the chair. Brady's nails scrabbled against the wooden steps as he raced back up at the sound of her distress.

God, what was she doing? She was supposed to be out here clearing her mind of the nightmare, not reliving the accident yet again. Her hands were bone white in the moonlight, shaking with tremors and clammy with perspiration. Her pulse pounded in her temples. She dragged her fingers through her hair as if the motion could push the last of the horrifying images from her mind.

Sighing, she picked up the mug. At least it hadn't broken. She unclipped Brady and led him back inside by his collar. "It's okay," she assured him again, even though it was still a lie. In truth, she was a mess. She locked the back door and carried the mug into the kitchen, setting it in the sink before wiping her feet with a dishtowel.

She paused, rubbing the cotton against her right ankle. She'd broken it in the accident, although adrenaline and terror had masked the extent of the pain until the paramedics arrived and began assessing her injuries. Her mother, meanwhile, was fighting them, rambling about enemy spies and mind control. Malorie's heart had sank, knowing that this was the incident that was going to change their lives.

And it did. Malorie did her best at first to maintain that it was just an accident, that her mother had simply lost control of the vehicle on a winding road. But her mother's bizarre rant, along with her medical history, told a different story. Despite privacy laws, the rumors spread. Soon everyone in town was whispering about how Isabelle Montgomery had tried to kill both herself and her daughter while in the grips of a crazy and violent delusion.

Russ Montgomery was not about to allow his family to remain in a town where embarrassing and painful gossip would hover over them permanently like an inescapable noxious cloud. He went into damage control mode immediately. Isabelle was moved to a private facility for serious mental illnesses in the UK, where she remained to this day. Malorie was homeschooled as she recovered, and she and her father moved here later that spring.

She pulled the towel away and rolled her foot around, eliciting a few small pops from her ankle. The injury had put an end to her gymnastics career, but it hadn't been something she would have been able to pursue at uni, anyway. College-level competition was a whole different thing. Still, she'd done her best to continue with the exercises that kept her strong. Somewhere, beneath the horror of the accident, she knew her quick thinking and physical conditioning had saved their lives.

But the bigger fact remained, like a raw wound that would never heal: her own mother had tried to kill her.

Chapter Twenty-One

Malorie followed Julia out of the spacious barn, blinking against the sudden glare as they emerged from the cool, dim interior back out into the bright July sun. She was receiving the formal tour of the future Friendship Farm, now that the closing date had been set. The property really was beautiful.

"It's perfect," Malorie said, sliding her sunglasses from her head to cover her eyes. She followed Julia along a little pathway that led them beneath a vine-covered arbor and into a small garden. Wildflowers sprung up haphazardly inside a ring of lacy hydrangeas. A stone birdbath sat in the center, surrounded by dark green groundcover, and wrought iron benches formed a square around the sides. "Wow. This might be my favorite spot so far." A small tree with white blooms threw dappled shade over the closest bench, and she sank onto it with a sigh that was meant to convey contentment but came out more like a groan.

Julia returned to the bench, her brow furrowing as she stared down at her. "Are you okay? You seem...down, lately. Unhappy."

Uh oh. Mal could see her slumped form reflected in Julia's mirrored sunglasses, and she indeed resembled a sad ragdoll. She straightened, pulling off her own glasses and rubbing her eyes. "I'm just tired, is all." Her pulse spiked erratically as she flicked a glance back up. She had not yet told Julia about everything that had happened between her and Dean, and with each passing day, the idea of revealing the bombshell she'd been keeping from her best friend grew more daunting. Figuring out how to share the secret now, after she'd kept it in this long, was weighing on her almost as much as the pain she'd caused Dean.

"Tired." Julia slid her glasses into her blonde hair and crossed her arms. "I'm not buying it. You can't possibly be jetlagged anymore. You haven't started your classes yet, and they're at night, anyway. Once upon a time, you tasked me with keeping an eye on your health. Clearly, something's up. So I think you'd better come clean."

Bloody hell. Julia had a point. She heaved out another sigh. "I do have something to tell you. But you're going to be mad." *And not just because I waited to tell you.* Malorie knew her friend was not going to like the choice she'd made.

Her lips pressed into a thin line. "Hmm. Well, let's get to it, then." She uncrossed her arms and dropped onto the bench next to Malorie, turning toward her. "Spill."

A bumblebee droned nearby, and she watched it alight on a tall purple blossom as she gathered her courage. *Here we go.* "I slept with Dean." The words tumbled out like water breaking through a dam.

Julia's mouth dropped open. "Holy crap," she finally said, shaking her head in disbelief. "When?"

"Two weeks ago."

"Two...weeks? Are you kidding me with this?" Julia's expression turned stormy.

"I know, I know. I'm sorry." She dropped her gaze, staring at her twisting fingers.

Julia spread her hands in a gesture of disbelief. "But...how could this even happen? After everything he did?"

"I found out some things that changed everything. Sort of."

"This is unbelievable. How could you hold out on me like this?"

"I know. I'm really sorry I didn't tell you before, truly." She forced herself to lift her head. In the center of the garden, a turquoise dragonfly hovered above the birdbath. It shone like a jewel in the sunlight. "It's just...things didn't go well, and I couldn't bear to talk about it. Even to you."

Julia huffed out a breath, pinning her with a penetrating stare. "Didn't go well? What do you mean by that? If things changed enough for this to even become a possibility, then I'm having trouble picturing sex with Dean Slater as something unpleasant."

"No, no...that's not what I mean. The sex was great. Incredible, actually." Heat seeped into her cheeks, and she bit down on her lip.

"Okay, well, that doesn't sound so bad. But I can't help but return to the fact that he hurt you pretty badly in the past, so I'm having trouble wrapping my mind around this. Are you upset with yourself for doing it, then?"

"Well, yes, but not for that reason." She pulled in a shuddering breath. Did she have the right to tell Julia about what Cherry had done on prom night? *Screw it.* Swallowing past the tightness in her throat, she relayed everything Dean had told her about that long ago night.

By the time she'd finished the story, a lock of Julia's golden hair was wrapped so tightly around her finger Malorie was afraid they'd need scissors to free it. "So, yeah…he already knew at that point I'd been blind drunk, and once he explained what he'd been through with Cherry, we both realized we'd been wrong all these years. And then it just…happened."

"Well, I'm going to need more details than 'it just happened'. I mean…God. This is unbelievable. But we'll get back to that. So why are you so upset?" A thundercloud slipped over her delicate features as her mind put it together. "Oh, Mal."

She tensed, suddenly defensive. But this was her choice to make, and it was the right one. Whether Julia agreed or not. "I had to put an end to it right way, before things went any further. But I know I hurt him."

Julia sighed. "You know how I feel about this. You deserve happiness too. I don't think you're being fair to yourself."

She shrugged. "And you know how I feel about it. I don't think it's fair to subject someone to a potential lifetime of dealing with the most severe mental illness there is. The kind of illness that makes life hell. The kind of illness that makes people want to kill the people they love. And I know one night of sex isn't a marriage proposal, but this is Dean we're talking about. I still love him." A wave of shock hit her as she realized what she'd just admitted. *She loved him. Still.* "So even if we're just fooling around for a while, eventually I'd have to end it. It would only get harder." Her voice cracked on a sob.

A pair of sparrows landed on the birdbath, their gray and brown feathers blurring as she fought back tears. Julia's arm curled around her shoulders, warm and comforting. She leaned into her friend.

Julia gave her a gentle squeeze. "What did he say about the schizophrenia, then?"

She stiffened. "Nothing. I didn't tell him about that."

"Oh, no." The disapproval was clear in Julia's voice, even before she turned Malorie toward her on the bench, bring them face-to-face. "So you didn't tell him the real reason you don't want to be with him? That doesn't seem fair. You just said you love him. You're not even giving him a chance to change your mind."

"That's right, I'm not. Because you know what? Then he'd be trapped. He's a nice guy, Jules. If he knew about the schizophrenia and we started dating anyway, what would happen if he wanted to break up eventually? He'd feel too guilty. Even if it had nothing whatsoever to do with the possibility of my getting sick, he'd worry I'd perceive it that way. He's a caretaker. He took care of his mom, he takes care of his brother, and he's going to take care of his nephew. He doesn't need to be faced with the possibility of taking care of me. If we stayed together and I got sick, his life would be about making sure I took my meds, and dealing with my hallucinations when I didn't, and maybe even trying to stop me from being violent. And trust me, even if I stayed on the meds, I wouldn't be a good partner. The side effects are horrible. He'd be stuck with a very different version of who I am now." She gulped in air, trying to get it past the iron band constricting her chest.

Julia frowned, shaking her head. "But...you're making a lot of assumptions! The statistics might be higher for you, but they're still in your favor. There's a really good chance you won't develop it all. An over 85% chance you'll just stay healthy, right?"

"Yes, but, Jules…he wants kids. He said as much when we were talking about his brother's baby. He'd be a great father. And I am *not* having kids. I'm not risking passing this on, but more than that, I'm not risking a child's life. You know what happened with my mom. Even before the accident, my childhood wasn't great. I never, ever had friends over. Daily life was usually unpredictable at best. Dangerous at worst. So I couldn't even adopt…it wouldn't be fair to subject a child to that." A dull ache throbbed in her palms, and she realized she was clenching her fists hard enough to drive her fingernails into her flesh. *Relax.*

"What about what's fair for you? You're a good person, Mal. A great person. Look at everything you've overcome. And everything you're doing to help people…from teaching your new classes to all the paperwork you're doing for the farm." She made a wide, sweeping motion with her hands. "Look at all the volunteer hours you've put in already to help create a place for disabled kids. You deserve to be happy, too."

Her vision blurred again as more tears welled up, and she blinked, sending them rolling down her hot skin. "I *am* happy," she insisted, and then laughed weakly at the absurdity of the statement, given the fact she was sitting here crying. "I mean…I will be," she added, sniffling. "Once some time has passed, and I'm over what happened with Dean." She wiped at her eyes. "I know you don't like my decision, and that you're looking out for me, but this is just the way it has to be."

Julia sighed, pulling her into a hug. "You're right, I'm not happy with your decision, sweetie. But I do understand why you think it's the right thing to do." She rubbed Malorie's back for a moment before releasing her.

"Thanks." She blew out a shuddering breath.

A smile played across Julia's lips as she dabbed at a missed tear on Mal's cheek. "Hell, I'm getting more and more tired of Pete by the day. Maybe you and I should just shack up and spend our lives together. I mean, as long as you don't mind if I sleep with guys when I feel the need."

She giggled. "That sounds like a perfect arrangement, actually. I'm in. I'll be your back-up plan. If you don't get married, we'll retire here. You can take care of the horses and I'll try to cook."

Julia laughed with her, but then her blue eyes took on a serious edge. "You know that, no matter what, I'll always be here for you if you need me, right? Married or single. Now or in the future."

Her throat swelled with gratitude, and she swallowed hard. "I know, Jules. And I love you for it."

"Love you too," she replied, squeezing her hand. She stood, pulling Malorie up as well, and looked up at the sun. "Come on. It's five o'clock somewhere. There's a cute little restaurant nearby I've been wanting to try. Let's treat ourselves."

Chapter Twenty-Two

Damn it to hell. He was late. Yanking open the door, he scanned a sign listing classrooms posted in the hallway of the building. Room 239. He strode down the hall, checking his phone as he searched for a stairwell.

Five minutes past six. Class started at 6:00, and it was the first night, so a few minutes wasn't a big deal, but he ground his teeth in irritation as he jogged up the stairs. It was Matt's fault. Dean's class began at 6:00 p.m. every Tuesday and Thursday for the next six weeks, and when he'd signed up for it—months ago, when Mr. Firenze first mentioned selling the business—he hadn't foreseen an issue. But then Matt and Sharon had to sign up for four weeks of childbirth classes, and their Tuesday night class began at 6:30. Since Sharon's old wreck of a car was both unreliable and without a functioning air conditioning unit, they all had to share the truck. And while it shouldn't have been a big issue, since both the Cape Cod Community College campus and the Cape Cod Hospital were in Hyannis, Matt didn't seem to have felt any pressure to leave early enough to get Dean to class on time. Matt had always put his own needs first, that was nothing new, but his utter lack of concern for anyone else, combined with his general belligerence, was testing Dean's patience lately. He didn't know how Sharon could stand being around his brother, to be honest. Hopefully, things would change when the baby came. Perhaps it was just the stress of change: both an infant and a wife were in Matt's near future, and his new situation carried a lot of responsibility.

There. Room 239. The door was closed, and a fresh wave of annoyance spiraled through him as he tucked his phone into his pocket and reached for the handle. Easing the door open, he focused on making his tall form as unobtrusive as possible. A female voice came to an abrupt halt, and he glanced toward the front of the room as he closed the door behind him.

His heart stopped. Malorie. Standing behind a large desk in a sleeveless dress, her hair tied up in a loose knot, her finger frozen over an open laptop.

Their eyes locked, and the stunned expression on her face told him she was just as surprised as he was by this bizarre turn of events. An uncomfortable pause hung over the room, and the heads of the other twenty-some students swiveled between them, searching for clues to the sudden silence.

Shit. She was the instructor. Malorie was teaching Intro to Business. How was that possible? His mind spun. When he'd signed up, he was pretty sure the teacher had been listed as "To Be Determined" or some other vague phrase.

Her mouth gaped, her cheeks flaming an almost neon scarlet. She looked completely, utterly bewildered, and the class was noticing.

The inescapable need to protect her took over, eclipsing his own discomfort. He spoke loudly, drawing attention to himself. "I'm sorry. Is this Intro to Business?"

She nodded slowly, a mix of comprehension and gratitude washing over her features. Clearing her throat, she gestured toward stacks of papers on a nearby empty desk. "Um…yes. I didn't realize we were missing anyone. Can you sign in on the sheet?" Her hand shook slightly as she reached for a plastic bottle of water. "And it's fine, we're just getting started. There's a handout there too." She lifted the water toward her lips and took a small sip. The furious blush began fading from her face.

He made a wide circle around the desks, staying near the walls, calculating the best way to maximize the distance between their bodies as he approached the vacant desk. Clearly she had the same thought, because she took a few steps away while he signed his name on the last line and collected the stapled packet of papers.

He took a seat far to the right, out of her sight line if she looked straight ahead, and she slowly regained her composure, returning her focus to the slide displaying the course outline. He sat very still, as though that might help her forget he was in the room. And maybe it did, because her voice grew stronger and her body language grew more relaxed.

Or maybe he was a fool to think it even mattered at all to her that he was there. Why should she care? She didn't want anything from him beyond 'friendship'. She was probably just shocked to run into him here, of all places, and embarrassed about what had happened the last time they were together. His presence simply churned up all the regret. He was a distraction, reminding her of a night she'd prefer to forget. That's all.

If only that was all it was for him. He wanted to forget that night, too, but for different reasons. For over two weeks, he'd been burning with anger. Anger at her, for rejecting him with such a vague, weak explanation. Anger at himself, for not being enough for her. But beneath all that was something worse: pain, sharp and unrelenting. Now it stabbed at him with renewed vigor, tearing at his heart. Every time he looked at her, he pictured her beneath him, her hair a mahogany halo on his pillow, her hazel eyes smoldering with desire for him. Had he imagined her passion? The thought had plagued him on a regular basis these past few weeks, but now it buzzed inside his head like a trapped wasp.

Being this close to her was torture. But he was here to learn, to become more familiar with the basics of running a business. So he forced himself to focus on the material, clenching his jaw with grim determination every time his mind drifted.

After one of the longest ninety minutes of his life, he grabbed his things from the desk and hurried out the door, determined to avoid spending one more second in a small room with her. Until Thursday, that was. *Christ.* How could this be happening? For the twentieth time that night, he wished she'd never returned to Cape Cod.

He jogged down the stairs, losing momentum as he approached the building's exit. His speedy departure from the classroom had been necessary for his sanity, but now, he had nowhere to go. Matt and Sharon's class didn't end until 8:00, and then it would take them a good ten to fifteen minutes to get to him. He was stuck here for at least 40 minutes. With a sigh, he strode over to a bench set away from the main entrance and sat down.

The sky was a dark gray, and the last of the sun's rays struggled to penetrate the blanket of heavy clouds. The weather pretty much summed up his mood, he decided, pulling out his phone to check the forecast for tomorrow. Heavy rain in the morning could impact his schedule for Wednesday. A total washout might even mean a day off, although that wouldn't be the case when—if—he became the owner of the business. There would always be something to do: sharpen tools, pay bills, work on promotion...

"Are you...waiting for someone?"

Gritting his teeth, he looked up. Malorie stood before him, arms crossed in front of her chest, hands rubbing her tanned skin against the damp air. A brown leather bag hung from one shoulder. Lifting her brows, she waited for an answer, something like hope flickering in her eyes.

Ridiculous. What would she be hoping for? That he was hanging around after class in order to tell her how happy he was that she was the instructor?

"Just waiting for my ride. Matt and Sharon had a childbirth class at the hospital tonight, and they're picking me up after." Why was he even offering her this info?

"Oh." She hesitated, glancing toward the parking lot. "Well...you could get a ride with me, if you want."

"That's okay. But thanks."

Her face fell, and she looked away again, chewing on her bottom lip. She took a step away, then tilted her head. "Are you sure? It's literally right on the way." A weak smile curved her mouth. "And I wouldn't mind some company."

It was a bad idea, but he paused for a moment, considering it anyway. It had been a long day and he was hungry. Knowing Matt, he'd probably stop at a drive-through after class, making Dean's wait even longer while also failing to order something for his brother.

He shrugged. "Yeah, okay, if you're sure you don't mind. Let me just text Matt." He tapped out a quick message as he stood. "Thanks," he added.

Her smile brightened, but a hint of uncertainty remained etched across her features. "Sure." She motioned toward the lot, and he grabbed his notebook off the bench.

She drew in an audible breath as they stepped off the curb. "I'm sorry that…things are awkward. I would really like us to be friends." She sighed, adjusting the bag over her shoulder. "I mean, we're neighbors. My family is one of your clients. And now," she swept her hand toward the building in the distance, "we'll be in class together, for the next six weeks, anyway."

Intermittent drops of rain fell from the leaden sky as they crossed the parking lot, and a gust of wind carried her scent in his direction. His insides tightened. This was a really, really bad idea. "That's fine," he said.

Her heels clicked on the pavement as they picked up their pace. "I was just…surprised to see you, in class. They had told me I had a full class, but I didn't get the sign-in sheet until today, and I didn't really look it over. I was too nervous about getting my laptop connected to their technology."

"I was surprised too," he said as they approached her car. "I signed up for the class a while ago, when Mr. Firenze first mentioned possibly selling me the business. I don't think they listed an instructor name at that point."

"Well, now we know." Her voice rang with forced optimism. "And the class should be helpful in terms of running a business." The taillights flashed as the doors unlocked with a chirp.

As he opened the passenger door, he caught her gaze. "Listen, it's not a done deal yet, so I'd appreciate it if you don't tell anyone. About me buying the business."

She nodded, sliding into the driver's seat and shutting the door. "I understand. I won't say anything to anyone." Rubbing her hands together, she shuddered. "Crappy weather." She smoothed her dress over her legs before starting the ignition. The pale lilac fabric had a constellation of tiny dark spots from the rain, and a few drops glistened in her hair.

He dragged a hand through his own hair, brushing away the moisture. His phone vibrated, and he checked the screen. A one-letter reply from Matt: 'K'.

"It's supposed to be a really nice weekend, though," she said as she pulled onto the main road through the campus. The wipers screeched across the windshield, triggered by the mist, and she flicked them off with a grimace.

He pulled his attention back to her. "What?"

"This weekend. It's supposed to be nice. In terms of weather, I mean." She glanced at him as she checked for traffic, then made a left onto Route 132.

"Oh." This was crazy. They'd been reduced to talking about the freaking weather. He scrubbed at his jaw and looked out the side window. Beyond a stretch of trees, the fast food signs near the highway ramps marked the rest area on the hill.

"Julia and I are going to go to the Vineyard on Saturday. Just for the day."

He appreciated her attempt to keep the conversation going, but he couldn't come up with anything beyond, "Sounds fun." He and Malorie had gone to Martha's Vineyard together once, in the spring of their senior year. They'd taken the ferry from Falmouth to Oak Bluffs. They'd ridden the Flying Horses carousel, the oldest in the country, and Malorie had joked about how much more fun it was than riding actual horses with Julia. After they'd visited the shops and the gingerbread houses, they'd eaten fried seafood overlooking the water.

"What about you? Any good plans for the weekend?"

She was trying really hard—he had to give her that. "Um, yeah, actually. Going to a wedding Saturday night."

She brightened, lifting her brows. "Oh! Your brother's?"

A wry laugh escaped as he shook his head. "No. Matt's dragging his heels on that one as hard as he can."

Frowning, she blinked. "Aren't they sort of…running out of time?"

He sighed, working at his knuckles. "Yep, they are. But short of what I've already done to encourage him to do the right thing, I'm not sure what else I can do. I can't really drag him down to the courthouse and force him to say vows. But I feel bad for Sharon, she actually seems to want to marry him." He sighed and shifted in the seat. "I'm afraid he might be cheating on her, though. I heard him get up in the middle of the night the other night, and when I couldn't get back to sleep, I went downstairs. The truck was gone."

The whole subject pissed him off, and he wasn't sure why he was telling Mal of all people. But it felt good to tell someone, and he knew she'd keep it to herself. She'd never been one to gossip.

She turned down the radio. "Oh, no. That sucks. Did you ask him about it?"

"Yeah. He said he couldn't sleep either, and went for a drive." He shrugged. "Maybe it was the truth...I'm sure he has a lot on his mind lately."

She nodded in agreement. "Well, I hope it all works out for the best. I really like Sharon."

"Yeah." Gesturing toward an upcoming turn, he added, "You can take that right to cut through to 28." Directions had never been her thing, and despite their apparent ability to discuss neutral topics with civility, he still wanted to make this ride as short as possible.

"Oh, right. Thanks." Flicking on her blinker, she glanced into the rearview mirror before switching lanes. "So...whose wedding then?"

His muscles tensed, and he scrubbed at his jaw. "Oh. Well, I don't really know the couple, actually. They're sort of friends of friends." He chose his next words carefully, despite the fact that it really didn't matter. "I'm just going as someone's guest."

A rosy flush crept up her neck as she stared out the windshield, the rising color highlighting taut cords. Her pearl earring glowed against her skin like a tiny full moon. "So…a date?"

He shrugged. "I guess." He was going with his old girlfriend, Nicole, but he decided to leave that part out. They'd run into each other at The Boat House last weekend, and she'd been lamenting over a recent break-up that now left her dateless for her friend's upcoming wedding. When she'd asked him if he'd go with her, he'd hesitated for only the briefest of moments before he decided, *Why the hell not?* He was single.

"Oh," she said, her voice flat. She swallowed, blinking rapidly.

Oh, no. His gut clenched. She was trying not to cry. Even after all these years, he still knew her well enough to read the signs. But why? It made no sense. She'd told him in no uncertain terms that she wasn't interested. Frustration bubbled up, warring with the inexplicable guilt twisting through him. "Do you have a problem with that?"

Her hands tightened on the wheel, her knuckles turning pale. She shook her head, biting down on her lip. "No, of course not." Her voice broke slightly as she added, "It's great."

Shit. He sighed. *Just leave it alone*, his inner voice commanded. But the reckless part of him that needed to know what the hell was going on took over. "You don't sound very convincing."

"Sorry, I'm just tired." Her eyelashes continued to flutter as she guided the car along the winding back road. Then she lost the battle, and tears slipped down her face, rolling down her profile.

Jesus Christ. "Malorie," he said, fighting to keep his tone level. "What's going on? You said you wanted to be alone. Those were *your* words. *Your* decision." He blew out a breath, uncurled his fists. "So why are you upset now? Do you want me to be alone, too? Is that what you want?"

Her hand flew up to stifle a sob. "No." Sniffling, she brushed at the tears on her cheeks. "It's just…hard."

"It's hard?" *What* was hard? Emotions roiled through him. He wanted to punch something. He wanted to tell her to stop the car so he could yank her into his arms. "Why? God, this is insane."

She stilled, the delicate line of her jaw hardening as her breath caught. A heavy pause, thick and solemn, hung in the air between them. Her pulse jumped in her neck. When she finally turned toward him, her face was closed, her eyes shuttered, their hazel depths revealing nothing. "Just forget it. I don't want to talk about this. I don't even know what I'm saying. I've been speaking in front of a class for nearly two hours tonight, and that's stressful."

Stress was making her cry over the news that a man she wanted nothing but 'friendship' from was going on a casual date? It didn't add up, and he was torn between backing off and pushing her further. The protective instincts in him wanted to do as she'd asked, to drop this conversation that was clearly distressing her. But there was something deeper going on here, and he couldn't protect her from what he didn't understand, so those same instincts were telling him to find a way to unlock the truth.

The rain picked up its pace, drumming against the roof, sliding down the windshield. She flipped on the wipers, and they slapped at the water rhythmically.

He swept his gaze between her rigid posture and the curving road. The cloud coverage was accelerating the evening's transition into darkness, and there were no streetlights to help cut through the shadows. "Mal, pull over. Let me drive."

"I'm fine."

"You said you're stressed, and you're clearly upset about something."

"I'm—"

She cried out as a fox darted into the road. Slamming on the brakes, she swerved to the right, and the car careened over the soft shoulder toward the woods.

Chapter Twenty-Three

The car rattled through the underbrush, snapping branches and tearing vines, lurching to a stop in front of a spindly pine sapling. "Oh my God," she wailed, throwing the gear shift into park. "We have to get out!"

What? Before he could ask her if she was okay, she had flung open the driver's side door and scrambled out into the rain.

Throwing off his seatbelt, he inhaled through his nose, expecting smoke or gasoline, some dangerous scent to explain her panicked exit. But he only smelled damp earth, drifting in from the open door, mixing with traces of her perfume. As far as he could tell, the car hadn't even hit anything substantial enough to cause damage—she'd braked to their sudden stop. So what was going on? *Was she hurt?*

He was at her side in seconds, fear burning through his veins. "Are you okay?" Seizing her shoulders, he scanned her body, searching for injuries.

"I'm sorry I'm sorry I'm sorry," she wailed, the breathless words running into each other like a protective chant. The rain plastered her hair to her head as she ran her hands over his arms, as if checking to make sure he was actually there, in one piece. Her eyes were wild, her wet skin pale.

"Are you hurt?" he demanded, shaking her slightly, aware that his fingers were digging deep into her skin.

She shook her head, still trembling violently. Then she threw herself into his arms.

His breath caught in a mixture of relief and confusion, but he pulled her close, shifting their bodies closer to a large pine, beneath a massive bough that provided a bit of shelter from the rain. "It's okay then. Everything's fine," he murmured, over and over again, rubbing her upper back. The car's headlights cut into the misty shadows, and raindrops trickled through the branches, pattering against the fans of needles, beading on their exposed skin.

Her muscles slowly relaxed, and her body melted into his, her head pressed against his shoulder. Although they were barely moving, he felt something change between them.

She lifted her chin, nuzzled his neck. He sucked in a breath as desire flooded through him. *Christ.* A moan rose in his throat, and he clenched his jaw against it. This felt wrong, like he was taking advantage of her, even if she was the one taking the embrace to a different level.

But he couldn't deny her. Didn't want to. He bent his head, brushing his lips over hers with the barest of pressure, tasting the rain and her tears, giving her time to withdraw, to change her mind. But she arched up to him, seeking his mouth, straining for more.

His hand moved to the back of her head, holding her fast as he ravaged her lips. She responded with her own urgent hunger, turning the kiss into something so powerful, so primal, he felt as though she were trying to convey some wordless message.

The hum of a second engine registered. A dark car approached, slowing down, breaking the spell. Reality came crashing in. *Damn it.* He groaned as they drew apart, forcing himself to try to ignore the arousal pulsing through his groin. *What had they been doing, anyway? And where could it have gone?* It would have had to end at some point, unless they planned on climbing back in the still-running car and having sex by the side of the road. He shook his head to clear it, adjusting his jeans in an attempt to hide the swell beneath the denim.

He and Mal turned toward the other car, fingers lacing for a lingering moment before they separated completely. The passenger side window rolled down as the driver craned his neck toward them. "Everything all right?" he asked, moving his gaze between the two of them and the idling car parked in the trees.

"We're fine." He raised his hand in a polite wave before raking it through his scalp, scrubbing the moisture from his hair. "Thanks, though."

The car drove off, and there was a beat of silence as their eyes locked. Her hair had escaped its loose knot and hung in long, damp waves around her face. Her color had returned, but she wore a slightly bewildered expression, like someone who had just woken up in a strange location.

"I'll drive," he said, his tone firm.

She nodded, crossing her arms over her chest, hugging herself.

Her vulnerable posture made his heart ache, but he kept his distance, gesturing toward the curb. "Let me pull the car out so it's easier for you to get in." His door had opened into a tangle of brush, and a few fresh scratches stung the skin of his arms.

When they were back on the road, he turned on the heat to warm her up, angling the vents in her direction. "Well, aside from a few scratches, the car seems to be okay. So that's good." He paused. "What about you?"

She nodded, a small shiver traveling through her. Leaning forward, she held her palms in front of the vents.

The air grew steamy as the heat inside the car mixed with the humidity outside. He hit the defrost button, clearing the fogged windshield. The rain had begun tapering off, and the clouds were tearing apart, revealing small patches of indigo sky.

With a sigh, she pressed herself back into her seat. "I was in a bad accident once." Her hands twisted in her lap, plucking at her dress. "In case you're wondering why I sort of freaked out back there."

"Oh." That explained a lot. "What happened?"

"I was with my mom," she said slowly, reaching for the plastic water bottle sitting in the cup holder. She took several long swallows, seemingly gathering her thoughts.

He'd never met her mother—Mrs. Montgomery had already left for England by the time he'd met Malorie—and she had never talked about her much. She hadn't talked about her father much, either, at least with him...probably because it had been clear by the beginning of their relationship how Russ Montgomery felt about Dean, well before he'd spelled it out to his face after the prom fiasco. Dean had understood the pressure Malorie felt, the expectations she'd been saddled with in terms of the family business, but Mal had claimed her mother had little interest in intervening in the plan for her future.

So, while he'd done his best to support her back then, any discussion of her father not only put Dean on the defensive, but reminded them both of their impending separation. Plus, they'd been teenagers, wrapped in their own world. The adults around them had barely registered in their lives most days.

Exhaling, she capped the bottle. "We…our car went into a lake."

"What?" He cut his gaze toward her as his hands tightened on the wheel. "Jesus. Everyone was okay, though?"

She hesitated. "Yes. Physically. Well, I broke my ankle, but it healed."

"And this happened in England?"

"No. In Connecticut. A few months before I moved here."

The words hit him like a punch in the gut, sucking the air from his lungs. "In Connecticut?" he repeated, struggling to process what she was saying. He stared at her for a moment before turning his attention back to the road. "But that would mean it happened the same year we met. Why didn't you tell me?"

She shifted in her seat. "It was traumatic. I didn't—I don't like to talk about it. It's the reason I'm afraid to go in the water now."

He frowned, his mind still reeling with the revelation. "But…you were a lifeguard. At the Club."

"That was before the accident. I switched to working the snack bar afterward. I didn't lifeguard at all that summer before senior year."

He slowed to yield at the rotary, flicking his glance toward her as he merged with the traffic. Her cheeks were flushed, her eyes downcast. His chest clenched, and he clamped down on the urge to berate her further for not telling him about this back then.

But...why hadn't she? After all the things they'd shared with one another? He had the niggling feeling this was the tip of a murky iceberg, a small piece of a deeper truth.

And why had she kissed him by the side of the road? She'd needed comfort after the scare, that was understandable...but the kiss was something else entirely. Something she'd denied she wanted only weeks ago.

A wave of exhaustion suddenly crashed over him. He was tired after a long work day followed by a tense hour-and-a-half class. He was still starving. He was confused about the kiss, about the secret accident, about Malorie's behavior. When her guard was down, her actions were not matching up with her words.

They were almost home now. He turned left into Sandalwood, choosing his own words carefully. "I think there's something you're not telling me, Malorie. And maybe you have a good reason. I don't know. But I do know *you*. And I know you're hiding something." He glanced at her as he tapped the brakes, turning onto Beach Plum. She stared at her lap, not meeting his gaze, her expression hidden by her hair and the shadows.

He plunged ahead. "So I just want you to know that you can trust me. Not trusting each other is what got us into trouble in the first place, all those years ago. So, if you need to tell me something…even as just a friend…you can trust me."

"I know I can." Her voice trembled with conviction and some other heartbreaking emotion. Something like sorrow. "Thank you," she added in a near whisper.

An exterior light glowed from her porch, a beacon among the mostly dark houses down here at the end of the street. The car's beams cut into the inky woods as he circled the cul-de-sac. Pulling into her driveway, he checked her visor for a remote garage opener. No clickers that he could see, but he could always jump out and use the code. "Do you want the car in the garage?"

She shook her head, smoothing her dress. "It's fine here. I'd like to think nothing else is going to happen to it tonight." She offered a shaky laugh. "I'm glad I got the long-term rental insurance."

"Okay." Shifting into park, he cut the engine and they both gathered their things from the back. "I'll make sure you get in," he added as they climbed out of the car.

She hitched the bag over her shoulder. "Thank you." Her fingers drifted to her lower lip as she paused. "And, um, I'm sorry if I made things…weird again."

That was one word for it. A thread of heat pulsed through him at the reminder of their kiss, but he shrugged it off. "No worries. I'll see you Thursday, I guess."

With a nod, she hurried up the walkway and clicked up the porch steps. When she'd fished her keys from her bag and twisted them in the lock, she turned to wave. "Thanks again."

"Say hi to Brady for me," he called out, waiting for the door to close behind her before he headed down the dark road.

***

He woke Sunday morning with a dull throb in his temples and the tug of trepidation in his gut. The headache was primarily the result of a late night at the wedding, complemented by a healthy dose of guilt over his repeated rejections of Nicole's increasingly blatant advances. The anxiety stemmed from a decision he'd eventually made as the night wore on, and the possible repercussions of following through with the plan. But he had to know.

After Tuesday night, the week had gone surprisingly smoothly. Thursday's class held no surprises. He was able to concentrate, and he learned some useful things. He had his truck, so there were no awkward rides. On Friday, he grabbed a few beers with the guys from work right after they finished up, then called it an early night.

Then came the wedding, a celebratory event designed to be fun, even if he didn't know the couple; an opportunity to prove to himself that he was just fine. He even knocked off a few hours early on Saturday to attend. But during the lakeside ceremony, as the couple took their vows, his thoughts kept turning to Malorie. During the reception, he found himself trying to avoid being alone with Nicole, as his hot ex-girlfriend—with whom he'd parted amicably—went from subtle flirting to suggestive comments to literally throwing herself at him, because he couldn't stop thinking about Malorie. On the tense drive home, Nicole's anger had filled the cab of his truck like a thunderhead, thick and ominous. She'd nearly jumped out before he came to a complete stop, muttering a terse goodbye as she slammed the door.

Christ. He dragged a hand through his messy hair, curling his fingers and yanking until a flare of pain rose in his scalp. He was damn well going to get to the bottom of whatever was going on with Malorie—today.

After a quick shower, he jogged down the stairs, the restless impatience growing with each passing minute. The coffee had been brewed, and he sent up a silent thanks to Sharon as he poured a steaming cup. He could see her through the windows, sitting outside on the deck, but he didn't want to engage in any conversation right now. Carrying his phone and his coffee, he retreated instead to the small study near the front of the house and sat down at the desk.

Eight forty-five a.m. Was it too early to start? With a shrug, he opened up his social media apps. If people were asleep, they should have their phones turned off. It wouldn't hurt to start sending messages now.

He scrolled through contacts, looking for mutual friends. A half hour later, he had the phone number he was looking for. He returned to the kitchen, poured another cup of coffee, and texted Julia.

Chapter Twenty-Four

The midmorning rays warmed her skin, and her eyes drifted closed behind her sunglasses. She settled her book against her chest. Could she really justify a nap, at this hour? She hadn't even been awake that long. But it was Sunday, she had nowhere to be, and yesterday had been a whirlwind of activity.

She and Julia had crisscrossed Martha's Vineyard, shopping, sightseeing, and eating. They'd even rented a moped, which Julia had fearlessly guided through traffic as Malorie clung to her waist, eyes screwed shut. But even as she admired the breathtaking clay cliffs of Aquinnah and ate ice cream overlooking Edgartown Harbor alongside her best friend, she'd had to constantly struggle to tamp down the memories of a similar day spent with Dean, years ago. By the time they'd shuffled off the ferry and driven home, she was both physically and mentally exhausted.

So what would be the harm in a little snooze? She dragged one eye open to check on Brady, but he was already a step ahead of her, curled in a patch of shade beneath the big table.

Her eyes flew back open as a trio of knocks echoed through the house. She and Brady jumped up in unison, her book sliding to the wooden planks of the deck, his barks answering the raps on the front door. *Who on earth could it be?* She unclipped Brady and followed him through the French doors into the house, pausing by the dining table. At the moment, she was wearing a red bikini…probably not the best attire in which to greet a visitor. The shopping bags from yesterday were still sitting on one of the chairs, and she fished through tissue paper to find her biggest indulgence—a gauzy white cover-up that had cost more than she should have spent, even on sale—and pulled it over her head. It would do.

Yanking the tags from the sleeve, she dropped them on the hall table and joined Brady at the front door. Her dog stood on his hind legs, peering out the window, his tail wagging violently. That was a good sign, anyway. She peeked out over his head as she reached for the doorknob, and her breath caught.

Why was Dean here? Anxiety rolled through her stomach even as her heart did a traitorous flip. "Is everything all right?" The question tumbled out as she yanked the door open. "Sharon?"

"Everything's fine," he assured her, leaning forward to greet Brady as he eased his way inside.

She backed up a few steps, her mind spinning. If there was no emergency, maybe this was just about class. Maybe he wanted to ask a few questions about the business acquisition he was considering, outside of the classroom. Or maybe it was about their landscaping contract.

He stood, and a small frown crossed his lips. "Actually, that's not true. I've just come from Julia's."

Fear gripped her with iron claws, paralyzing her lungs. "What's happened?" She looked around wildly for her phone—

where had she left it? Kitchen. She turned and ran, Brady at her heels.

"Julia's fine!" he called after her. "I just went over to talk to her."

She grabbed the phone off the island and flipped it over. A single text popped up when she lit the screen: 'Please don't hate me. I want you to be happy.' Rows of emojis followed the words.

The floor lurched beneath her feet. *Oh, God, Julia, what have you done?* She whirled around, smacking the phone back on the island. "What did she tell you?"

He held his hands up in a placating gesture. "Nothing, really. Don't be mad at Julia."

"Don't tell me how to feel!" Her voice was high and brittle, her body shaking. Brady whined. *How could Julia betray her like this?*

"Okay," he said softly, taking a step closer. His green eyes were wide with concern. "Just, hear me out for a sec, okay?"

She nodded, choking back a sob.

"Julia didn't tell me anything personal. No details. Just that there is something you're keeping from me, something that might explain why you believe we can't be together."

A mix of primal emotions shuddered through her. "She had no right."

"I went to her, Malorie. I didn't leave her a lot of choices."

Tears pricked her eyes, blurring her vision. She shook her head as she swallowed against the swelling lump in her throat. "There are always choices."

"Then why won't you give *me* one?" he demanded, his voice rising. "Why can't you tell me whatever it is you're hiding, so I can stop living in constant torture?"

She bit down on her lip. "It's…complicated."

He sighed, raking his fingers through his hair. "I can handle complicated." Closing the distance between them, he reached out, settling his hands on her shoulders. "I care about you, Mal." He shook his head. "Shit. That's not right. I *love* you, Mal. I loved you six years ago, I've loved you every second in between, despite what I thought had happened, and I love you now. And that's what I told Julia, too. That's why she admitted there was a reason you believed we can't be together." His fingers tightened. "So just…tell me. Tell me what this awful thing is, so we can work through it. Together."

She couldn't hold back the tears, and they dribbled out, hot and humiliating, as she dropped her head. *He loved her.* Still. But he didn't *know* her. Not really. He didn't know about the hidden time bomb that might be lurking in her genes, waiting to change her into an entirely different person. A person who would make life a living hell. A person capable of trying to kill the people she loved. An agonizing mass expanded in her chest like a tumor.

"Please. Just let it go," she whispered, her voice trembling. She pulled away, wiping at her cheeks.

"No."

Crossing to the sink, she splashed cold water on her face and grabbed a paper towel to dry off. When she turned back, he was standing by the counter, holding the broken picture frame that she'd left lying on a pile of papers for weeks. His gaze moved from the shattered glass to meet hers.

She stilled. "It fell off the table," she said needlessly. She knew that wasn't the reason he'd picked it up; she could see his mind turning ideas over, trying to fit them together like pieces of a jigsaw puzzle.

"Is this your mom?"

Swallowing, she nodded. She turned back to the sink and filled one of the glasses in the dish drainer.

"She's beautiful." He peered closer before setting it back down gently. "You look like her."

"Thanks," she managed as she brought the glass to her lips with a trembling hand.

He pinned her with a steely gaze. "You never talk about her. Where is she?"

"The UK." The pressure in her chest was building. It was going to tear her apart at the seams. She gulped at the water, as though it might be able to douse the turmoil inside her.

"Does she have something to do with…?" He trailed off, unable to articulate exactly what he was referring to.

Oh God oh God oh God. This was unbearable. He was getting dangerously close, and he seemed to sense it. He wasn't going to give up. Thanks to Julia, he knew she was keeping a secret. She could lie—make something up—or she could tell the truth.

She didn't want to lie. Not to Dean.

Tremors quaked through her. She didn't so much crack as shatter. "She's in a mental hospital." She sagged as the admission finally tumbled out, a cathartic rush of five words that could never be reined back in.

His mouth dropped open. "She's in—" He stopped, rubbing a hand over his forehead as he processed the information. "God. I'm so sorry, Mal."

Her limbs felt numb, and she dug her fingernails into her palms. "Paranoid schizophrenia," she said, answering the unasked question. "My father had her institutionalized after the accident." A faint rushing sound whispered in her ears.

"Jesus, let's get you sitting down." He was beside her in seconds, curling a strong arm around her waist.

She leaned into him, allowing herself these few moments of support. Physical connection. It might be the last time they touched.

He thought she was strong, but she was weak. She'd kissed him that day after class. Hell, she'd made love to him at his house. Now she'd told him about Isabelle. He was going to feel obligated to her now, and she couldn't let that happen.

With heartbreaking tenderness, he helped her onto the couch. He returned with her water glass, refilled, and sat down next to her. Deep furrows of concern etched themselves across his handsome face. "I'm so sorry about your mom," he said carefully. "But I don't understand...why didn't you tell me? Did you think I would judge? *My* dad's in prison, remember?"

She took a shaky sip of water, fighting to regain some composure. "My father didn't want anyone to know. I was basically forbidden from discussing it. He didn't want something like that associated with his business."

His brows pulled together. "But...your mom didn't work there, did she?"

"No, but I did. And schizophrenia...," she trailed off, drawing in a deep breath. "Well, there's a hereditary component."

A hard look passed across his features. The muscles on his arms tightened, revealing taut cords of tendons. "Tell me that's not why you're here," he ground out. "Tell me he didn't make you leave the business, after everything he did to force you into becoming a part of it."

She bristled, even though he was right. For the most part, anyway. "It was sort of mutual," she said, hoping to avoid fanning the flames of dislike for Russ Montgomery that already simmered in Dean. This conversation was already emotional enough without stirring up the old animosity between them. "I made a big mistake and lost a client a lot of money. It was entirely my fault. Brady was sick that day—really sick—and I'd been up all night with him. When the vet called and said they could fit him in, I forgot about the trade I was supposed to make. It completely slipped my mind."

"Everyone makes mistakes."

"I know, but this affected both our client and my father's business reputation. It scared me, and it scared my father too. Even though the mistake was simply the result of worry and exhaustion, we both ended up coming to the same conclusion—that maybe the pressure of the job was too much. Stress and trauma can trigger schizophrenia. I was devastated and there was nothing I could do to fix it. He saw what it was doing to me, and we decided it would be better for my health if I did...something else." The words were pouring out now, like lake water through a window.

Dean stayed silent, but his green eyes sparked with anger.

"It was the right choice, really. The only choice. What if I did become delusional while I was employed there? Not many people would want someone like that handling their finances and personal information."

He took her hands, the warmth of his skin a shock against the chill of her own. "Malorie…I'm sorry about the mistake at work. But it was just a mistake. And I'm sorry about your mom. But you're saying things like 'what if' and 'hereditary component', which tells me that inheriting this illness is only a possibility." He released her left hand and raised his arm, cupping her cheek, forcing her to meet his gaze. "There's a possibility I could get cancer. My mother did. There's not a single person on this earth that can say with complete certainty that nothing bad will happen to them. You can't live your life in fear of a 'what if.'"

She dropped her eyes. "But I do," she whispered. "It could happen anytime. And I wait for that first delusion, or that first hallucination, and I wonder whether I'll even recognize it for what it is." Shaking her head, she covered her face as she choked out her next words. "I thought you were a hallucination. That first day, in the woods…I thought my brain was conjuring you up from my past." A sob escaped, and she tried to muffle it with her hands. The tears were returning, clogging up her throat, pricking the corners of her eyes.

He gathered her in his arms with a force that bordered on rough, tangling his fingers in her hair, rubbing her back. "It's okay," he murmured. "I'm right here. I'm not going anywhere."

Her heart sank. Those were the words she'd been trying to avoid. Sharing the awful truth had led to this...now he was making promises he shouldn't. She had to make him understand.

Sniffling, she pulled away, wiping at the moisture on her face. Brady was sitting by her side, his black fur pressed against the white couch, his soulful expression making it clear he knew she was in distress. She reached out and scratched his head as she gathered her thoughts.

"Dean, schizophrenia is a devastating mental illness. Even if it's caught and diagnosed, a lot of people go off the meds, because they come with significant unpleasant side effects. And because the person thinks they're cured. This disease affects the thought process, which is the very thing a person relies on to gauge whether they're okay. A schizophrenic's brain doesn't recognize the symptoms as abnormal. The things that person thinks and sees and hears are real to him or her."

A queasy fist tightened in her stomach, but she hesitated only for a second. She had to get this out. "I lived with it for years, and it was horrible. I wouldn't wish it on anyone. And there *is* a genetic component that puts me at higher risk to develop it." Her fingers found a knot of matted fur behind Brady's ear, and she worked at loosening it, grateful to have something to do with her restless hands.

He reached out to stroke Brady's neck. "But that doesn't mean you will."

"No. But while the general population has about a 1% chance of developing it, the children of an affected parent have a 12% chance."

"That's an 88% chance you'll be fine," he said firmly.

She nodded. "I hope so. But it's not something I'm willing to expose anyone to," she added, hoping to match the steel in his voice. With a sharp tug, she extracted the stubborn clump of fur, and Brady shook his head, scattering crinkled black hairs into the air. Outside, a thudding sound rattled overhead, and a few moments later, an orange and white Coast Guard helicopter whirled over the ocean. She watched its path, hoping that if it was a search and rescue, the lost would be found. Alive and safe. A shiver rippled through her spine as she fought back images of icy water rising over her chest.

"So you're never going to be in a relationship?"

The question brought her back to the present. "Not one that binds someone to me forever." Warmth flushed her cheeks. "Sorry, I realize that sounds presumptuous. I'm just trying to explain that I'm not going to marry, or have children, because I can't take the chance of putting anyone through what I went through."

His full lips pressed into a thin line. "But...that's ridiculous. Life is about taking chances. There's a much greater chance you'll live a happy, healthy life." He inhaled, lowering his head until their gazes locked. "What if I want to take the chance that we could have that life together?"

A bittersweet ache bloomed in her chest, nearly stealing her breath away. *Say yes*, an inner voice pleaded. But she shook her head. "It wouldn't be fair. You deserve so much better."

"Better?" He blew out a frustrated breath and stood up, dragging his hand through his hair as he paced the room. "Better than the girl I've loved since I was 18? Better than the one person who makes me feel complete? You're the only one I want, Mal. You're all I think about." He balled one fist inside the other and brought his knuckles to his mouth when he stopped in front of her, then let his arms fall to his sides. "Listen to me. Only one thing really matters here. Do you love me?"

Oh, no. She was trapped. If she said no, she'd be lying...and she would hurt him deeply with that lie. But if she admitted how she felt, that she did love him, he was going to keep fighting for something he shouldn't want.

She swallowed. The silence spun out, the only sound the thrum of her pulse in her ears. "Yes," she admitted. "But—"

He cut her off. "No 'buts'. That's all that matters." Kneeling down in front of her, he tucked her hair behind her ears with exquisite tenderness. Closing his eyes, he brought their foreheads together. Their breaths mingled in the small space between them, warm and shaky with emotion.

She wanted to stay like this forever, suspended in this moment of pure, raw connection. Every cell in her body seemed to pull toward him, as though he were a planet exerting a gravitational force. But invading thoughts broke into her rapture, tugging her back to reality. He loved her and she loved him, and in a perfect world, that should be all that mattered. But it wasn't that simple. Not for her. For her, loving him meant letting him go.

She squeezed her eyes shut, shifting backwards, breaking the connection. Her heart teetered, preparing to fall. "No, it's not," she said softly. "Other things matter. You want kids. If we stayed together, that wouldn't be possible."

"I want *you*." He gripped her hands as he emphasized the word. "That's all I need. We'll have nieces and nephews to spoil. Matt's kids. Julia's kids."

That he was including Julia as family only sharpened the pain ripping through her. She hesitated for a heartbeat, studying his features and flaws, committing them to memory. The rugged shadow of scruff along his unshaven jaw. The pale crescent moon scar on his cheek, the remnant of a long-ago cut from a chain-link fence. The copper streaks in his tousled hair. The mix of kindness and strength shining in his sea glass green eyes. The clean, male scent of his skin.

"You don't understand," she said, her voice fading to a hoarse whisper. "If it happens, if I get sick…it's not just that I might behave strangely. It's much worse than that. I could pose a risk to anyone I'm around." She dropped her gaze as she forced out the words. "I could be…dangerous."

Chapter Twenty-Five

What? He blinked, rewinding what she'd said in his head. *Dangerous?* The idea of his sweet, compassionate Malorie as dangerous was impossible to reconcile. But an icy spike of fear traveled through him as he studied her grave expression. "I don't understand, Mal."

Her face crumpled. "My mom...tried to kill me. The accident..." She trailed off, drawing in a shuddering breath. "She thought I'd joined the enemy. It wasn't an accident. She drove into that lake on purpose, to kill me. To kill both of us."

A dark red rage burned through him, his muscles tensing instinctively, as if he could protect her somehow from the past. No words came to him, though, so all he could do in his speechless despair and fury was drop her shaking hands and haul her into his arms, shifting himself back onto the couch. Her back hitched with silent sobs, and he smoothed her hair as she clung to him.

God. He could barely wrap his mind around what she'd said, and yet, it explained so much. All the mysterious pieces began to solidify, random particles becoming a malignant mass. And yet, she'd survived, overcoming the terrifying and painful tragedy, seemingly unwilling to wallow in the unfairness of it all. She hadn't let it destroy her spirit. Her ability to love.

He'd always known she was strong, but this was beyond what a person should have to endure.

Sensing she still needed time, he lowered their locked bodies down into the cushions, until they were lying on the couch, her head on his shoulder, her tremors reverberating through him.

He would absorb them. Take away whatever pain he could. Whatever shame and fear and loneliness that he could. From now on, whatever happened, they would face it together.

Eventually, she quieted, her breathing slowing down, evening out. They remained like that for what could have been minutes, or hours. The early afternoon sun moved softly across the floor. Brady slept, twitching and whimpering at one point, chasing a rabbit or a squirrel in a canine dream world.

He was drifting somewhere on the edge of consciousness, stroking her temple, when she finally stirred.

With a small sigh, she lifted her head. "Sorry."

"Nothing to be sorry about." He squeezed her, reveling in the solid warmth of her body cradled in his.

"But…you understand now, right?"

He could feel her muscles tense as she once again braced for rejection, and he framed his words carefully. "I understand you survived a difficult childhood and a terrifying, traumatic event, and still became a strong, kind, capable woman whose first instinct is to protect the people she loves. Whose goal in life is to help disabled kids for no financial compensation. I understand why you were trying to keep all this secret." He paused, bending his neck to kiss the top of her head. "But I do wish you'd told me sooner."

She sighed. "I know. But it's a painful thing to admit. Especially when *your* mom was so loving."

"Your mom was sick, Mal."

"And it could happen to me," she reminded him again.

He frowned, tightening his arms around her. "We're not going back to this. Yes, it's a possibility—a small one—but there are no guarantees in life for any of us. If you didn't love me, I'd simply promise to be there for you, as a friend." His heart contracted as he reminded himself the sentence he was about to speak was true. "But you *do* love me, and I love you. I'm not going to let you push me away, so you may as well stop trying."

He could almost hear her thinking, deciding whether to continue to argue. *Trust in this*, he urged silently. *Trust me.*

Finally, she nodded, her hair sliding against his chin. "Okay. But you have to promise me something." Shifting her weight, she pushed herself up until she could look him in the eyes. "Look, I know I'm projecting way into the future when I talk about us staying together long-term, having a life together. It's silly, but I guess because it's you..." She bent her head slightly, her gaze sliding away as she trailed off.

He reached up and tucked a lock of hair behind her ear. "I get it," he said softly, swallowing past the tightness in his throat.

Her body rocked gently as she gave a silent nod. When she met his eyes again, two bright pink spots colored her cheekbones. She caught her bottom lip in her teeth for a lingering moment before she tried to speak.

"My fear, though, is that what if we date for a while," she began, clearly struggling to keep her voice steady, "and you don't want to be with me anymore? I'm scared you won't break up with me out of fear that it might look bad. Or that you just don't want me to have to spend my life alone."

His heart throbbed, aching with incredulity that she could even think that. With sorrow that she felt she *had* to think like that. And with relief that the promise she'd referred to was something he could agree to. He traced his thumb over the faint freckles dusting her skin. "You think I'd stay with you solely out of obligation? That's—" He stopped himself before he said 'ridiculous'; he didn't want to diminish her concerns. Besides, she had a point…people stayed in relationships for the wrong reasons all the time. Wasn't that what he was encouraging Matt to do? His brother had made it pretty clear he didn't want to marry Sharon, but Dean had been insistent. That was different, though, wasn't it? A child was involved. Still, maybe he needed to give up that fight. It hadn't happened yet, and maybe if they all just let the legalities go, things would be less tense. Maybe without all the additional pressure, Matt would stop being such an asshole all the time.

He exhaled. "That's not going to happen," he finished, cupping her cheek with his palm. "But I see your point. And I promise. After everything you've said, it seems like you were completely prepared to live your life on your own. I know you're perfectly capable of that, and knowing you, you probably had a plan in place in case you did get sick."

"I did. I mean, I do. Julia knows." The flush returned as she dropped her gaze. "I told her everything after the accident. I had to talk to someone other than the weird therapist my father made me see in Connecticut."

That stung. She'd trusted Julia with the truth, but not him. But he pushed his petty jealousies away. She'd had a history, after all, with Julia—they'd been friends for years before Mal moved here. And the nature of their relationship had been very different.

"So now she knows the initial signs and symptoms," Malorie continued, sinking back into him. "She knows what type of behavior she should be looking for. If she notices anything, she'll get me to a doctor immediately. Hopefully before I'd be beyond trusting what a doctor said."

His fingers settled on the back of her neck, and he kneaded the taut knots of muscle. "At least we know what to look for, then, to catch any issues early. A person could become an alcoholic, or a drug addict, without showing a lot of outward signs at first, and become equally dangerous to the people around them."

She moaned softly as he moved up toward her scalp. "I guess that's true," she murmured.

A thread of desire pulsed through him as she continued to make little sounds of pleasure, and he did his best to tamp it down. This was not the time or place, despite his body's growing insistence. They were still in the middle of a serious conversation—an emotionally draining one, as well—and there was something else he wanted to know.

"Your mother," he began before hesitating, unsure how much pain his question might cause. "How is she…now?"

After a beat of silence, she answered, her voice thick with emotion. "She's safe. Like I said, she's in an institution in England. My father moved her there right after the accident, before he moved the two of us here so I could finish high school in the States. The fact that she was already over there is one of the reasons my father wanted to move the rest of the family so quickly after graduation."

"So…you were able to see her?"

A small, sad sigh escaped. "I've tried to keep up with visits over the years, but it's hard. The medications she requires now are very strong, and she sleeps a lot. But she has to stay on them, because otherwise, she regresses quickly, and starts to think everyone is out to get her. When I show up there, it brings up memories and unwanted thoughts, and she gets very agitated. The staff say she's…content…for the most part, when things stay in a routine. So I try to avoid disrupting things." She swallowed audibly. "I do make sure I send her favorite flowers, though, once a month. And my father makes sure she has everything she needs in terms of care and necessities, even though they're divorced. He makes sure she has top-of-the-line art supplies, because she still enjoys painting."

"That's good." He felt an unlikely flash of respect for her father, despite everything the man had done to keep him and Mal apart. Clearly there was some part of Russ Montgomery that was decent. And any control he'd once wielded over the two of them was now in the past. He and Mal were together, again. He tightened his grip around the curve of her waist, inhaling the alluring scent of her: the familiar citrus of her shampoo, the intimate musk of sleep, the tropical coconut of sunscreen.

"Yeah," she agreed, her shoulder moving in a small shrug as she settled her palm on his chest. "I actually need to call him and check in. I usually do on Sundays."

"Do you need to get up?"

She laughed, the sound soft and musical. "Oh, no, not now. It can wait. I don't want to talk to my father right now. In fact, I don't want to talk *about* my father right now, or my mother, either, for that matter."

He buried his nose in her hair before kissing the top of her head. "What do you want to do?"

"Maybe stay just like this all day. Would that be okay?" She rubbed his chest lightly.

"I'm good with that." His eyes drifted shut, and he listened to the rhythm of their breathing, enjoying the feel of her touch. When her stomach made a small protest of hunger, he chuckled. "We might have to move, eventually, if only to get you something to eat."

"Umm," she replied, stretching her legs out before burrowing back into him. "I'm not really that hungry. For food, anyway." Her hand slid lower, her fingers slipping beneath his T-shirt. "I have some other ideas, though."

He stilled, his abdominal muscles quivering beneath her touch, his groin tightening as hot blood surged low in response to her sultry tone. *Oh, God.* There was nothing he'd rather do than make love to her right now. His body ached to claim her. But was it a good idea, after the emotional toll this day had already taken?

A groan formed in his throat as she nuzzled his ear. *Yes.* Maybe this was the perfect idea...a way to push everything else into the background. Focus instead on the two of them, right here, in this moment.

Still, he forced the strangled words out. "Are you sure?"

"Hmm. Let me think about it," she teased, her fingers dipping beneath the waistband of his shorts.

His breath seized as she lightly traced the length of his erection. He closed his eyes. Pulled the gauzy fabric of her cover-up past her hip. Splayed his hand over her warm skin. "Any decisions yet?"

"Still thinking." He could hear the playful smile in her voice. "You seem sure, though." The pressure increased as she stroked him, their flesh still maddeningly separated by a layer of fabric.

He groaned again, tugging at the band of her bikini bottoms. She shimmied out of them, and the movement of her body against his nearly drove him wild.

"I've decided I've never been more sure of anything in my life," she murmured, rolling on top of him. She gasped as he hauled her forward in one sudden motion, bringing her face above his. As she leaned down, he tangled his fingers in her hair, holding her to him, capturing her mouth with his.

He kissed her urgently, possessively, as if he wanted to brand her as his. Which she was. *She was his again, after all this time.* And she returned his kiss with equal passion, their tongues exploring, their teeth scraping the tender flesh of each other's lips. White heat burned through him as she nipped at his earlobe, sucked on his neck.

Gathering the sheer cover-up to her upper back, he unclasped the bikini top and slid his hands along her bare skin.

She rose up to allow him to pull the last of her clothing over her head, and the pieces landed on the floor soundlessly. He reached behind his head to help as she clawed at his shirt, returning his hands to her waist so quickly it was as though he was afraid she might vanish.

Then she was straddling him, her thighs around his hips, her eyes glazed, her hair tousled, her lips swollen. His love. He wanted to draw the moment out, gaze at her perfection, but he was nearing his limit. He had to have her. *Now.*

His hands slid up her ribcage until his thumbs grazed the sides of her breasts, and she leaned forward, letting out a small gasp as he drew her nipple into his mouth. He managed to unbutton his shorts, and she helped slide them down with her legs, the friction of her movements both torturous and tantalizing.

Her fingers closed around his erection, and the jolt of pleasure nearly took his breath away. Angling her hips, she guided him inside her slowly, forcing him to grit his teeth against the unbearable ecstasy of each deliberate movement. Every cell in his body was demanding release, and he had to resist the urge to grab her waist and plunge inside her. *Stay in control.* He would let her set the pace.

Bracing her arms against his chest, she began rocking gently, her eyes fluttering closed. *God, she was beautiful.* As she moaned with pleasure, his last thread of restraint broke, and he gripped her hips, pulling her down, thrusting upwards, deeper with each stroke. She leaned forward slightly, her hair falling around them like a curtain. With a whimper, she arched her back, digging her nails into his shoulders as she shuddered, her muscles contracting, her thighs clamping around him. He came right after her, the force of his release crashing through him like waves in a violent storm.

She collapsed on top of him, and their hearts pounded in unison beneath sweat-slicked skin. The shallow rasp of their ragged breathing filled the room. His fingers played across her back, drifting along the depression of her spine.

"Damn," he murmured, when he could finally speak.

She made a small, satisfied sound, and he could feel her cheek curve into a smile against his chest. "Yeah."

"That was…" He trailed off, unable to find a word that would do it justice.

"Yeah." She shifted her weight, kissed his neck. "We're really good at that."

He laughed, smoothing her hair. "No argument here."

"Do you realize that's only the third time we've made love in…seven years?"

How was that possible? She was right, though. He cleared his throat. "Clearly we're going to have to work very hard to make up for lost time. I'm up for the challenge, though."

She giggled. "Me, too."

"Give me another few minutes."

Still laughing, she rolled to her side. "Don't get any ideas right now. I actually *am* hungry, now. For food," she clarified.

A cold nudge against his ribs made him flinch. He turned to see the dog sitting upright now, looking at him expectantly with hopeful brown eyes. "Oh, hey Brady." Reaching over, he scratched him beneath his bristly chin.

"I think he knows the word 'food'."

"It's an important word in a dog's vocabulary. Along with—"

"Don't say it," she interjected. "I'm too hungry to go for a W-A-L-K right now." She spelled the word in question out, lifting her head to check if Brady had cracked the code.

"Okay, we'll save that for later. Let's go find something to eat. We should celebrate."

"I feel like that's going to require getting up," she said with a playful sigh, stretching.

"Probably. We're not really in appropriate attire to go out at the moment, either."

"Excellent point. But, I'd hate to starve to death here on the couch, and I have next to nothing in the fridge. Grocery shopping was supposed to be this afternoon's main activity."

"I think this was the better alternative."

She laughed again, wiggling forward to kiss him. "Definitely."

Untangling their limbs, they sat up, and he scooped their clothes from the floor. "Where do you feel like going?" he asked as he pulled on his shirt.

"How about Baxter's? It's close, and we can sit by the water." She put on the cover-up, setting the bikini on the coffee table. Standing, she peered down at the see-through material. "Think I'll need a different outfit, though."

He slid an appreciative gaze over her body, lingering at the point where the fabric hit the tops of her tanned thighs. *So gorgeous.* So tempting. "I don't know, I kind of like it." His lips curved into a wicked grin as he reached for her.

Her eyes widened, and she jumped out of the way, startling Brady. "Oh, no you don't. Food first," she said, giving him a mock stern look as she ruffled Brady's fur.

He sighed and stood. "Fine. You'll need to keep your strength up, anyway," he added, lifting his brows suggestively before lunging for her. She squealed in surprise, but he caught her this time, drawing her in for a quick kiss while Brady attempted to squeeze between their legs. "Baxter's it is. Go get changed. I'll give Brady some F-O-O-D, if that's okay."

"That would be great. It's on the floor of the pantry. Can you grab my phone and keys from the island, too?"

"Sure. I can drive, though. I drove here from Julia's."

Her lips pulled into a frown. "Hmmm. I believe I have a few choice words for her regarding her secret-keeping skills."

He grinned. "And I believe I owe her a nice dinner. Maybe a giant bouquet of flowers."

She rolled her eyes, feigning exasperation, but failed to suppress her answering smile as she turned toward the hall, and he called to Brady, whistling under his breath on his way into the kitchen.

Chapter Twenty-Six

In the end, she couldn't really be mad at Julia, given the outcome. Plus, Julia hadn't really told Dean anything…she'd just admitted there was something to tell. So she'd texted Julia a "I could never hate you! All is good, going out with Dean now, will call later!" message with a string of heart and smiley emojis while they drove to Baxter's.

They'd made love again when they'd returned to her house, more slowly and tenderly this time, but no less passionately. Then she'd reminded him she needed to get some paperwork done, both for the farm and for class, which was true, and that she was going to have trouble focusing on that with him in the house, which was also true. She had no idea how long their new-found insatiable sexual appetite would last, but she was already looking forward to tonight, even though she was sore in a few intimate places. She smiled to herself as she gingerly sat down at her desk. *Worth it.* Maybe she'd take a long bath later, before Dean came back. He was going to do some things around the house, and then go for a jog through the trails. She marveled that he had the energy. He'd tried to convince her to go with him, but she'd shut that down immediately. Not happening. Her leg muscles felt shaky enough as it was, and she still had to get Brady his walk at some point this evening.

Maybe later they could order something to be delivered for dinner—she'd never made it to the store—and then go together afterwards.

After forty-five minutes, she came to the realization that focusing on work wasn't going to be easy after everything that had happened today, whether Dean was in the house or not. With a sigh, she minimized the blank presentation slide taunting her from the laptop's screen. At least she'd managed to get a few simple forms filled out for the farm and to create an outline for Tuesday's class. She could get more done tomorrow.

The image of her soaking in a warm bath floated through her mind once again, and she checked the time in the corner of the computer. Almost five o'clock. Maybe she'd pour a glass of wine to sip while she soaked. *Was there any bath oil in the house?* She chewed on her lip, trying to picture the contents beneath the sink in the master bath. At some point, she should also touch base with her father. A short conversation would be fine…no need to discuss her renewed relationship with Dean yet. That could certainly wait for another day.

Crap! She still hadn't called Julia and filled her in! A tiny wave of shame washed over her. What a horrible friend she was being…Julia was going to kill her. Jumping up from the chair, she rifled through the forms and folders on her desk, searching for her phone.

Bloody hell. Where was it? She checked the table in the front hall and the kitchen counters before jogging up the stairs, trying to remember the last time she'd seen it. In the truck. She'd typed the quick text to Julia, then set it down to hold Dean's hand. She hadn't brought it into the restaurant. And by the time they'd arrived back here, they'd already been groping each other in the cab of the truck. Her only thought had been getting into the house before they tore each other's clothes off on the walkway. She flushed at the memory, smiling to herself.

Okay, so her phone was probably still in his truck. And she couldn't call and ask him to check, obviously...although she was embarrassed the thought *had* flitted through her tired mind before she'd realized the problem with it.

She headed back downstairs and paused at the front door, slipping on her flip-flops. Did she need to grab her keys? Brady was out on his lead on the deck, sleeping in the evening sun. Still, it probably wasn't necessary to lock the door to run down the street to her neighbor's house for a few minutes. Thankfully, she'd heard no more news of dead bodies or missing women.

Pulling the door closed, she descended the porch steps and started down the cobblestone walkway, picturing how she and Dean must have looked just a few hours ago as they fumbled their way along this same path, trying to both kiss and navigate their way to the house at the same time. But as she glanced around, she was relieved to note that most of the nearby houses appeared vacant already...weekend residents often packed up early on Sunday, even when it was a nice day, in an attempt to avoid the nightmarish back-up of traffic that stretched for miles on Sunday evenings in the summer, as hundreds of cars from all over the Cape tried to funnel over only two narrow bridges leading back to the mainland.

So…maybe no one had witnessed their behavior. *Who cared, anyway*, she decided with a shrug. She was an adult, she was in love, and she wasn't trying to impress anyone around here. It was just the last vestiges of her father's preoccupation with maintaining some kind of spotless reputation that made her even worry about it in the first place. As far as she was concerned, the world—or at least the Sandalwood community, at this point—could learn she was in love with Dean Slater, again—*still*, actually—and that they were having difficulty keeping their hands off of each other at the moment.

The truck was parked in the Slater's driveway, but the doors were locked, and she couldn't see her phone as she peered through the front windows. A flicker of anxiety wound its way through her. She wasn't attached to her phone like some people—not anymore, at least, thanks to her departure from her old job—but she really couldn't afford a new phone right now. Hopefully it was somewhere in there, out of sight.

She climbed the three stone steps up to their porch, rapping her knuckles against the front door. Hopefully Dean was still around. But after her second, and louder, knock, the door opened to reveal Matt, his face clouded with barely-concealed annoyance.

"Dean's out running," he informed her in lieu of a greeting.

Unease bubbled up inside her, but she pushed it down. For some reason, he always made her slightly uncomfortable, although she'd never mentioned it to Dean. Matt had rarely been around when they were younger, and now…well, she'd never seen the point, since she'd never imagined she and Dean would end up together again. Maybe, once Matt knew about their relationship, he'd warm up to her. Or maybe, like Dean said, it was the stress of the baby, and had nothing to do with her personally.

"Oh, okay. He said he was going to go for a run. But I think I left my phone in the truck earlier, and the doors are locked. Can I grab the keys and check?"

His mouth scrunched to one side, and she was struck again by how different the two brothers—step-brothers, actually—looked. They shared their mother's dark, thick hair and prominent cheekbones, but aside from that, their features were unalike. Matt's lips were thin and pale, while Dean's were full and sensual.

She shook her head slightly to clear it. What was she doing, thinking about Dean's lips? God.

"Hang on," he said with a sigh, leaving her waiting by the door. Peering inside, she searched for a glimpse of Sharon, but she couldn't see past the kitchen into the great room. Voices from a television show floated down the hall, though. *Should she go in and say hi?* She hadn't exactly been invited.

"How's Sharon doing?" she asked when Matt returned with the keys.

"She's fine." He brushed past her and went down the steps, aiming the fob at the truck. Lights flashed as the locks clicked open.

She followed Matt as he continued toward the truck. Why was he going with her? Did he think she was going to steal something? But her question was answered as he explained, "I need to get some stuff out of the back. Baby stuff I forgot to bring in yesterday," he added, his voice relaying more exasperation than excitement.

She felt a small pang of envy—she would never be a mother. But she shoved the thought aside, unwilling to allow anything to ruin her good mood on this amazing day. And hopefully, she and Sharon would get closer, and she could help out when the baby came. "It won't be long now," she pointed out, unnecessarily, just to make conversation.

He grunted in response, moving around to the back of the truck and lowering the tailgate.

Fine. She shrugged to herself and bent over the passenger seat, searching for her phone. It wasn't on the center console, but maybe it slipped between the console and the seat.

It wasn't stuck there, though, so she lowered her head all the way down to the floor to check beneath the seat. Yes! The phone was lying there, and as she reached for it, her eyes caught the glint of something metallic. She snagged it with her fingers and pulled it out, and a gold chain unfurled. A necklace. It was broken, but the fastened clasp kept a curved pendant from slipping off. A few long blonde hairs were twined in the links.

"Found my phone. And some jewelry," she called out. Closing the door with her hip, she walked toward the end of the driveway.

Matt looked up as she approached, a strange expression on his face. "What jewelry?" he asked gruffly, shifting the large, brightly-colored box in his arms. A motorized baby swing, it looked like, and the box already unloaded appeared to be some kind of play mat with soft toys hanging from overhead arches.

"A necklace," she answered, dangling it in front of him. She frowned, noticing the pendant—a capital letter 'J'. Huh. Not Sharon's.

Something like panic flashed in his eyes, and her insides twisted. *He's cheating on Sharon.* Just like Dean suspected. He'd mentioned Matt had been disappearing in the middle of the night.

He set the box down. "It's Sharon's," he said, his voice hard.

She was about to point out that it couldn't be when a memory tugged at her brain, struggling to surface. The description of a necklace with a gold 'J'. Inexpensive, but sentimental. Given to a big sister as a gift.

Missing from a dead body, found nearby, dumped in the woods.

Jessica Cole.

Her thoughts raced as time slowed. *No.* This had to be a coincidence. But…Matt shared that truck with Dean. He was taking it somewhere in the middle of the night. And now, he was staring at her, his features set into a cold, menacing mask.

He took a step forward.

Her heart seized, the ground pitching dangerously beneath her feet. Fear sliced through her. *He knows.* Dean had probably told him the reason Mrs. Cole had come to their house that day, the reason she'd wanted to talk to both him and Malorie. The missing necklace.

She took a corresponding step backward, gesturing toward the house. *Please, Dean, get home soon.* Even if this was a misunderstanding, she did not want to be alone with Matt for one more second. Maybe Sharon was inside. "I'll just go give it to her, then, so I can say 'hi'," she said, fighting to force a casual note into her tone.

"No. Give it to me." He held his hand out expectantly, his narrowed eyes piercing into her like lasers.

Scream, her inner voice demanded. But who was around to hear? She glanced around wildly at the quiet houses. Even Dean's nosy neighbor was missing from her window. And what if this was a misunderstanding? She'd never live down the embarrassment.

A flicker of doubt coursed through her. Could this be it, the beginning episodes of paranoia that would herald her descent into schizophrenia? But no, the body had been there. The police had come to her house, as had Jessica's mother. And she'd forgotten all about the necklace…it seemed too elaborate a trick for her mind to manufacture. Still, she pinched her fingertips together, pressing the metal links into her flesh as though feeling it would serve as physical proof. And she didn't think she was imagining the mix of anger and panic emanating from Dean's brother.

Even so, she hesitated, searching for a way out that would still allow her to save face if this was all some bizarre coincidence. It *had* to be. There had to be some explanation other than the one her overworked brain was envisioning. *Think.* "It's broken." She nodded toward the bottom end of the necklace. "But I have a chain I'm not using that would work. I'll grab it from my house and put the pendant on it. Then I can return it to Sharon so she can wear it," she added, swallowing past the tremors in her throat.

"You don't need to do that. Just give it to me."

She began backing away, her pulse pounding in her ears. "I have to go," she said shakily, ignoring his last comment.

He glared at her before swiveling his head, checking the surrounding area. A calculating gleam shone in his green eyes, and the tendons along his arms rippled as he opened and closed his fists.

Was he looking to see if there were any…witnesses? The alarm bells jangling in her head grew louder, begging her to listen. And to react. *Get away from him now. Ask questions later.*

Licking her dry lips, she added, "I left something in the oven. I'll drop by later." Then she turned and walked away, glancing back over her shoulder.

"Just give me the necklace, Malorie." He moved around the box and started following her. "Listen, we have to talk." The words were edged with steel. Deadly serious.

She picked up her pace. What was she going to do? There was no one around to help. Adrenaline poured into her veins, sharp and bitter, urging her to run. But he could easily outrun her. She was no runner. She was wearing flip-flops, and she had a tricky ankle. His legs were much longer than hers. He'd catch her before she made it to the safety of her house.

Her door was unlocked…if she could just get a head start, she might make it before he could catch her. Hurry! Pivoting around, she glanced behind Matt and called out, "Oh, hey, Sharon!" He faltered, looking over his shoulder, and she kicked off her flip-flops and cocked back her arm. As he turned back, she hurled her cell phone at his face. The corner of the hard plastic case caught him in the temple, and she heard his grunt of pain and surprise as she spun away from him. *Go!* With a burst of speed, she fled toward home.

"Shit!" he yelled from somewhere behind her.

How far a head start did she have? Her chest heaved, jagged breaths searing her lungs. *Faster!* One more house to pass before hers. Sweat poured down her back, and her feet flew over the hot asphalt, each stride sending a jolt up her bones.

Terrifying images spun through her brain...his hand clamping on her shoulder, yanking her down...his hands around her throat, her lifeless body in the woods.

"I'm not going to let you talk to Dean about this."

The declaration came as a furious, insistent growl from behind her...but how far behind? She couldn't afford to turn her head and check. Terror hammered at her breastbone, and she pushed herself harder, veering at an angle into her next-door neighbor's yard. Praying her ankle would hold out, she leapt over a border of low bushes and into her own yard. Almost there.

Her porch had no railing; it was only a few feet off the ground...if she came at it from her diagonal path, she'd get there faster. But could she clear the jump up without falling? Her gymnastics training would help, but her muscles lacked the strength they once had.

She had no choice but to try. If she swung around the porch to climb the steps, he would likely launch himself up from the side and cut her off at the front door. Adrenaline surged in her veins as she neared the corner of the porch. Gathering her strength, she sprang forward and up, stumbling as her bare feet hit the wooden planks, flailing her arms to keep her balance. A distant twinge flared in her ankle, but it held as she hurled herself toward the door.

The thump of his weight vibrated through her bones, and panic nearly paralyzed her. Get inside. Her hand shook violently as she reached for the knob, her numb fingers slick against the metal. *Open it, dammit!* The latch turned and she burst through the door, spinning to slam and lock it before he pushed his way in.

Gasping for air, she collapsed backward into the door, bracing herself for the thud of his body against the wood. What was happening? Was she really just running for her life from Dean's brother, because she'd connected him to a murder? Oh, God. This had to be a nightmare.

No forceful twists shook the doorknob—Matt wasn't even trying it for some reason. She cringed, trying to make herself invisible from the side windows framing the door. If she peeked out, would he be leering in at her? Worse, would he smash something through it?

Another sound registered past the pounding roar of her pulse and the desperate wheezing of her lungs. Brady! His frantic barks traveled down the hall.

Shit! Brady was outside on the back deck. She had to get him in and lock that door, before Matt got around back and did something to Brady in order to get to her.

She pushed herself forward on rubbery legs, then froze as another noise rose above the barking. A mechanical rattle. Her heart seized. The overhead garage door. Matt knew the code because he took care of the property, just like Dean.

Indecision swirled through her mind, rooting her feet to the floor. Any second now, he would be inside the house—she was certain the interior door leading in from the garage wasn't locked; it was her failsafe against locking herself out. She stared helplessly down the hallway, her thoughts racing. If she tried to make it to the back deck, she'd run right into him. If she turned and ran out the front door, she'd be back where she started…easy prey with no safe destination to escape to. *Do something! Run!*

The door leading in from the garage banged open, and a scream tore from her throat as she scrambled up the stairs. Brady's answering barks increased in pitch and intensity, and a sob built in her chest. What now? Bolting down the upstairs hallway, she swerved into her bedroom and punched the flimsy button on the knob as she slammed it. It wouldn't hold long, but it would give her a little time.

With a silent shriek, she backed away as the knob rattled, refusing to twist beneath his grasp. The door shuddered in its frame, and he ground out a string of curses. Retreating steps pounded away.

It was too much to hope he was giving up, leaving her alone. Most likely, he was heading into the kitchen or the garage to find something long and thin enough to pop the lock. Brady's yelps continued, and she prayed he wouldn't try to hurt her dog as she spun around the room, fighting to come up with a plan.

The room was sparsely decorated, and nothing stood out as a possible weapon. Why, why had she thrown her phone? There was no working landline in this house anymore. The windows would open, but would anyone hear her cries for help?

She ran to the window facing the woods and knocked out the screen so she could lean her torso out. "Help," she screamed into the thick tree branches. Would Dean hear her? "I need help!"

Steps thundered back up the stairs. She tightened her grip on the sill. Should she jump? She would probably survive, but it was a big house with high ceilings. At the very least, she would break some bones—and that would only serve to make her an easy target, unable to run away. He could even make it look like an accident...

Fear churned in her belly like boiling acid. She needed more time. Whirling from the window, she raced to the master bathroom. There was a lock on that door, too, and a window as well. She would have a few more seconds to try to think.

She locked herself in the bathroom just as the button lock on the bedroom door popped out with a soft click. She looked around the room wildly, terror and frustration blurring her vision. She had seconds.

And she had an idea.

Chapter Twenty-Seven

Her palms were slick against the cool porcelain. Please, let this work. She perched on the vanity counter, squeezed into the corner, her legs trembling beneath her. Pulling in a shuddering breath, she listened to his footsteps cross the room.

The doorknob jiggled, unyielding. A heavy sigh. "Malorie, are you in there? We need to talk. I'm not going to let you show that necklace to Dean."

She stifled a moan. The necklace was somewhere near the neighbor's bushes—she'd dropped it as she fled. Hopefully, someone would find it and put things together if...if something happened to her. It was doubtful, but she'd needed her hands free, and she hadn't wanted Matt to get hold of it.

She fought against both the panic ripping her apart and the urge to scream, 'Did you kill that girl?' She knew the answer. He wouldn't have chased her, wouldn't have entered her home, wouldn't be breaking into her bathroom to find her if he hadn't. As horrible as it was, nothing else made sense.

The lock popped. The knob turned, and she steeled herself. Instead of barreling in, he paused in the doorway, his gaze shooting to the open window with the missing screen.

She just needed him to come in a little farther. *Please.*

But he sensed her presence a moment later, his head starting to swivel toward her. She was out of time. *Now!* With a grunt, she swung the heavy lid of the toilet tank down from over her shoulder. His roar of anger and surprise was cut off as it connected with his forehead with a horrible crack, and the impact of the blow traveled up her arms like seismic tremors. He fell to the floor as his knees buckled, the toilet tank lid crashing on the tiles beside him. The forward momentum of her attack threw her off balance, and she tumbled off the vanity counter, landing on top of him with a bone-jarring thud. Pain exploded along her right side, from her ribcage to her temple, and the air left her lungs in a painful rush. For a few stunned seconds, they lay in a crumpled heap, neither of them moving. *Please, let him be unconscious.*

Her heart sank as she felt his body twitch beneath her, and a low groan turned into a furious growl. "You fucking bitch!" he bellowed, rearing up. The sudden move flipped her onto her back, and she blinked up at the ceiling, struggling to focus. Brady's frantic barks drifted in through the open window.

He scrambled on top of her, straddling her chest, pinning her to the floor with his crushing weight. Blood ran down his face in crimson streams. His lips parted in a triumphant grin as he clutched at the neck of her shirt. "Dean will be better off without you anyway." His fingers formed a fist as he drew his free arm back.

White hot agony erupted as his knuckles slammed into her jaw. Her head snapped to the side, a coppery warmth filling her mouth. *Better off without her?* The words sank past the ringing in her ears. He was going to kill her. She was going to die…on the happiest day of her life. Twisting wildly beneath him, she slapped at his chest. "No! Dean loves me!"

He caught her forearms and wrenched them above her head, looming over her. His eyes burned from a macabre mask of blood and sweat as he shook his head. "You're just a piece of ass." A spray of pink spittle accompanied the words. "Easy to replace." He clamped down on her wrists, grinding the fine bones into the floor until she yelped.

Her heart thrashed as terror surged through her. "No!" she cried again, her voice breaking with her pleas. "Your brother needs me. We'll get you help."

He barked out a cruel laugh. "No one needs you." Leaning down closer, he hissed, "And I told you, you're not going to tell my brother anything."

"You can't do this!" She squirmed and bucked, drumming her bare heels against the tiles. "Dean will be here soon. He's coming back here soon, you know." Her breath came out in raspy pants as she struggled for freedom.

His eyes narrowed dangerously. "Don't tell me what I can't do! I'm the one in control of this situation." He shook her arms. "I'm in control!"

A drop of blood slid from his chin and landed on her cheek. She cringed, but the sticky warmth triggered a thought. Glaring at him, she tamped down the hysteria rising in her throat and challenged him. "What are you going to tell him, then? Your DNA is all over me. Your *blood* is all over my bathroom."

His features tightened before curving into a ghoulish sneer. "The person who's been killing women came after you. He found you, alone in the house, and I heard your screams for help. I fought him off, but I was too late. Like I said, I'm in control."

She was about to point out it would never work, that there would be no mystery DNA to corroborate his story, but his hands suddenly clamped around her neck. Fighting for breath, she instinctively latched onto his wrists to try and pull him away, but she knew on some level it was futile. He had the strength and leverage.

The pressure built quickly, around her neck, in her lungs, behind her eyes. She twisted like a wild animal, battering him with her hands, clawing at exposed skin.

Need. Air. Flames licked at her chest. This was it. All that time she'd wasted worrying about something that might happen in the future, and she wasn't even going to have a future. A crushing sadness joined the tortuous pain and the raw, primal fear.

The world turned gray as the vise beneath her breastbone tightened. Her remaining strength was slipping away with her consciousness. But a stray thought fluttered through her mind, determined to break through the murky surface.

Something's…changed. Beyond the pounding rush in her ears and the strained breath of her attacker, it was quiet. The lack of sound registered as significant, and then it came to her, along with a tiny shred of hope.

Brady had stopped barking.

Chapter Twenty-Eight

Maybe she's just in the shower, he told himself as he soothed Brady. But his heart was racing, and he knew it wasn't simply from exertion, although he had pushed himself to his limits to get back to the beach once he'd heard the familiar, continuous barking.

It was the only reason he could think of for Malorie to ignore Brady, especially when he was being this persistent. But it didn't feel right. If she was in the shower, why would he suddenly be so anxious to get inside? Why would he be running back and forth in front of the French doors, stopping to frantically scratch at the glass?

Because he needs to get to Malorie. Because something's wrong. A blade of fear sliced through him, and he saw it reflected back in the dog's dark eyes as he crouched before him, stroking his fur. "What's the matter, boy?"

In response, Brady whined, spinning around and practically throwing himself against the door. Dean was right behind him, his damp palm seizing the handle. Unlocked. He didn't bother to knock—if Mal wasn't responding to Brady's barks, she wouldn't respond to that.

The moment the door opened, Brady barreled through it, his toenails clattering against the wood floor as he tore through the great room. Dean's heartrate skyrocketed, adrenaline pulsing through his veins like bursts of gunfire. He resisted the urge to shout her name as he chased after Brady. The dog seemed to know where to go, and if there was someone else in the house…

No. His mind clamped down, trying to reject the thought, but the image of Jessica Cole's lifeless body shot to the surface. No, no, no. Please, God, let Mal be okay. He bounded up the stairs behind Brady, just catching a glimpse of black fur disappearing into the master bedroom. A roar of surprise and outrage followed. From a distinctly male voice.

Fury and terror ignited in every cell of his body, turning his vision red. Following the snarls and curses, he charged into the master bath. Through the scarlet haze, his brain struggled to process the scene in front of him.

Malorie, lying on the floor, pale and limp. Blood smeared across the tiles. Brady's teeth flashing white against tanned flesh. A man straddling Malorie, punching at the dog's head with the arm not locked in powerful jaws.

Dean froze as recognition slammed him in the gut. Matt? What the hell was going on?

But there was no time for that right now. "Get the hell off her!" he bellowed, catching Matt's arm in mid-swing and yanking violently. A popping sound accompanied Matt's howl of pain, and he tumbled off of Malorie, spinning onto his back with a thud, his flesh tearing away from Brady's teeth.

Dropping to his knees, Dean cradled Mal's head in his hands. "Mal?" he begged as he leaned over her, his eyes catching on the imprint of fingertips circling her throat. Jesus Christ. His heart careened into a free-fall.

But then he noticed something else—a flicker of rhythmic movement beneath the angry red splotches. A pulse! Malorie was alive! "Wake up, Mal," he murmured, his thumbs pressing into her temples. "I need you to wake up, baby."

Her eyes fluttered open, her hands clutching at her neck as she coughed. She moaned.

Oh, thank God. He wanted to haul her up, pull her into his arms, but he settled on lowering his head until their foreheads touched. "You're okay." He whispered the assurance for both their benefit, closing his eyes for one brief moment of gratitude before snapping his head back up at the rumble of Brady's growls.

Matt had curled himself around the base of the toilet, his back to the dog, but now he was trying to pull himself up. His right arm hung from his shoulder at an awkward angle, and his left arm oozed fresh blood from torn flesh. *Injuries he'd received because he'd tried to strangle Malorie.*

Dean jumped up and grabbed a fistful of Matt's T-shirt, hauling him up against the wall. "What the fuck were you doing to her?" he roared, pulling his brother forward and slamming him back against the wall with savage force.

Beneath the layer of crusted blood, Matt's face was white and expressionless. His eyes darted around the bathroom as though looking for answers—or escape—but he remained silent.

"I asked you a question! Why were you hurting her?" When no explanation came, he let his fury take over, driving his knuckles into Matt's jaw. Sharp pain exploded through his hand, but it was quickly swallowed by the tumult of emotions raging inside him.

"Answer me!" he shouted again, because there had to be an answer to the questions crashing through his brain. Things were happening too fast—there was something he wasn't getting. A reason he'd found his own brother pinning the love of his life to the floor, in her own house, and choking the life out of her with no remorse. Because that would make him a monster. He was an irresponsible asshole, yes. An angry young man with a boulder-sized chip on his shoulder and nothing but contempt for everyone and everything. But a maniac capable of hurting—killing—a woman? Horror warred with disbelief as his muscles bunched, his arm cocking back again.

"He didn't want me to tell you what I found!" Malorie cried, her voice rough and rasping. She was sitting up now, leaning against Brady as he stood guard. His normally sleek fur rose in a ridge along his back, and his canine glare remained on the man who had hurt his owner.

Shit! "Don't move," he warned Matt, pressing him against the wall. "Do not fucking move." He released his grip on the shirt and spun around toward Malorie. "Careful, now." He helped her up from the floor, supporting her weight as she sat on the wide corner tile around the bathtub. Stealing a glance back at Matt, he added, "What did you find?"

She pulled in a labored breath. "I found...a necklace." Her wild eyes darted over toward Matt, and she cringed as she continued. "In the truck. I left my phone in there, and when I went to find it, I also found a broken gold necklace under the passenger seat. It had…the letter J on it. Like the one Jessica Cole's mother told us she always wore."

His blood turned to ice water as the words sunk in. No. It couldn't be true, what Malorie was trying to say. But why would she lie? If she said she found a necklace with the letter J in their truck, then he believed her. But that didn't mean it had to belong to the murdered girl. Necklaces with initials weren't exactly uncommon. It couldn't be Sharon's, but maybe it belonged to one of her friends. Or…maybe it belonged to one of Nicole's friends, and it had been in her purse. Maybe it belonged to one of Malorie's friends! Julia!

But then Malorie would have recognized it. And if the necklace had landed under their passenger seat by innocent means, by some mishap Matt knew nothing about—then *why*? Why try to silence Mal in the most brutal—and permanent—way possible?

"Did you hurt that girl?" Despite the mounting evidence, he still couldn't bring himself to say *rape* and *kill*. Oh, God.

"What girl?"

"Don't play dumb. I told you about the woman who came to our house, the day Sharon was sick." Mentioning Sharon's name caused the barbed wire already encircling his heart to tighten. If this was true, how would she handle it? "The woman looking for her dead daughter's 'J' necklace. The daughter that was found strangled in the woods." His gaze left Matt's for a moment as his eyes were involuntarily pulled toward Mal's neck. A wave of nausea roiled his belly. "That girl."

Matt stared at them from his spot against the wall, a small sneer his only response.

"The necklace had hair in it," Malorie said breathlessly. "They can test it for her DNA."

Dean nodded. "I could turn the truck over to the cops, and they could test *that* for her DNA, too. So answer the question. Did you do something to Jessica Cole?"

Matt lifted his uninjured shoulder in a shrug. "She was a junkie."

"So what? She was someone's daughter!" Despite the burning rage flooding his system, an icy shiver slid down his spine. Matt's statement sounded a lot like an admission. Of rape. And murder. He scrubbed a hand over his face. "We have to call the cops."

"No!" Matt's eyes widened, glinting with panic. He shook his head. "No, you can't call the cops." His arm spread in a pleading gesture. "Look, that one was an accident."

He stilled. Behind him, Malorie gasped. "What do you mean, an accident? And 'that one'? Does that mean…have there been others?" His fingers curled into fists at his sides. *This couldn't be happening.*

Matt's chest rose and fell in rapid, shallow breaths. "You can't call the cops on me. You're my brother." His voice rang with disbelief, but he had the look of a trapped animal.

"You're my brother, and you just tried to kill the woman I love to keep her quiet! I have to call the cops. You're sick. You need help." He glanced back toward Malorie. "Mal, is your phone around?"

She shook her head. "It's—"

A sudden movement caught the corner of his eye at the same time Brady sprang to his feet, and Dean spun around.

Matt clambered up onto the toilet as Brady lunged toward him, and Malorie's scream filled the room. Dean instinctively moved in front of Malorie, but Matt wasn't charging at them. He turned toward the back wall, grabbed the windowsill, and launched himself out the open window.

"Oh my God! Oh my God!" Malorie sobbed, clutching his arm as they raced together to the window. Her sharp intake of breath rattled in her swollen throat as they craned their heads to look outside. On the ground two stories below, Matt's body lay still and lifeless in the dappled shade from the nearby trees.

He closed his eyes. "Shit." Emotions he couldn't identify tore through him, and he sighed. "Will you be okay for a second?" he asked, swallowing past the boulder in his throat.

She tightened her grip on his biceps. "I'm going with you." Her bloodshot eyes shone with sympathy and steel.

He nodded. "Let's go."

Clinging to each other, they descended the stairs and exited the house through the open French doors, closing Brady in behind them. They made their way from the deck to the side of the house in silence, each lost in their reeling thoughts. As they approached Matt, Dean searched for any movement. A twitch. A breath.

Nothing. And once they were closer, he could see how Matt's head was twisted at an impossible angle. The trees beyond blurred and tilted.

Matt was dead.

Chapter Twenty-Nine

Malorie emerged slowly from the thick veil of slumber, struggling to get her bearings. The bed beneath her felt strange, but familiar as well. She dragged her heavy lids open. For some reason, she was in the bedroom she'd used as a teen. *Odd*. Then the memories of everything that had happened on Sunday night came flooding back, and she groaned and closed her eyes again as the events replayed in her mind.

In a state of shock, she and Dean had trudged back to his house, collecting the necklace and her shattered phone along the way, and called 911. They'd had to break the news to Sharon, helping her deal with her horror and denial as they waited for the police and EMTs to arrive. Eventually, both she and Sharon were transported to the hospital—Malorie to have her injuries checked out, Sharon to have her pregnancy monitored as her hysteria grew to an alarming level—with Dean following behind in Malorie's car, since his truck had been seized.

She'd been subjected to interrogations, exams, and tests, and at some point during the night, Julia had shown up, barely concealing her distress behind a brave smile and a comforting embrace. A lot of it was a blur, which was probably a blessing. She knew Sharon's mother had arrived to stay with her daughter, and to take her back to their house. Once Malorie had finally been discharged, Dean had driven her back home as the first gray streaks of dawn began to lighten the sky.

They'd been unsure where to go, once they turned onto Beach Plum Drive. Both houses seemed tainted. But Brady was at Malorie's, so they'd ended up there, closing off the master bedroom and curling up together in her old double bed after swallowing prescription sleeping pills.

But where was he now? She slid her arm across the empty space beside her, frowning at the cool pocket of air between the sheets.

The darkened room gave little indication of what time it was. Or what day it was, for that matter. She pushed herself up to sitting, her stiff muscles and leaden limbs protesting each move as though she were asking them to scale the final summit of Mount Everest. Ugh. A new bottle of water sat on the night table, and she reached for it eagerly; her throat felt like it had been paved with asphalt during the night. Once she'd swallowed a few blissful sips, a sharp ache in her bladder made her realize she was going to need to get up, and fast. She nearly expected her joints to creak as she climbed out of bed and hurried to the hall bathroom.

She inspected her reflection as she splashed water on her face. God, she looked horrid. Tiny red spots in the whites of her eyes, purple bruises around her neck, hair a tangled rat's nest. For all she knew, a rat may have in fact moved in. She sighed, turning away. Nothing to be done about it now. She was more concerned with finding Dean, making sure he was okay.

But downstairs, she found Julia, standing over the stovetop in the kitchen, Brady at her feet. A phone on the counter played soft music. Malorie's brows pulled in as she glanced around. Golden light filtered through the windows, and the large wall clock read 7:30. "How long have I been asleep?" she asked, tugging her fingers through a matted knot of hair.

"Oh!" Julia started, twisting toward her. "I didn't hear you! How are you feeling?"

Brady left his hopeful watch for falling food and trotted over, tail wagging. "Hey, buddy." She scratched his head as she sunk onto a stool. "I'm okay. Where's Dean? Is it still…," she paused, thinking for a moment. "Monday?"

Julia laughed softly, stirring the contents of the big steel pot as she lowered the flame on the burner. "Yes, it's Monday. Monday night." She tapped the wooden spoon against the rim and set it on a holder by the stove. "I think Dean said you guys went to sleep around 5:30 in the morning, so you've been asleep for 14 hours."

"Good Lord." She shook her head slightly, rolling her shoulders. "And…Dean?" The prickle of unease she'd felt since she woke up alone intensified, lodging itself in her chest like a spiky mass.

Julia reached for a box of teabags on the counter, holding them up in a silent question. When Malorie nodded, she pulled one out. "He called me around…let's see…4:00. Said he had some things he needed to do, but he didn't want to leave you alone. I stopped by the store on my way over so I could make some chicken soup." She tipped her head in the direction of the simmering pot as she filled a mug with water.

"So he's at his house?" She stood back up. "I'd better go check on him."

"Whoa." Julia held a palm out, her voice firm. "I get that you need to see him, but you're going to have something to eat first. Non-negotiable." Her gaze swept over Malorie, lingering on her hair. "And maybe a quick shower. Just saying."

She sighed, closing her eyes. Her nerves sang with tension, but she knew this was an argument she wouldn't win. Julia's delicate features were set in that determined expression that Malorie knew well. And Julia was right, of course. When was the last time she'd eaten anything? Her stomach felt hollow, and her muscles shook with hunger.

The warmth of the tea and the soup soothed her throat, and the fact that Julia had prepared these things for her—and was sitting here beside her—soothed her soul. But she couldn't stop worrying about how Dean was coping. She had the terrible feeling he would try to pull away, at the very time he needed her most.

"That was delicious," she said as she finished her bowl. "You didn't need to do all this," she added, waving her spoon toward the stove, "but it was exactly what I needed. I think I'll take your advice and grab a really quick shower, and then..." she trailed off, not wanting to sound like she was kicking Julia out after everything she'd done.

But Julia just laughed. "I get it. You need to be with Dean. I'm glad you guys have each other through all this."

Her heart contracted. *Please let that be true.*

Julia took the bowl from her hands as they stood up. "How about this? I'll clean up down here while you shower. I can pack up some soup for you to take to Dean's too."

"You've already done so much, Julia. I can do the clean-up."

She lifted a pale eyebrow. "You think I can't see how anxious you are to get over there? It's fine. I'm not leaving until I deposit you at Dean's door, anyway."

Malorie shook her head, feigning exasperation. "It's only five houses away. I think I can make it. I'll take Brady, too. He probably could use the exercise."

"No way. Not on my watch. Dean put me in charge of making sure you're okay, and I'm not taking any chances. If you want to walk, I'll follow you in the car."

She rolled her eyes playfully, but she couldn't suppress her smile. A swell of gratitude rose in her chest, and she thanked her lucky stars once again for blessing her with such a friend. "Okay," she said, heading for the stairs. "I'll be ready in ten."

It was more like fifteen—her sore muscles made everything take longer. But she felt a thousand times better, she decided, as she gingerly slid a cotton T-shirt dress over her head, pulling her damp hair out from the collar. She doubted she looked much better, but there was no time for that. Besides, her makeup and toiletries were in the master bathroom, and she wasn't going in there yet. It had been bad enough just walking by the closed door to grab something from her closet. Thank God she'd stocked the hall bathroom with the basic necessities a while back, in case Julia ever spent the night.

A plastic shopping bag with a large container of soup was already waiting by the front door, and she found Julia sitting at the island in the clean kitchen, scrolling through her phone. Malorie sighed inwardly at the reminder that her own phone was a lost cause. Replacing it wasn't high on her current to-do list, but since she'd been awake, her fingers had been itching to text Dean.

She'd be over there in five minutes, though. Less. "I'm all set," she said, trying not to sound too anxious. But the need to see Dean was becoming unbearable. *Was he okay?*

Julia looked up from the screen. "Kay. Pete says he hopes you feel better soon," she added, nodding toward her phone as she stood.

"Oh, that's nice. Tell him thanks."

"I will." She pressed her lips together, twisting a lock of blonde hair around her finger.

"What?" Shoving her feet into flip-flops, she collected her keys off the hall table, along with Brady's leash.

"Oh, nothing." Julia gave a little shrug as she handed Malorie the plastic bag. "It's just...the past few days..." Her forehead crinkled. "How do I say this? I know a lot of terrible things happened these last few days. I mean, my God, we almost lost you. But some good things happened too. From yesterday morning when Dean came over to my house, determined to figure out what was keeping you two apart, to last night at the hospital, how he could barely leave your side. The look on his face when you were taken away for tests was pure torment. Then his concern over leaving you today, and how desperately you need to see him now...it just keeps reminding me how much you two love each other. What you guys have is special. You're soulmates. I just hope I find mine one day, because I'm quite certain it's not Pete."

Tears stung her eyes. Never in her life had she imagined she might have something others yearned for. Leave it to Julia to remind her of the positive things during the dark times. *Please, let their love be strong enough to make it through this.* "You will," she assured her friend, gripping her hand. "You're too wonderful not to."

Julia's lips curved in a wan smile. "I hope so. But, ugh…I can't imagine getting back into the dating scene," she added, wrinkling her nose.

"So…you're definitely breaking up with him?"

With a shrug, Julia picked up the plastic bag and followed Brady out onto the porch, weaving to avoid becoming entangled in the leash. "I mean, I think it's just going to be a mutual decision. Originally, I'd thought maybe we'd move into the farmhouse together, once it became a reality. But he's not going to be happy that far away from his gym. And I'm going to need to live at the farm, with all the animals. I *want* to live there."

"Have you asked him if he'd consider it?" She pulled the door shut behind them, testing the lock.

"That's the thing. I'm not really sure I'd want him to. I just think we've sort of…reached our expiration date." She made a sound between a laugh and a sigh.

"Ah," she said, nodding. "Well, I'm here for you. Whatever you need." She felt bad that Julia would have to go through a break-up—change was hard, especially when couples lived together. But she couldn't bring herself to feel any real dismay over the end of the relationship; Julia deserved true love. If a twenty minute commute was a deal-breaker, this wasn't it.

"I know." Julia perked up again, flashing a smile as they stopped beside her SUV. "Who knows? Maybe I'll end up hiring a hot stable hand who'll want to be there for me, too."

Malorie laughed with her as they embraced, holding tightly to each other, drawing strength from their silent exchange of support and love.

"Okay," Julia said, handing off the plastic bag. "Are you sure you don't want me to drive you there?"

She nodded. "The walk will do me good. Besides, I have him." She tilted her head toward Brady, who was already tugging her toward the street.

"Please. I'm going to live on a farm. I think I can handle a dog in my car for two minutes." But the glint in her eyes told Malorie she understood. "Go check on Dean. I hope he's okay. Text me if you need anything. And I'm still making sure you get to his house safely."

"Thank you, Julia. For everything," she added, lifting the bag of soup as she allowed Brady to pull her a few steps away from the driveway.

Julia blew her a kiss as she climbed into her SUV, then, true to her word, she braked at the turn off of Beach Plum and waited in the middle of the deserted road, left blinker flashing like a heartbeat.

The warm evening air whispered with a slight breeze off the ocean, and orange streaks stretched across the sky. A rabbit on the neighbor's lawn froze as they approached, and she braced herself to reel Brady back from his lunge. Thankfully, he didn't notice the tiny animal, and she relaxed her grip on the leash's handle. Her fingers tightened again as her gaze slid over to the row of bushes where she'd dropped the necklace, and she looked away, drawing in a steadying breath. Nightmares were no stranger to her, and she was sure her desperate flight back to her house would be a new theme. As would the struggle on the bathroom floor, and her frantic fight for life. She'd deal with it as it came. Right now, she was much more worried about Dean's mental demons than her own.

She knew he'd need time to grieve: for the loss of his brother, for the loss of who he'd thought his brother was, for the loss of the lives Matt took. It would also take time to accept the enormity of what Matt had done. She'd give him all the time he needed, but she was determined to remind him that he wasn't alone. To offer any comfort she could give. Just two days ago, he had shown up at her door and pressed her until he learned the brutal truth about her mother, about the accident. Then he had held her as she cried, shared her sorrow and pain. She would do that for him now, be there in any way he needed, as he began to face the complicated emotions that would come with this tragedy.

A movement from across the street caught her eye; the curtains twitched as the nosy neighbor peeked out from her window. Malorie sighed, frowning. Where had this woman been the other night, when her snooping could have been useful? *Mind your own bloody business.* She shot the neighbor a nasty look as she turned into Dean's empty driveway.

His house looked deserted, dark and shuttered against the falling shadows. A wave of trepidation flowed through her as she climbed the stone steps to the porch. What if he'd gone somewhere? He didn't have his truck, but there were other means of transportation. Or what if he was asleep? But he'd told Julia he had things to do. Rolling her shoulders back, she pulled in a breath and knocked on the front door.

No footsteps approached, but she swore she detected some small hint of movement from inside the house. Brady's cocked ears and tilted head seemed to confirm the muffled sound was not a product of her imagination. "Dean, it's me," she called out, tapping her knuckles against the door again.

The sharp tang of whisky hit her as the door opened to reveal Dean, bare-chested and barefoot, clad only in worn jeans hanging low on his hips. His complexion was pale and slack beneath his tan, his rough stubble well beyond the five o'clock shadow stage. "Hey," he said, dragging a hand through his disheveled hair. His eyes were glassy, but concern still shone in their green depths as his gaze swept to her neck.

Her heart clenched. He reminded her of a wounded wolf, deeply hurt but still fierce and protective. The agony that crossed his face as he stared at her bruises tore at her insides, and she berated herself for not finding a summer-weight scarf to hide the marks.

But my injuries are not his fault, she reminded herself. And yet she knew misplaced guilt was probably eating at him like poison. Her instincts told her to be careful, but her body took over, and she threw herself at him, wrapping her arms around his waist.

He crushed her to him, squeezing her as though she were a lifeline, and his chest heaved with a shuddering breath. Then his muscles went lax, and gripping her shoulders, he pushed her away.

She caught the haunted look in his eyes before he dropped his gaze. Reaching behind her, he shut the door and bent slightly to run his fingers over Brady's head. He brought his hand back and folded it into his other fist, pressing at the joints as he turned away. The hollow pops seemed to echo in the still air of the hallway.

Biting her lip, she watched as he walked toward the kitchen, Brady at his side. Despite the potent smell of alcohol, his gait was steady, the muscular planes along his back rigid. Yet something about his posture gave the impression of turning inwards; a hint of defensiveness that would protect him against the outside world. She hoped—prayed—that didn't include her, but the fact that he'd released her so suddenly, pushed her away so firmly, did not bode well.

She followed him into the kitchen, growing dark now as the last of the light left the sky. The open bottle of whisky sat on the island, along with a lowball glass half-full of the amber liquid. As he reached for the glass, she glanced at the papers spread across the counter. Print-outs of listings of houses for sale in Sandalwood. Information on local realtors. She glanced up at him, her brows lifted in a silent question.

He met her gaze over the rim of the glass, the column of his throat moving as he swallowed. "I'm going to sell the house. Give the money to Sharon."

Her eyes widened, but the shock was quickly surpassed by a surge of warmth. *He was so kind.* "Wow. That's very generous of you. I'm sure it will help her out immensely." She exhaled, pressing a hand to her quivering belly. "You can...come live with me."

He blinked, his brows furrowing into a deep V. "What?"

She shrugged. "I know it's a bit soon, since we just got back together, but it makes sense." When he continued to stare at her, she added, "You said you wanted to be with me."

He closed his eyes with a sigh, lowering his head. "That was before."

Ice crystals formed in her blood. At first, the words wouldn't come, but after a few tries, she found her voice. "So...now you don't want to be with me?"

"Things are different now." He knocked back the rest of the whisky, poured another. The neck of the bottle clinked against the glass. "My brother was a rapist and a murderer."

"Half-brother."

Lifting a bare shoulder, he took another swig.

She eyed the bottle, biting back the desire to tell him he'd probably had enough. That might only serve to swing the conversation in a different direction, and she wasn't about to get sidetracked. Whether he was drunk or not, he needed her. She needed him.

Twisting her fingers, she plunged on. "Even if he was your full brother, it doesn't matter. You are not him. *You* are a good person."

His bark of laughter held no humor. "Am I? I was responsible for him." He shook his head in defeat as he scrubbed a hand over his face. "I promised our mother I would take care of him."

Oh, God. "You are not responsible for what he was. And you *did* take care of him. He was sick, Dean. You said so yourself. But you didn't make him that way. And you didn't know." The words rushed out, and she pulled in a shaky breath.

"I should have."

"No," she said sharply, shaking her head with enough force to make the sore tendons of her neck throb. "That's ridiculous. He worked hard to hide that side of himself. But in the end, you saved me from him. That's what matters."

"Brady saved you." He bent forward slightly, spreading his palms on the island, staring at the granite countertop.

"You both saved me. You knew Brady was sounding the alarm—you said so to the police. You raced back and saved me. People know you're a hero."

He gestured toward the listings. "I'm not staying here, Malorie," he said, his voice quiet but firm.

What? Her heart seized. "What do you mean?"

"Once I sell, I'll move somewhere else. Here, I'll always be the brother of a serial rapist and killer."

Pain lanced through her at his torment. "No," she repeated, filling her tone with conviction. "He does not define you. We're not going to let him define you."

The muscles along his arms tightened, cording beneath his skin. "Stop saying we."

She struggled to hold her trembling limbs steady as she shot him a stubborn glare. The hell she'd stop saying 'we'. Crossing her arms, she put extra emphasis on the pronoun. "*We* are not letting him define you, and *we're* not running away. That's what my father did, and it nearly ruined my life." It was a dangerous ploy, comparing him to her father, but she was desperate. She held her breath, wishing his expression wasn't so difficult to read in the deepening shadows.

His eyes narrowed, a defiant gleam flickering in their depths for a moment before fading away. He pushed his weight off the counter and looked away, arms hanging by his sides. "There's nothing else I can do."

"Oh yes there is." She closed the distance between them, reached out to touch him. "You stay here, and we fight through the terrible times together. That's what people who love each other do."

He took a step back, his jaw a hard line as he shook his head.

"What does that mean?" Panic squirmed in her belly, hot and slippery. "That you don't love me?"

"No, it means I'm not going to saddle you with this. You don't want me."

Anger bubbled up even as her knees went weak with relief. *He still loved her.* She straightened her spine, planting her fists on her hips. "Don't tell me what I want. I know *exactly* what kind of person you are." She clutched her hands to her chest, locking her eyes with his and softening her voice. "I *see* you. I've always seen who you are, even when others couldn't. When we met, I saw right away that you weren't a screw-up or a trouble-maker. I saw how you cared for your mother, how you took care of the family and helped out, without ever complaining.

"I saw how you treated me from the very beginning. Helping me find that bracelet. All the things you did for me when we were dating. Going to all that trouble to make our spot in the woods perfect for prom night." Swallowing back a sob, she swiped at the warm tears dribbling down her cheeks. "Even in these past few months, even when you were still mad at me, I saw how you treated me. Watching out for me that night at the bar. Making sure I got home safe even after we fought the night of the cookout here. For God's sake, you were willing to let your brother's pregnant girlfriend live here. Even now, you're thinking of her needs." The words rasped against the swelling in her throat. She took another step toward him and laid her hand on his arm. "You don't hurt women. You protect them."

He flinched at her touch, his muscles going rigid. "And I'm trying to protect you now," he said gruffly. "Go home, Malorie."

The words tore at her heart, but she recognized his cold directive for what it was. Did he think he could scare her away? She was stronger than that. He'd said before that he knew she was strong, but he had no idea how hard she was prepared to fight. She bit down on her lower lip, registering the faint taste of salt along with the anchoring flare of pain. Her fingers tightened around his bicep as she shoved herself into his field of vision. "So, what...you're going to break all your promises to me? You fought for us only days ago! You said you weren't going to let me push you away, remember? Well, I'm not going to let you push me away."

"You don't have a choice."

"The hell I don't. We've been down this road already. I tried to protect you from me. You made me see I was wrong. You told me you loved me, wanted to be with me. You gave me hope that I could be happy—truly happy—and share my life with the man I love. And now you're going to desert me?" Her voice rose, breaking with emotion. She clutched him as she shook her head. "No. I need you. We need each other. So I'm going to ask you the question you asked me, the one you said was the only thing that matters. Do you love me?"

The question hung in the air, stretching between them, the sound of her ragged breathing growing thunderous in the silence. Finally, he responded with a heavy sigh. "I love you. But—"

"Good," she said, cutting him off. "I love you too. We belong together, and I'm not going anywhere. We're done protecting each other from ourselves. From now on, we face everything together. And if we can get through everything that happened on Sunday, then I'm pretty sure we can get through anything."

She knew him well enough to see that his resolve was weakening, and she leaned into him, wrapping her arms around his waist. After a few agonizing beats, his hands settled on her shoulders. Then in one rough motion, he pulled her even closer, crushing her to him in a fierce embrace until their bodies felt like one. Fresh tears pooled where her cheek met the bare skin of his chest, but this time they were tears of relief, and she welcomed the cleansing release.

"Okay," he murmured, stroking her hair. "Okay."

They remained like that as time slid by, locked in each other's arms, swaying slightly, until her body felt as though it could not hold her up for one more second, even with the support of his strong arms. Despite sleeping so many hours, she was suddenly exhausted again. *What must he feel like?* He'd had much less sleep than her, and a lot of alcohol. She eased back a little, tilting her head up to him. "Let's get some rest."

He nodded, and they moved apart, but their hands remained clasped, as though they were each other's life boats, and to break the connection would be to risk being swept apart. She grabbed a bottle of water for him from the fridge, then led him upstairs, Brady a silent sentry at their heels.

Chapter Thirty

Twilight washed the sky above the farm in shades of blue and violet as they shared their first dance as husband and wife. The colors were magical, just as the wedding had been. The early summer sun had made its descent as they took their vows on the emerald lawn, and now lanterns and fairy lights glowed around the temporary dance floor Dean had installed with the help of his landscaping employees. The initial smattering of applause faded, leaving only the soft music of their song.

I can't believe this is happening, she thought for the hundredth time that evening, and she opened her eyes to assure herself once again that she wasn't dreaming. The smiling faces of their guests surrounded them, and her heart swelled with joy. The Pearson family stood in a proud cluster: Julia's parents, Julia's sister and her family, and Julia and her new beau. Behind them were some of the staff and volunteers of the farm, who'd quickly begun to feel like family. Dean's employees were all in attendance as well, even Mr. Firenze, who was beaming like a proud papa.

As they turned a slow circle, she caught sight of her own father, standing with his arm around Holly, and she marveled again at his presence here. Her near-brush with death had shaken him, and he'd come to accept her relationship with Dean, especially since Dean had been the one to save her. Even the twins were here, and her adorable English half-brothers had served as ring-bearers. Now, they were likely still in the bounce house they'd had set up for the children, under the watchful eye of a teenage girl whose younger sister received riding therapy at Friendship Farm. The boys had been running around all day; they were going to sleep well tonight.

Even Sharon was here, with their 10-month-old nephew Ryan, although she'd recently moved to New Hampshire with the money Dean had given her to help her child avoid any stigma. Malorie wished she'd stayed on the Cape, but she understood the need for a fresh start after everything that had happened. Thankfully, Dean had received mostly support and sympathy from people here, and no one seemed to be holding him accountable for his brother's actions. Firenze had lost a few accounts in the aftermath, but Mr. Firenze had stood behind his most valued employee—and been unwavering in his intention to still sell Dean the company—and business was steady now.

Dean's arm tightened around her waist. "I love you, Mrs. Slater." He dipped her back, leaning down for a kiss.

Warmth surged through her, ignited by both the tender touch of his lips and the sweet sound of those five words. "I love you, too," she said, smiling up at him. He pulled her back into a tight embrace and she sighed happily as she settled her head on his tuxedo-clad shoulder. *I wish I could bottle this feeling.* It was almost a bit frightening, being this blissful and content. But didn't they deserve it, after everything they'd been through in the past eleven months?

How far they'd come in a year. Moving in together. A fairytale proposal at their secluded spot in the woods. And now, marriage. She'd been offered a full-time job at the college, and Friendship Farm was doing so well, Julia insisted on giving her a small paycheck for her work doing the accounting and financial reports.

Malorie had even discovered that horseback riding was therapeutic for her as well, and she went trail riding with Julia—and sometimes even Dean—as much as she could. There was something intensely soothing and peaceful about weaving through the woods on horseback, immersing yourself in nature, escaping technology.

Of course, she and Dean were in regular therapy as well, to make sure they had professional support as they dealt with the tragedies of their lives, both recent and past. They'd both come to terms with a lot of things, although it would always be a work-in-progress. Especially her fear of getting sick, but now she had even more people ready to step in if she began showing symptoms: a safety net of Dean, Julia, and her therapist.

But today—tonight—she felt glorious, and she would not worry about 'what-ifs'. She would dance with her husband, spend time with her friends and relatives, indulge in the hors d'oeuvres and desserts covering the buffet tables, eat her wedding cake, and drink champagne.

Breathing in, she savored the heady mix of his masculine scent, fresh bouquets and garden flowers, and burning candles. The velvety night air was just beginning to cool, and she sent up another prayer of thanks that the weather had cooperated for their outdoor wedding. The ceremony had been magical, and Dean's vows had brought tears to her eyes. Thank God there was such a thing as waterproof mascara, too.

Dean brought his lips to her ear. "I can't wait to get you out of this dress," he murmured, pressing his palm into her lower back.

"I thought you liked my dress." Her mouth refused to curve into even a fake frown, but she managed to inject mock indignation into her voice as she glanced up at him.

His eyes sparked with both playfulness and desire. "It's beautiful. I just happen to like what's underneath better."

Heat shot to her cheeks and pooled in her belly. She couldn't wait to be alone with him, either. "Well, we can't exactly rush out of the reception just yet. In the meantime, we'll just have to try to enjoy the anticipation," she said, returning his wicked grin.

His shoulder lifted beneath her hand. "I don't know...we could always disappear for a little while." He titled his head in the direction of the barn, adding, "The hayloft seems cozy and somewhat private."

"Stop," she said, suppressing a giggle. Another round of applause rang out as their song ended, and the DJ invited everyone else to join them on the dance floor.

It was a whirlwind from that moment on, with time passing in a delicious blur of laughter, dancing, conversation, and food. After what felt like minutes rather than hours, they found themselves in the back of the limo, heading back to the house, where they'd agreed they wanted to spend their wedding night. It was home. It was where they'd started their life together, where they'd begun their second chance. It was where Brady and Champ, their new rescue dog, were. They'd even managed to find enough money in their budget to remodel the master bedroom and bath, in an attempt to reclaim it from the tragic memories as much as possible. While they would never be able to erase the past, they were doing their best to live in the present.

There was no formal honeymoon planned at the moment, either—the summer months were just too busy for Dean's business for him to get away for too long. Especially during this first year of ownership. But they'd managed to clear both their schedules enough to enjoy a few quiet days together at home, doing nothing but celebrating their marriage. Relaxing on the beach. Maybe even swimming in the ocean—she was working on conquering her anxiety. Walking the dogs. Watching the stars come out over the water. Cuddling on the couch. Making love…

Already, Dean was nuzzling her neck, his hand sliding over the curve of her breast. A shiver of pleasure hummed through her as his fingers traced the line where her flesh met the strapless bodice of her gown. She squirmed and squeezed her thighs together, wondering how she could possibly wait even five more minutes to tumble into bed with him.

"This driver had better hurry up," he murmured, echoing her thoughts. His teeth grazed her ear, sending a jolt of scorching heat to the parts of her that were already smoldering with need. She pressed her palm against the rigid bulge beneath his black pants, eliciting a tortured groan from deep in his throat.

He nearly flung the door open before the limo came to a complete stop, and they hurried up the walkway, keys already out. But once he'd unlocked the door, he only turned the handle and opened the door a crack. Then she was lifted off her feet as he caught her around the waist and swept her up into his arms.

"Oh!" she gasped as she latched on to his neck. She'd forgotten about this part. Laughing, she clutched her bouquet to her chest as he maneuvered her through the door while attempting to keep the ecstatic dogs from considering escape.

"Hey, guys! We're married!" she informed them giddily. The two dogs swirled around Dean's legs, and Chance, a rescued lab mix, took off on his usual celebratory run down the hall and back.

She fully expected Dean to set her down so they could attend to their furry babies, but he continued up the stairs. "But—"

"All taken care of. For now, anyway. I had one of my clients come over a few times to secretly meet them, and she came over this evening. They've probably just come in from their evening walk."

She lifted her brows, her throat tightening with emotion over the fact that he'd thought to do that. And that he'd anticipated being that anxious to take her to bed. Blood thrummed in her veins as he carried her down the hall.

"And, just in case they need something to keep them busy," he said as he set her down gently in their bedroom, "here we go." Plucking two rawhide bones from the top of the dresser, he waved them in the dogs' view before rolling them out onto the hallway floor, shutting the door as they followed the treats. "Sorry, guys. I need some time alone with my bride."

She laughed and set her bouquet of purple blooms on the nightstand, then turned back toward him, her heart pounding, her nerves tingling. There was no reason to be nervous, and yet, here she was, suddenly overwhelmed with the weight of their wonderful new reality. They'd done it. She was married, to the one man who had always had her heart.

His gaze ran over her, and she pressed her palms against her fluttering stomach. Only the bright moonlight illuminated the room, turning the skirt of her white gown into liquid silver.

He took a step forward and raised his arms, touching his fingertips to the veil floating around her face. "You're beautiful." He brushed the tulle back behind her bare shoulders, along with her hair, and cupped her face in his hands. "You're my world." Stroking the rough pads of his thumbs across her cheekbones, he lowered his head and brushed his lips against hers. He kissed her slowly and tenderly, each time lingering a bit longer, claiming a bit more of her mouth.

Oh, God. She clung to him as flames licked her insides, begging to be stoked. *More.*

His hands slid down her back, and his fingers found the zipper of her dress. With agonizing deliberation, he pulled it down a few inches as he continued to kiss her senseless. Then he pulled away and turned her around, sweeping the veil and her hair away from the back of her neck. Her breath caught as he brought his mouth to the sensitive flesh at her nape. He unzipped the bodice the rest of the way, and her gown fell in a pale pool around her feet. She was left clad in only her heels and a white lacy thong, and his palms glided from the curve of her waist to cup her breasts.

How could he endure this sweet torture? Her own need was becoming unbearable, and she turned back to him, pulling his crisp white shirt from the black cummerbund around his waist. The tuxedo jacket had long since been discarded, and he hurriedly released his bowtie and cufflinks as she worked at the buttons. Each item joined the growing pile on the floor, and as she kicked off her heels, she pulled out the pins that secured her veil, shaking out the cascade of loose waves she'd left unstyled.

He plunged his fingers into her hair, seizing her mouth again, urgency now edging out tenderness, his intense control fraying. His kisses moved down her neck and over her breasts, and she gasped when his lips tightened around her nipple. He continued down along her quivering belly, nuzzling the soft skin as he slipped the lacy panties down her thighs. Then he was kneeling before her, cupping her buttocks, exploring her with his tongue, and she was on fire.

A delicious pressure built as he tasted and teased. Her body quaked, begging for release, and a sound escaped her throat, something between a moan and a cry. *Now. Please.* "Dean." Her fingers gripped his hair, tugging upwards. "I need you."

He worked his way back up until their mouths met again and walked her backwards, supporting her loose limbs with his strong arms. She sank onto the bed, reaching for him as he held himself above her. Digging her nails into the hard muscles of his shoulders, she arched her hips, desperate to feel him inside her.

He entered her slowly at first, drawing out each moment, each sensation, as she trembled and moaned beneath him. Then with a powerful thrust, he filled her completely, and she wrapped her legs around him. Every coherent thought disappeared from her mind, replaced by primal need and bright pleasure, as their bodies rocked in urgent rhythm. When she tightened around him, bucking and shuddering, he came with her, and they rode out the powerful waves together, his groan answering her whimpers, their ragged breaths mingling, their hearts thudding in unison.

When she could finally speak, her voice came out in a raspy whisper. "That was…" No acceptable word came to her pleasure-soaked brain. "Wow," she finished, sliding her hands over the hot skin of his back.

"Yeah," he agreed as he leaned his forehead against hers. "I love you, Mrs. Slater." He kissed her and rolled to his side, gathering her into his arms.

"I love you too, Mr. Slater." She settled her head onto his chest, splaying a palm across the hard planes of his abdomen. "We did it."

He stroked her hair, smoothing it away from her temple. "We did." His lips brushed the top of her head.

She snuggled into his embrace, a sigh of contentment bubbling up from her chest. Despite all the obstacles fate had thrown in their way, they had officially joined their lives, promising to spend forever together. She knew it wouldn't all be as blissful as this moment, this day. There would be trials. Pain and problems. But there would also be triumphs. Joy and passion. And they would go through it all as partners. As friends. As lovers. Together.

The End

About the Author

Kathryn Knight spends a great deal of time in her fictional world, where mundane chores don't exist and daily life involves steamy romance, dangerous secrets, and spooky suspense. Her novels are award-winning #1 Amazon and Barnes & Noble Bestsellers and RomCon Reader-Rated picks.

When she's not reading or writing, Kathryn spends her time catching up on those mundane chores, driving kids around, and teaching fitness classes. She lives on beautiful Cape Cod with her husband, their two sons, and a number of rescued pets.

Please visit her at
www.kathrynknightbooks.blogspot.com.

Made in the USA
Columbia, SC
14 December 2020

28212526R00178